World Without Love

Betrayed

Book One

Jaye Frances

World Without Love – Betrayed

Copyright © 2015 - Jaye Frances

All Rights Reserved

Redstone Press

ISBN 978-0692541937

Printed in the United States of America

www.jayefrances.com

We're all captives,
in one way or another . . .

Prologue

I'm awakened by the sounds of creaking wood and straining rope—constant protests to the unsteady pitch and roll of the darkness.

Dizzy and disoriented, I take a breath, trying to dispel the nausea. But the air is laced with the pungent smell of damp rot, and its raw bite forces me to shallow my breathing.

Staring into the darkness, I search for a shape, a silhouette—anything to give me a clue about my surroundings. But there is only a thick layered blackness, as endless as the grave.

I'm plagued by the sensation of motion, of being rocked up and down. A flash of impaired logic tells me to dismiss it as a specter, an artifact from the nearly depleted dose of Halcion.

A minute passes—or an hour. I can't tell which.

I hear something—a garbled voice, remnants of disconnected conversation. And from much farther away, the plaintive cries of a bird. The sounds seem genuine, missing that phantom-like quality associated with suspects from a barbiturate daze.

I take it as a sign—the drugs are finally leaving my system.

A prickly thaw sweeps the surface of my skin, bringing with it the nagging sensation that something is pulling at my limbs, tugging at me from both ends.

It's not an after-effect of the drugs, I'm sure of that. It's too strong, too constant. I have the sense it's been there all along, waiting to break through the chemical cloud that kept me unconscious.

It's growing stronger, getting worse, becoming a piercing burn stretching from my shoulders to my hips, cutting me to the quick.

I try to turn, to get away from the waves of searing heat raking at my arms and legs.

I can't move.

The realization is as damning as if I'd awakened in the sulfur pits of hell. I'm bound like an animal, my wrists tied above my head, my legs strapped at the ankles—my body a living bridge of straining joints and wrenched sinew.

Even as my muscles scream at the draw of the restraints, I feel the bite of riveted steel against my back, the harsh, unforgiving surface running the length of my spine.

I'm naked.

It's no accident. Whoever did this intentionally stripped me, leaving me exposed and vulnerable, determined to violate my mind as well as my body.

The blackness rolls then plunges, releasing something new into the shifting darkness. Slithering against me, it touches my skin with a bitter cold that breaks through the unrelenting agony of the rope. I hear my own tortured wheeze catch in my throat as I feel it scoring my stomach, the freezing nip and sting quickly followed by the unmistakable seeping of liquid, collecting in the hollow of my belly, running down my sides.

A rush of useless adrenalin floods my bloodstream, my chest threatening to explode as my racing heart frantically pumps blood to an unseen wound.

Even through the suffocating surge of panic, a vision of what I cannot see crystalizes with vivid detail: My arms and legs are tortuously drawn on a makeshift rack . . . a pendulum of biting chill slices across my naked torso . . . tiny rivers of fluid trickle down my sides.

I barely hear it over my pounding heartbeat—the sound of sloshing liquid.

In seconds, it becomes as familiar as it is terrifying.

I'm lying in water.

I take a halted breath as I realize the truth: The fluid running down my sides is not blood, but ribbons of over-wash from the frigid pool that surrounds me.

Rope and water.

Pain and fear.

It's deliberate . . . to break me.

Again, the darkness lurches and rolls, churning the water, splashing it over my breasts and thighs. And although the icy burn forces me to gasp for air, it also sparks a moment of fleeting recognition—a vague memory from my past, a connection to the rise and fall of everything around me.

I've felt it before.

But where? When?

Stray thoughts flood my mind—the gentle climb, the momentary sense of weightlessness, the sudden drop . . . the unique motion of the sea.

It isn't much, but it gives me something to hold on to, a starting point in remembering what has happened to me.

Chapter One

"Cards?"

My husband, Carl, was betting strong, challenging the table. He knew better. He'd warned me on more than one occasion never to bet strong this early in the game.

Carl had met the four men this morning. Crewmen from a large schooner docked in the harbor, they were in town to buy provisions and spare parts from the marine supply store where Carl worked. He'd offered them a few tips on installing an upgrade to their GPS, and in return, they had extended him an invitation to join them for lunch.

Their offer wasn't unusual. Carl was one of the best marine diesel mechanics on the island of Sri Lanka. And the price of a meal in exchange for his opinion of the newest oil additives and cold-weather starting tips was a frequent occurrence.

Lunch had been followed by several pitchers of dark beer, and the discussion had quickly transitioned to one of the men's favorite pastimes—cards. At sea it was a common activity, helping to fill the empty hours. Often taking the place of internet-provided entertainment, a round of poker was an onboard ritual.

The suggestion of a game was more temptation than Carl could stand. He loved to play, but the locals had nothing to bet. And wagering for poker chips that had no value beyond their plastic content made it impossible to win—or lose.

That was Carl's world. Strictly black and white. He hated the idea of pretending. 'Life is not a spectator sport,' he'd said. 'You either jump in with both feet or not at all.' To a naïve twenty-year-old it had sounded like scripture, the missing truth I was searching for.

Carl and I met in San Diego during one of his leaves from the Navy, where he worked as a diesel mechanic in Little Creek, Virginia. I was two years out of high school and marriage was the last thing on my mind. But he was seven years my senior and immediately impressed me with his plans for the future.

With eleven months remaining of his four-year enlistment, he was already making plans to travel the globe—this time as a civilian. After dating less than five months—he visiting me on leave, and I making one trip to Virginia—he made it clear he wanted to marry me.

His proposal had come Navy-neat and methodical. 'We'll coordinate everything for an effective and timely execution,' he'd said, quoting from one of his management textbooks. At the time, we'd laughed. But I knew there was a part of him that was already systemizing every detail. With my own dreams of marriage constructed from bits and pieces of TV sitcoms and dozens of happily-ever-after movies of the week, it wasn't quite the whirlwind romance I'd hoped for.

That's not to say the prospect of sharing our future wasn't exciting. If I joined Carl as his wife, we would see the world together, a carefree couple without the usual constraints of kids, a mortgage, or a car payment.

'That can come later,' he'd said. Carl's version of the American dream had nothing to do with climbing the corporate ladder or ass-kissing his way into a corner office. His idea of success was lying on a tropical beach or trekking through an Asian rain forest while thinking about ways to boost diesel engine horsepower without increasing engine displacement.

Did I love him? I told myself I did. We got along well and had similar interests. We liked the same music, clothes, films, and food. And after all, he was older and more experienced. There was a lot he could teach me. Independent and ready to live life at full speed, Carl was a proverbial open book, and I never had to second-guess him. He had a no-bullshit, bottom-line approach to everything—including our relationship. If something was important, he told me about it. If it wasn't—and he was always quick to remind me that most of it wasn't—he didn't waste the words. Maybe Carl wasn't as romantic or affectionate a man as I'd hoped to find in a husband. But instead of flowers and candy, Carl brought something else into my life—self-confidence. He'd made me realize it was okay to accept the attention I'd always received from others.

In high school, I'd been nominated for homecoming queen. But I had a shy streak that sent a huge wave of relief through me when I lost to perky cheerleader Sharon Burgess, who we all knew would win anyway since she did such a nice job of taking care of the football team on those out-of-town games.

Truth was, I was much happier being out of the limelight. Accepting compliments about my appearance came with a lot of reluctance, and I'd never been comfortable being called 'pretty' or 'beautiful.' As far as I was concerned, the flirty comments were simply the boys hitting on me, hoping I would let them fondle my breasts or allow their hands to linger on my ass. And flattery from my girlfriends came with the territory, a social requirement of sisterhood, even though a few of them made it clear they wouldn't mind exploring the possibilities. Regardless of the source, I never let myself think I deserved more attention than any of the other girls.

My epiphany finally came during one of those late night conversations with Carl. After watching a rented movie and a half-hour of sex, I'd asked him about his past girlfriends, wanting to know who they were and what they'd looked like. He'd brushed the question aside, saying there hadn't been anyone significant before me.

That was worrisome.

Without having previous relationships with other women, how did he know I was the right one? He must have sensed my concern, as he reassured me he'd always wanted a golden-haired, green-eyed California surfer girl with tits that could throw their own shadow.

Discovering I was the realized fantasy of his youth gave me the courage to knock down the wall I'd hidden behind since I was thirteen. I gained a sense of how others saw me—a pretty blonde with a nice body that received a twice-weekly aerobic tune-up. More important, I learned that how others perceived me didn't have to influence the way I acted around them. I could be a bit shy, enjoy the quiet times, and choose my friends based on their personality and sincerity.

With his outspoken honesty and support, Carl had given me every indication he would be a loyal and faithful husband. Plus, his Navy training gave him the kind of education and experience that assured a successful career. Even with all that, I'd asked myself, *is it enough*?

Looking back, I suppose I'd hoped my love for Carl would blossom while we pursued the exciting future he'd laid out for us. In spite of my doubts, I knew one thing for sure. He was going on a great adventure . . . with or without me. And If I married him, we would travel to places I didn't even know existed. On the other hand, if I stayed behind, my choices weren't nearly as exciting—take a stab at college and tolerate four years of tedium or, worse, continue my entry level secretarial job while sharing my two-bedroom apartment with three other girls.

During the last six months of Carl's hitch in Little Creek, our endless emails and nightly phone calls helped to crystalize our future.

We set the date.

Seven days following his discharge, he flew to San Diego where we had a quick ceremony followed by a weeklong honeymoon driving up the northern California coast.

I was anxious to begin our new life of travel, but Carl insisted we work another year. 'We need to save at least twenty thousand dollars,' he'd said. 'Then we can take our time to explore, decide which part of the world we want to live in.' It wasn't just the journey that appealed to Carl. He wanted to experience other cultures, people, and lifestyles. And as I listened to him, I convinced myself it was what I wanted, too.

We left the States four months after my 21st birthday.

Sri Lanka had never been one of our top five destinations for an *extended sleepover*, as Carl called it. But by the time we arrived, we'd been traveling for eight months and we both needed a break.

Like anyone in our situation, I was a little nervous. Would the locals accept us? Would we be able to find a decent place to live? Carl countered my apprehension by reminding me of the pretty scenery, gentle people, and a fairly large ex-pat population. And he also saw a real opportunity to make some decent money as a boat mechanic.

The main port on the island was in the bustling city of Colombo, about a twenty-five-minute drive south of the village of Kandana, a sleepy residential area where we'd found a two-bedroom cottage on a large wooded lot. It was the last house on a dead-end road and offered the rare privacy of a much larger and more expensive property. The monthly rent was at the upper end of our budget, but we both agreed the cozy hideaway was a place we could call home—at least for a while. That had been nearly a year and a half ago, and in that time, I'd grown to love the place, with its covered front porch where I often sat for hours reading cheap romance novels as the warm rain dropped lightly on the coconut palms. I'd even started a garden by the side of the driveway—in spite of Carl's prediction the weeds would quickly overtake the flowers.

With Carl's work schedule—six days a week and often ten hours a day—I had a lot of time to myself. Carl had encouraged me to enjoy the freedom of exploring the countryside and its people. 'You'll have plenty of time to work later,' he'd said. 'And when the right job comes along, you'll know it.' He was referring to the low-paying and frequently available clerking and waitress jobs he adamantly discouraged me from taking, since they typically required shift work and would reduce the amount of time we could spend together.

The warm reception we'd expected to receive from the ex-pat population had been disappointing. While a few would wave or even speak politely when passing on the street, most kept to themselves. Like many displaced Americans, they had a common desire for seclusion and privacy, and went out of their way to maintain it. Even so, we'd managed to make a few friends, most of them native to Sri Lanka.

We still talked about continuing our adventure. But as the months passed, our passion to explore new destinations gave way to the comfort of home and the surprising security of routine. I also knew how much Carl enjoyed his work. He'd not only acquired the reputation of being an expert mechanic, he was also a bit of a "magician"—one of those rare technicians who could squeeze another thousand hours out of a thirty-year-old engine.

Personally, I felt *settled*. I enjoyed my weekly hikes into the rainforest, and driving to the south end of the island to spend the day at the beach. I especially liked Saturday mornings, when I drove to the Kālu Grill, the little café where I'd eaten my first meal in Sri Lanka—a roti pancake stuffed with eggs. I'd even shown the cook how to put yeast in the batter to make a traditional American pancake, adding pecans for flavor.

Now a regular customer, I ate there every weekend, looking forward to seeing the owner's old brown and white dog lying across the entrance, the trusting mutt hoping patrons would understand his silent request to step over him and not disturb his sleep.

The quick double-tapping of cards on the table brought my attention back to the game. It was Carl's turn to deal. He was showing off with two quick taps, one to the top of the deck, and another to the bottom. He said it brought the cards into alignment. In truth, it had nothing to do with straightening the deck. It was all swagger and fanfare, a display of his dexterity. I'd watched him practice the move for hours—a quick flip of the deck and a twist of his wrist. 'In the world of poker,' he'd said, 'confidence with the cards is just as important as skill.'

I'd never wondered how much truth there was in Carl's logic—until now.

"Anybody know what time it is? My watch stopped." One of the men at the table—he'd introduced himself as Roy—was thumping at the diver's chronograph on his wrist. He'd been the last one through the door and the first to take a seat. With long scruffy hair nearly touching his shoulders and a full beard covering his face, I couldn't begin to guess his age. His manner seemed unthreatening, and I didn't give him a second thought.

"For what you paid for that thing, it should have come with a Swiss watchmaker and a handful of batteries." It was Wiley, a small wiry fellow with protruding bottom teeth that kept his mouth from completely closing, the gap forcing me to look in another direction every time he'd taken a bite of the apple cobbler I'd offered the men as a snack. As sarcastic as they come, he never seemed to miss an opportunity to get in a jab at someone else's expense.

"Doesn't use batteries. It's a self-winder," Roy said proudly.

"That must be why it's keeping such perfect time." Wiley chuckled.

"It's two-thirty," Carl said. "Shank of the evening."

"Now that we've confirmed the time, you two think you could shut up long enough to play out the hand?" Victor's irritation was obvious. A brown-skinned man with a narrow nose and chiseled jaw, he seemed overly serious and a bit edgy, as if he were hiding something sinister. From the few times our eyes met, I was glad he kept his secrets to himself.

The older man—everyone called him Captain—sat through the entire exchange without blinking. Mid-fifties, too much over six foot to measure, and sporting a full head of gray hair fringed with coal-black tufts at the temples, his commanding presence made it clear he was in charge, and not the least bit interested in the men's petty squabbles.

Carl had invited the four men back to the house, where the game had gone on for hours. There had been too many hands to count, and so far, only small amounts of money had moved back and forth across the table. Carl had managed to stay about even.

That was his strategy. Take a little. Give it back. Then ramp it up. Never let them see it coming. Blindside them with skill and they'll invariably think it was luck—and want to play again.

I couldn't fault Carl's ability with a deck of cards. Regardless of whether it was a private game or a tournament, he regularly came out on top. And that's what made it so difficult to defend my argument against his desire to pursue gambling as a career. But Carl's obsession was tantamount to addiction—something I refused to live with. And although he adamantly denied it, I was convinced the lure of a full-time gambling gig could easily override his desire to travel and experience third world cultures. In fact, one night he'd talked about his fantasy of living in Vegas and working the tables, ultimately playing the high rollers to make that once-in-a-lifetime score. I'd gently reminded him we still had lots of world to see, and Vegas was a long way from Sri Lanka.

He'd quickly agreed, partly to placate me, and partly because it was true.

"I want to be clear of the harbor an hour after sunrise," the captain said. "So we best make this our last hand. I don't want to see your butts dragging on the deck when it's time to weigh anchor."

"Right you are, Cap'n." Wiley nodded, his allegiance to his master—at least on the surface—obvious and absolute. "Last hand it is."

"Let's raise the ante," Roy suggested. "Make it count." He looked directly at my husband, asking for agreement.

"Sure, no problem," Carl said.

Wiley and Roy glanced at the captain, as if he always had the final say. The captain's assenting nod lifted the previous twenty-dollar limit.

Like the rest of the men, Carl had been drinking. And it didn't take long before he had pitched every penny of last week's paycheck into the pot.

That's enough, I thought. *You need to stop*. But Carl was a rotten mind-reader.

The betting continued, the stakes increasing with every round. Finally, Carl was draining our savings. I had to speak up.

"Carl, can I see for you for a second?"

I felt awkward bringing it up. He had been the sole provider for over a year and had never complained. By rights, it was his money to do with as he chose. But he was in over his head, betting money he didn't have. That was stupid—and dangerous.

"Uh-oh," Wiley chided. "Looks like the missus is pulling back on the reins." He started to say more, but a quick glance from the captain stopped him cold.

"Not to worry, babe," Carl assured me. "Everything's under control."

"It's a lot of money," I said. "And I know how hard you have to work for it."

Carl smiled and gave me his trademark wink as he pushed the last of his chips into the middle of the table.

I knew he was good; he wouldn't be this confident if he didn't have an excellent hand. But I could also see his quiet anxiety. The money had pushed him over the edge, the lure of easy cash more important than the fun of playing. It was exactly why I had such an aversion to Carl's gambling. At some point, the game always seemed to evolve from harmless entertainment into a mythical siren of temptation, turning the players into ruthless competitors.

Another round of bets brought the ante back to Carl.

"What about a little credit?" From Carl's flippant tone, I knew he was trying to hide his frustration. He desperately wanted to stay in the game.

"Credit? You've got that good of a hand?"

Carl backpedaled. "Just want to keep the ball in play, keep things interesting."

The captain took a deep breath and frowned. "Don't know if you're good for it. And I don't want you turning me into a debt collector. If you can't play, you need to fold."

"I'm not asking for much," Carl argued. "How about if I offer some collateral?"

The captain scanned the room. "I don't see much here that can be sold for quick cash."

I could have interpreted his comment as an insult. But he was right. Our belongings were second-hand and well-used, most of them purchased from a local hotel after the owner replaced the property's aging furniture.

"What about the mantel clock?" Carl motioned to the bookcase displaying the timepiece. "It's over a hundred years old," he added. "And there's also my mother's silverware, place settings for eight."

I cringed. The clock was a cheap reproduction and the "silverware" was stainless steel.

"What'd'ya say, Captain?" Carl asked. "Can you give me a thousand on the clock and silverware?"

"No more than I would give you a thousand for an hour of your wife's time." He paused to look up and lock eyes with me. "Even as lovely as you are, my dear," he added. Then turning his attention back to Carl, he said, "Although I will say she comes far closer to a fair exchange of value than that clock or set of steak knives."

I told myself it was a compliment, even though his words were wrapped in innuendo.

Carl was quiet. Maybe he'd taken offense, though that seemed unlikely. We were both used to his Navy buddies and their flirtatious comments, even their tendency to be a bit "hands-y" with me during their hellos and goodbyes.

I knew he'd been counting the cards, extrapolating the odds. No doubt he was determining the probability of whether the remaining face cards were still in the deck or in the hands of the other men.

Finally he broke the silence. "What *would* you pay for an hour with my wife?"

I hoped I hadn't heard him right. "Carl, can I talk to you?"

He looked at me with his familiar sly grin, his way of asking for permission and forgiveness at the same time. "You'll play along, won't you babe?"

"That's enough, Carl," I cautioned. "Maybe it's time you fold and we call it a night."

I could tell from his expression he was ignoring me. Either I wasn't getting through or he'd turned pig-headed stubborn. I would give him a piece of my mind later.

Focusing on the captain, I tried another tactic. "I'm afraid my husband has forgotten his manners. It's probably best to finish the game and end the evening on a friendly note And of course, if you're ever back in Colombo, you're welcome to—"

"But wouldn't it be fun to find out?" Carl interrupted. "Just for kicks?"

Until now, the captain had projected his usual quiet, commanding demeanor, his attention focused squarely on the cards. "What are you talking about . . . exactly?"

"I'm saying," Carl began, laboring over each word, "we put a price on my wife's favors, for fun, you know, to see how it plays out. We can freeze the money right where it is."

Jesus, the man has completely lost his mind. I was more embarrassed than worried. No one was going to take him seriously. The money was the only thing of importance—the only thing that mattered—to those holding a decent hand. Putting anything into the pot that had no redeemable value was pointless.

"Please Carl," I pleaded, "let's move on so we can call it a night. It's late."

"It's just to put a little spice in the game," he argued. "And we'd only be pretending. It won't involve you at all."

And there it was—*the look.* I hadn't seen it since I'd dragged Carl from a casino on St. Maarten.

"I'm not going along with this," I shot back—directing my words not only at Carl, but to every man sitting at the table. "You need to drop it."

The captain chuckled, seemingly out of character for the man, and it made me wonder if he was laughing at me or the situation. "The

22

universal currency, eh?" He brought a hand to his chin. "That's a creative proposition, and while it would certainly make the game more interesting, it's obvious the little lady is not in agreement."

He was talking as if Carl's suggestion was made in good faith. I felt the muscles in my neck and shoulders tighten, a sudden attack of anxiety sending a stream of acid to my stomach.

"The captain is very perceptive," I said. "The lady is *definitely* not in agreement."

Carl bristled. "But it's our last hand and I'd really like to play this one out. Please, babe, go along with me so we can get back to playing."

I started to object, but Carl cut me off. "Besides, it's just a friendly game. No one's going to take advantage of the situation."

The captain scanned the table, then shifted his gaze to me, his steely eyes giving me the once-over. His scrutiny seemed more facetious than perverse.

Either way, he was waiting for an answer.

I could see Carl wasn't going to give up. And if he eventually took *no* for an answer, he'd be ticked off at me for a week.

I shook my head, the way a frustrated parent might display their irritation with a misbehaving child. "All right. But make it fast. I'm getting tired and our guests have an early sailing."

The captain drew a noisy breath. "The lady's right. Let's finish it."

There was a sudden buzz between the men, the air reeking of bravado and testosterone.

"First, we have to set a value on my wife's favors." Carl was unable to hide his excitement over striking some credit—even if it was only Monopoly money. "We have to get specific," he added. "You know, how much for what."

The idea of putting a price on my body—even in jest—was as degrading as it was unsettling. I glared at Carl. More than irritated, I was ready to explode. But it was too late. And I refused to be one of "those" wives—the kind that agreed to go along with their husband's wishes, but made it clear they were plenty pissed about it . . . in other words, a bitch.

Besides, I was probably over-reacting. There had been flirtatious banter all evening, and this was nothing more than a suggestive joke—albeit a bad one. Soon the game would be over, the men would leave, and I could get some sleep.

I went back to the kitchen, wiped down the counters, and began putting away the dessert plates. The men's conversation faded into the background.

". . . and the value of the pot, it stays or floats?" I overhead the captain asking Carl a question, talking in a lowered voice.

Carl mumbled, too soft for me to hear.

"You're sure? No changing your mind later."

I heard Carl again, a word here and there, with gaps of silence between—too much silence to understand what he was saying.

Poking my head around the corner, I saw him nodding.

What the hell is he doing now?

"Can I get you anything?" I walked into the living room, hoping my return didn't seem like the obvious ploy it was.

Carl shook his head, the cryptic exchange between him and the captain having come to a suspicious and immediate halt.

Although my husband remained quiet, the captain reacted automatically. "No thank you," he said. "We have everything we need."

He wasn't just placating me, the man was glossing over the awkward hush. I had the sense I'd caught him mid-sneak, before he had put everything back in place—before he could close the lid on his own personal Pandora's Box. And yet, even with the possibility I had seen a flash from the darker side of his character, he seemed consummately satisfied with the situation.

I wanted him out of my house—the sooner the better.

"Carl, don't forget. You promised you'd wrap it up, so no extra hands."

He hadn't actually promised, but I wanted him to think I'd interpreted it that way. And I planned to hold him to it.

I could tell my proximity to the table—standing next to Carl—was slowing the game. "I'll sit over here," I said, "by the breakfast bar."

There was no way I was returning to the kitchen, out of earshot.

Carl scribbled an IOU and pitched it into the pot.

The captain picked it up and shook his head. "That's way above the going rate. A hundred bucks for a hand-job? And you want twice that for a blow-job? I can get either one of those in town at half the price."

Carl bristled. "She's worth every penny of it and you know it."

The captain's lips narrowed into a frown. Rolling the IOU between his fingers, he seemed to be in deep deliberation. Finally, he pitched the scrap of paper back on the table. "Let's play."

"I'll raise," Wiley said.

Carl set his cards face down on the table to write another IOU.

I didn't know whether to be amused or concerned as the bets continued to escalate. More than once I thought of interrupting them, to reconfirm their bets were imaginary, without the remotest possibility of being redeemed. Yet I knew their earnest wagering was the very thing giving the game its edge—a reason to continue. I also knew part of their fun was watching my reaction, seeing me squirm over the prospect of paying off my husband's gambling debt with sexual favors.

Noticing another beer bottle had been added to the inventory of empties, I slipped off my chair, intending to gather them. A challenging glare from the captain stopped me cold. I tried to soften his dismissal with the suggestion of coffee, but my offer was immediately refused with a hand gesture—curtly directed and delivered with a scowl.

Five minutes passed. Another round of bets.

More IOU's.

Eventually, Carl was forced to convert the value of individual sex acts into full days of sexual servitude. A few rounds later, even that wasn't enough to stay in the game. Again, Carl and the captain renegotiated my value, calling it "full-service companionship," joking about how housework and laundry should be included in the week-long intervals of time.

As they bantered back and forth, the breaking grins and little smirks helped dispel my concerns. Secretly, I wanted to confront them, to make sure everyone still understood the idea of using my body as sexual currency was just man-whimsy, a virtual wet dream that would end when the last bet was made. But my interruption would be a full scale attack on Carl's masculinity. Especially now, since the game had taken on a life of its own—men playing in a man's world—something the "weaker sex" could never fully appreciate.

So I did what I thought Carl would want me to do—continue to watch, offer the occasional feigned smile, and attempt to convey my amusement over their game of pretend.

Eventually, the three crewmen folded, leaving Carl and the captain to play out the hand. There was a haunting sense about those three men and, for a moment, I wondered if they had retired from play as a collective strategy, motivated by some secret and pre-established signal.

I told myself I was being paranoid. If there was any collusion among them, it was more likely to reduce the game to its principle players, since the crew's money surely came from their employment and their contributions to the pot were simply extensions of credit from the captain.

I looked at the pile of chips and hand-scribbled scraps of paper in the pot, trying to estimate the value. It was close to twenty-five grand—with nearly a third of it from Carl.

The captain had also gone to IOU's written against an established credit line at the marine supply.

But why?

Neither man could possibly expect to collect.

I couldn't let it go.

"The captain is using IOU's?"

"More realistic that way," Carl said.

They were like little boys playing cops and robbers. I supposed from their perspective, it made sense. Carl's Navy buddies had often talked about the realism of the new computer flight simulators and how it gave the experience an extra kick, as if the mind had been tricked into believing the activity was real.

It was nearly four in the morning. I had to get some sleep.

"Carl?" I waited until I had his attention.

"Yeah babe, almost done here."

"It's late," I said. "You need to call this one a draw and let the men get back to their boat."

"On a roll here, sweetheart." His tone was dismissive and dripping with irritation.

I was about to push back. I decided to leave it alone, give him some slack. But soon I would insist he shut it down or I was going to bed without him.

Ten minutes later, I lowered my magazine with lots of rustling. I was done. "So how we doing, Carl?"

Their collective IOU's had bumped the pot to over forty-five thousand dollars, and from what I remembered about the last agreement over the rate of exchange, Carl's last raise had extended my "body-use collateral" to over three months of exclusive possession.

They're ending the night on a high note. Having some fun at my expense.

Carl nodded slightly, acknowledging my question, but not answering it.

The captain, however, was more than aware of my building irritation. He tapped his cards on the table. "Your wife has been more than patient." He looked around the table, then directly at Carl. "I call. Let's see what you've got."

Finally.

I looked around the living room. I'd straighten up the mess in the morning.

I glanced back at Carl, expecting to see his usual unrestrained gloating after setting his cards on the table. I planned on speeding the process along, reducing his savoring of victory to a minimum. I'd given him what he'd asked for—time to finish. Now I wanted him to focus on *my* needs, which were centered on the queen-size Beautyrest calling to me from the bedroom.

It took a moment to register—Carl wasn't gloating. In fact, he hadn't even shown his cards.

He was . . . *hesitating*.

Carl never hesitated. Unless he was bluffing.

"Let's see 'em," the captain repeated.

Carl's gray eyes were half-shuttered, the color dull and lifeless. A thin strand of brown hair fell across his forehead as the corners of his mouth began to twitch. With trembling fingers, he collapsed his hand on the table.

He was one card shy of a straight flush.

The captain leaned forward, never breaking his deadpan expression. "You kept playing with an empty hand?"

I didn't know if he was complimenting my husband or calling him stupid.

The captain slowly laid his cards on the table.

Three queens.

Carl dropped his head.

For a moment, the captain sat there, as if waiting for acknowledgement of the win. But Carl remained silent. The captain's authority was apparent and unchallenged, not only over his men, but now over my husband as well.

During the game, the captain had paid little attention to me. Now he looked at me as if evaluating a piece of merchandise, making sure it wasn't torn or frayed at the edges. "Do you have anything you want to take with you, clothes, shoes, that sort of thing?" His voice was dry and matter-of-fact, without a hint of play.

"What are you talking about?"

The game had been a joke. They all knew Carl's IOU's were nothing more than a ploy to keep playing. No one in their right mind would actually think they could win a twenty-three-year-old girl in a poker game.

The rest of the men turned toward me—I assumed to watch my reaction, to make sure they didn't miss the gag.

Except for Carl.

His face was white, his eyes locked on the table.

"I'm really tired," I began. "It's been a long day, so I'll say goodnight and my husband can show you out." I began nervously gathering up empty beer bottles and butt-filled ashtrays.

I wanted these men—especially the captain—out of my house.

"We're leaving," the captain growled. "I've give you two minutes to get whatever you want to take with you."

I felt my stomach tighten, my throat go dry. "Look, you've had your fun, and I didn't mind going along with the joke. But the game's over. It's time to call it a night."

The captain lowered his head slightly, his eyes burning right through me. It wasn't the reaction I was expecting. Judging from the sudden flush on his face, I had challenged his authority and he didn't like it. If there had been any part of him conveying the slightest bit of weakness, I would have scolded him for acting like a ten-year-old. But his skin was tanned and leather-tough from endless days on a sun-scorched ocean, and even though he was at least twenty years older than Carl, his arms were as big as my thighs and just as solid with muscle.

He was intimidating as hell.

Every instinct told me the same thing . . . *run.*

The thought of bolting through the back door and disappearing into the darkness lasted a micro-second.

They want me to run, I reasoned. *So they can laugh at me and make fun of the scared little girl.*

Fuck 'em.

I threw Carl my *I've had enough of this shit* look and raised my voice. "I'm going to bed. Leave everything the way it is. I'll clean up in the morning."

The sound of scraping chairs filled the room as the three crewmen rose from the table. I held my breath, waiting for one of them to break out laughing and say something that would untie the knot in my stomach.

"Good night, all," I chimed as I turned toward the hallway leading to the bedroom.

The captain rose from his chair and with a few quick strides, stepped in behind me. "I'm not going to ask again," he said, placing his huge hand on my shoulder.

An eerie chill seized the air in my chest. If this was still a joke, it had gone too far. I really didn't know him, and I didn't want his hands on me. I tried to brush him away, taking another step forward.

I didn't get far. Sinking his vice-grip deep into my shoulder, he spun me around and yanked me to within inches of his face. "That's the last time you'll ignore me," he barked.

I stared at Carl in disbelief. "Do something. Tell him it's a mistake."

Carl glanced up, then dropped his eyes back to the table, his face grimacing as he bit his lower lip.

"Carl, what the fuck? Tell this asshole to let go of me."

The captain tightened his hold, pinching my skin. "You got a real fast tongue in your head, don't ya, bitch."

I twisted back and forth, recoiling against the pain, trying to break free. "Stop it, you're hurting me!"

I was no match for a man the captain's size. I was in good shape, but at five-foot-three, my weight rarely exceeded a hundred and ten pounds. My efforts to defend myself were nothing more than a token display.

"Carl, help me!"

I kept waiting for him to pull the guy off and, if necessary, grab the .38 caliber revolver hidden behind our wedding picture on top of the bookcase. But in spite of my continued pleading, Carl remained frozen in his chair, mute and paralyzed, a look of sick acceptance contorting his face. Later, I would remember his expression hurting me more than the monster pinning my arms behind my back.

The memory of the captain dragging me from the house is still a hysterical blur of disbelief and savage fear. Once I nearly broke free, surprising him with a backward jab of my heel to his knee. But as I lunged toward Carl—believing his protective instincts would kick in—the big man grabbed me around the waist and lifted me off the floor, his powerful arm crushing me to the point of restricting my breathing.

With no resistance from Carl, the captain carried me through the front door. As we crossed the threshold, I caught the doorjamb and held on, still desperately believing this was some kind of sick charade and after the men had their fun, it would end. But the expression on the three crewmen's faces—their wicked smiles, nodding their heads in approval as the bastard slid his arm between my legs for extra leverage—told me otherwise.

"You can't do this," I screamed. "The bets weren't real!"

"You couldn't be that stupid," the captain shot back. "Why would we continue to play if we couldn't collect on your husband's markers? He knew the bets were genuine. It was the only reason we let him stay in the game."

36

I struggled to believe it—this Neanderthal actually thought I was his property.

And judging from the lack of challenge from Carl, my husband believed it, too.

Losing my grip on the doorframe ended my connection with my home—the place I'd thought was a safe refuge.

As the captain carried me across the yard, I continued screaming for Carl.

Only the crew followed. Like a pack of wolves driven by the promise of shared prey, they trailed closely behind, just out of reach of my flailing arms.

The truth—my husband having lied to me—was heartbreaking. But it couldn't compete with the sheer terror of realizing these men were about to carry me off into the night.

Any hope I had that the captain's behavior was a prank carried much too far, quickly surrendered to the tormenting ache in my groin. With his hand firmly planted in my crotch, he was squeezing—hard.

"Go on, Cap'n, show her whose boss."

"Take charge of that bitch."

The men were goading him on, wanting a show.

I shouted at Carl one last time. "For God's sake, get the gun!" I hoped the threat of my husband charging out of the house wielding a pistol would be enough to scare them off and make them realize he was only seconds away from dropping all four of them.

But Carl never stepped beyond the front door. Either too ashamed or embarrassed to show his face, he had gambled away his wife, and with it, his honor as a man.

Refusing to surrender, I pounded on the captain's back, clawing at his shirt, trading broken nails for the satisfaction of seeing small blots of blood spot the fabric. For a moment, I thought it was working—he loosened his grip. But he was only pausing to brace himself, firming up his stance to throw me into the back of our panel truck—now his, collected as part of the winnings.

The irony was fleeting but strong. Not only had Carl sold me to strangers, he'd supplied them with a vehicle to make the transfer of ownership more convenient.

I landed against the spare tire, the jolt of pain a convincing argument to the erroneous notion of soft rubber. Roy and Wiley were immediately on top of me, holding me down, slapping handcuffs on my wrists.

Screaming, kicking at anything within reach, I continued to fight back, hoping to catch the attention of someone passing by—someone who might call the police. But the privacy that both Carl and I cherished also came with seclusion. There was no one to hear—or see—my struggle.

"Victor, shut her up!" The captain was sliding behind the steering wheel.

Victor had been the silent one. I had intentionally avoided engaging him, his unflinching stare setting me on edge. Now he was crouching over my head, clamping my face between his knees. "This will quiet you down," he snarled, dangling a large rubber gag-ball in front of my eyes.

Even in my state of terrified panic, I understood—Victor was the captain's henchman, the one who did the dirty work. Not only did he obey orders without question, he was also well-suited to the task. His emerging wicked smile and clouded eyes smoldering with anticipation made it clear—he enjoyed his job.

I struggled to turn my head, to get away from the gag-ball pressing against my clenched teeth. But Victor kept up the pressure, the building strain on the back of my skull so excruciating, I was struck with the grisly possibility of snapping my own neck.

Determined to pry my mouth open, he pinched my upper lip and twisted the skin into a knot, his show of teeth a convincing argument he would tear my flesh if I didn't cooperate. My eyes wide with fear, I saw the thrill—the satisfaction—in his grotesque sneer as he used both thumbs to press the hard rubber ball deep into my throat.

I never realized how effective the threat of slow suffocation could be—forcing my lungs to wait, wavering on the edge of passing out—intensified by the horror of knowing I could die here and now.

Even as I struggled to suck air through my mucus-clogged nose, I nodded at Victor, letting him know I would cooperate. I was not willing to jeopardize my life over the threat of an unknown future.

He ignored my promise of submission, taking pleasure in watching me labor over each tortured breath. Only when he was sure my convulsions were real and I was on the verge of passing out did he lessen the pressure on the gag, allowing me to inhale a few times before retightening the strap.

It struck me with frightening clarity—the men's brash and controlling arrogance, the ease with which they produced and applied a set of handcuffs, their aloof detachment from another's suffering—*they had done this before*. Their collective attitudes and behaviors were the villainous traits of criminals, thugs, and outlaws. They had learned by repetition, with each new experience adding to an insulating veneer of indifference.

Despite my growing fear of what they planned to do with me, I began taking a mental inventory of what I'd last seen in the back of the truck—a few tools, some emergency flashers, and a small air compressor. Nothing with the deadly potential of a knife or a gun.

I remembered the advice our senior class had received during a safety presentation. The best time to flee from a kidnapper is during the initial encounter. Always fight. Always run. While I hadn't been able to avoid capture, I might still have a chance. I had to brainstorm, think of a way to escape.

The harbor was twenty-five minutes from our house. They wouldn't need to stop for gas. Carl always kept the tank full.

My chances would improve once we reached the marina. Even though sunrise was an hour away, the dock would be busy with locals loading their boats and heading out for a day of fishing. Certainly, a girl who was gagged, handcuffed, and being hauled across the docks would be noticed by someone. With any luck at all, a Good Samaritan would call the police.

Most of the locals—the ones sincerely wanting to help—would know better than to describe me as a blonde, white-complexioned American. Expatriates living in Sri Lanka rarely received much more than a token response from the authorities, and even less protection. The local law thought of us as outsiders, undeserving of their time and resources.

"You live here at your own risk," one of the immigration officials had told us, making no effort to conceal it.

But what could go wrong? I remembered thinking that.

Never in my darkest nightmare could I have imagined my husband betting—and losing—me in a poker game. Sure, I knew Carl could be a sucker for the promise of easy money. The temptation of striking a big win was so intoxicating to him that I'd often wondered if he'd been better off with a two pack-a-day habit or predisposed to Saturday night benders with a bottle of Jack Daniels.

Now I knew. And this time, his obsession had blinded him to the consequences of his actions. He had stamped a price on my head and thrown me on the table.

I decided right then and there—if I ever got out of this mess, I would track him down and tell him what a sniveling excuse of a man he was. And then I would cut him out of my life forever.

Wiley, the disgusting troll with buckteeth, leaned in close. He'd stared with rapt attention while Victor shoved the gag-ball down my throat, and for the last few minutes seemed fascinated with Victor's sadistic need to pinch my nose shut and hold it until I began to jerk and tremble in spastic suffocation.

"Hey, little girl, I'm going to put these in your mouth. You need to swallow them. If you try to spit 'em out, I'll hurt you. Understand?"

Bringing his face within inches of mine, Wiley waved his dirty, grease-stained fingers in front of my eyes, showing me the two tiny pills. Knowing the rubber ball would keep me from biting, he slipped his index finger into my mouth and held my tongue to one side, his bulging, blood-shot eyes confirming his own perverse brand of excitement. Ignoring my smothered whimpers, he continued to stretch the opening, in no hurry to get the pills down my throat. Unable to contain the building pool of saliva within his gaping mouth, a thick string of drool breached his lips, connecting his face to mine, his mucus-laced spit adding to the revolting taste and feel of his grimy digit.

I started to retch.

NO!

I had to control my convulsing stomach. Throwing up could aspirate the puke into my lungs—I could suffocate and die.

"Hold your breath," he said. "I don't want you coughing these up." He dropped both pills—Halcion—into the back of my mouth, watching me until he was sure I'd swallowed them.

He had just eliminated any chance of escape. In a few minutes, the opportunity to attract attention from those at the dock would be lost to the effects of the powerful tranquilizer.

Chapter Two

Pain. Water. Darkness.

Of the three, the darkness should have been the least of my enemies. Unlike my childhood friends, I'd never feared the night or the unspeakable monsters that it supposedly contained. To me, the summer's advancing twilight was a warm invitation to swim in the backyard pool. In the winter, it became a cool reminder of how good it felt to pull up a blanket just before inviting the dreams of a new adventure into my bed.

But this was not the welcome and comforting friend from my youth. This heavy cloak was an ominous death shroud. And rolling it back would reveal what they'd done to me—the gruesome details of taut rope and chain, of swollen joints and bruised muscle, and the trailing streaks of blood seeping from the forced marriage of steel shackles and weeping skin.

The Halcion had held the worst of it at bay, but with most of the narcotic leached from my system, there was nothing left to keep me from being fully aware of my captor's cruelty.

I quickly learned that crying was not an option. The draw of irregular breaths brought increased tension—and punishment—from the restraints. Sobbing in self-pity was a luxury I couldn't afford.

My final release from the mind-numbing narcotic brought all the cruel and heartless details rushing back—my violent abduction, the captain throwing me into the back of the van, my screams for Carl going unanswered.

Recalling the torturous ride to the docks required a boost of willpower and self-restraint—holding back what would otherwise be a steady stream of tears as I relived the anguish of the gag-ball, the cruel suffocation and, finally, Wiley sliding the Halcion down my throat, his thick rope of slobber spilling onto my face as he hovered above me.

The rest of the story wasn't hard to put together.

Drugged and unconscious, they had carried me aboard their ship, where they bound and stretched me out like of piece of hide.

I was sure they could hear me, because I could hear them. Occasionally I picked up a fleeting word or two, sometimes half a sentence.

More than once I thought of calling out, asking for release from the restraints. Yet a single thought frightened me even more than the pull of the shackles . . . once they realized I was conscious, what would they do to me?

Irrationally believing my silence would delay the inevitable—when I would have to face the worst of what was in store for me—I remained quiet. But ultimately, my resolve was no match for my tortured wrists and ankles.

Reluctantly, I cried out. "Is anyone there? Can someone untie me? How long are you going to leave me like this?"

My own empty pleas echoed in return.

The answer was as obvious as it was terrifying. They would release me when they were done reveling in my torment. My treatment was intentional, and the bastards meant to enjoy every minute of it.

A quick stab of pain shot up my right leg and lodged in my hip. I drew a breath, fighting the urge to howl.

Struggling to contain it, I let it escape as a barely audible whimper.

Depriving my captors of the pleasure they would receive from hearing my screams was, admittedly, a small triumph. But for the first time since regaining consciousness, I'd found a way to take back some control.

My victory was short-lived.

Ear-splitting throbs from the engine filled the air, penetrating my brain. While the deafening racket was irritating as hell, the thudding pulses also traveled through the rope, attacking my raw nerves with needling torment.

Twisting my head, I submerged one of my ears, assuming the surrounding water would block some of the noise.

I should have known better. While snorkeling, I'd often heard the chop of propellers long before the air-carried roar of the engine. This was no different. The liquid amplified the sound, battering my skull from the inside.

I heard a shriek from beyond the din and clatter, from outside the darkness. It came to me slowly, layered in chaos and confusion. The voice was my own.

It was a gut reaction, a primal response. I had reached the limit of my endurance. The tension of the rope, the chill of the water, the unbearable noise and vibration—all of it pushing me over the edge. I wondered if these were my final moments of sanity, before reason and judgment surrendered to sheer agony.

Thankfully, I never had to find out.

The grating hammer of the engine ended as abruptly as it began. Perhaps the captain was expediting a course correction or a short run of the diesel had been necessary to offset the diminishing wind. In any case, it was a safe assumption the additional battering of my senses was not intentional. I had to believe these men would not expose me to a level of discomfort beyond what I could physically and emotionally withstand.

Otherwise I was finished.

The short but intense ordeal made me realize how exhausting—excruciating—it was to lay motionless in this water-filled pit.

I wanted out. I had to get someone's attention, and I needed to do it now.

I began to speak. Not to anyone in particular, just to make some noise. If I could keep it up, they might grow tired of listening to my monotonous banter and free me.

I briefly considered the alternative. My captors could easily subject me to something far worse than the icy sting of the water and pull of the rope. I pushed the thought from my mind. Admittedly, my plan was a gamble, yet not as much a calculated risk as a choice between taking action or remaining a victim.

Beginning with my first recollections of childhood, I rambled on about my parents and how they had moved to a new city when I was seven, putting me through the ordeal of changing schools in the middle of second grade. Pausing only to stifle a moan, I described each juvenile memory with as much detail as I could remember.

I was ranting about my junior year of high school and the heartbreak of discovering how my boyfriend had cheated on me, when I first heard it—another voice, separate and apart from my own. It was like recognizing a radio or TV playing in the background. How long it had been there, I wasn't sure. And unlike the earlier fragments of quickly fading conversation, this voice was getting closer, increasing in volume, disclosing the subtleties of inflection and accent.

I stopped talking, wanting to hear more.

It didn't take long to recognize something unusual about the man's dialogue. After a few seconds, I realized his discussion was completely one-sided. He was talking to himself. And he didn't sound happy.

"Blasted bitch . . . going to be another pain in the ass, just like the last one."

My nonstop monologue had produced the response I wanted. But I wasn't sure if this man would release me or was here to punish me for irritating the crew.

The solid snap of a hatch lock and the hollow metallic draw of a deadbolt set my heart pounding.

He's coming in.

The piercing squeak of hinges preceded an abrupt flood of light. Like the sunrise reclaiming the interior of a coffin, the intense rays burned away the darkness, extinguishing every shadow. Except in this case, the occupant was still alive.

"You ready to shut up and behave?" It came from above, a disembodied voice hovering above me.

Squinting against the harsh glare, I could see the backlit outline of a man standing on an elevated landing. Although impossible to see him clearly, his burly shape suggested something less than human.

"You'd better answer me, and I mean *right now*, otherwise you can stay down there 'til we reach port." He was growing impatient. "And that's three days from now. I imagine you'll get plenty hungry before then."

Food! That's why he was here. He had to feed me, keep me healthy.

"Yeah, I hear you," I said.

"And?" he bellowed.

"And what?" I had no idea what he expected me to say.

"You gonna behave?"

I answered quickly. "Yes, I'll behave. I promise."

Hurry up, these ropes are killing me. It was all I could do to keep it inside.

He swaggered down the stairs. He looked to be late fifties, maybe early sixties. Wearing a faded blue work shirt and a pair of old jeans, his grizzly, red face was pock-marked and deeply lined.

He scanned me from head to toe, then bent down on one knee and produced a set of keys from his pocket. The unforgiving light left nothing obscured, and beneath his scraggly gray beard I could see a collection of scars confirming a defiant disposition and quick temper. I didn't recognize him as one of the men who had kidnapped me.

"Don't even think about giving me any trouble. You so much as look at me cross-ways and you'll spend the rest of the trip right where you are."

"I'll do whatever you say. I just want out of here."

The release of the lock at my feet provided immediate relief from the tormenting strain on my joints. I brought my legs up, testing them. My ankles were numb, the tattle-tale clinking of

52

chain confirming the leg restraints were still attached.

As he fumbled with the upper rope, a few long strands of dirty gray hair fell over his eyes. He carefully brushed them over his balding head, then untied the knot, releasing my arms. "Looks like you stayed wet most of the night."

I looked at him expectantly, holding up my handcuffed wrists.

"The cuffs stay on."

"What about my feet?"

"The shackles stay too."

I could understand his reluctance to remove the handcuffs, but the leg shackles were connected to a piece of trailing chain a good ten feet long. The thought of subjecting my sore ankles to more abuse was too much. "Why? I'm on a boat. Where am I going to go?"

He exploded. "This isn't some fucking negotiation. You give me any more shit and you'll spend the next three days in this pit. You got it?"

I nodded.

It wasn't enough.

"Say it," he growled. "I want to hear it."

"I got it. I got it."

He extended his free hand. "Grab on," he ordered.

The thought of touching him was repulsive. But without full circulation in my limbs, I doubted I could make it to my feet by myself. Fumbling for a grip, I skimmed over the thick tuffs of white, scrub-brush hair covering his forearm until I found his hand.

Even with my reduced sensation, I could feel the deformity. Whether damaged by accident or a genetic deformity, his palm felt like a thick plate of bone punctuated with gnarled stubs in place of fingers.

My wrenched shoulders hurt nearly as much as my swollen and bruised ankles. But at least I was out of the water.

I had spent the night in what appeared to be a recessed metal basin. About five feet wide and seven feet long, it was no more than four inches deep. At one time, it might have been an anchoring base for a large piece of equipment, perhaps a commercial refrigerator or freezer. Now it functioned as a natural reservoir, collecting excess water from leaking pipes and topside overflow.

"Where is this boat going?" I asked. "How long have we been at sea?"

He shook his head, talking to himself. "It's always the same, starting right up with questions." Then looking at me, he added,

"When it's time, you'll be told what you need to know. Right now, you need to shut the fuck up."

I felt myself breaking down, the tears beginning to flow. I brought my cuffed hands to my face, pretending to massage my temples, draining my eyes before they could overflow down my cheeks. I didn't want him thinking I was fragile or weak-willed.

The aging troglodyte picked up the loose chain trailing from my leg manacles and began coiling it around his arm. "Number one rule. You fuck with me and I'll yank your ass to the ground. Understand?"

I cleared my throat and answered quickly. "I won't give you any trouble." I reached out to steady myself against a nearby stanchion. "What do I call you?"

Bastard. Asshole. Cocksucker. They all came to mind.

"The crew calls me Butch."

"That doesn't sound like a real name."

He ignored me.

Motioning toward an opening in the bulkhead, he rattle-snapped the chain against the deck. "You first," he barked. "I'll be right behind you."

I was naked, wet, and cold. But if I hesitated, even to ask for a towel or blanket, it might give him the excuse he needed to slam me to the deck. I shuffled ahead, scanning the labels on a few of the crates, searching for details that might reveal more about our destination.

Butch realized what I was doing.

"Keep moving." It was more a threat than instruction. He jerked the chain again, making his point.

Passing into the next section, I hesitated. The only light in the room came from a dozen equipment dials and gauges, their dull illumination revealing the shadowed outline of what appeared to be some kind of heavy machinery.

"I can't see where I'm going. I could bump into something."

Butch reached through the opening and swept the wall with his hand. The click of a switch awakened a single fluorescent fixture, its twin tubes winking on and off before finally settling down to a dingy yellow.

We were in the engine room. From the simplicity of the equipment and open layout, I knew this wasn't a commercial vessel. But it wasn't a day-tripper, either. Based on the size of the engine and the internal beam of the boat, I guessed its length at two hundred feet, maybe more.

The construction was typical of an older ship, with obvious scars from several major overhauls and retro-fitting. Aging wood beams had been replaced with steel channel and support brackets, confirmed by the residual outlines of previously extracted timbers. Even the wooden hull was reinforced with steel spanner bracing, permitting the unforgiving marine diesel—much heavier and far more powerful than the original power plant—to push the boat beyond the limit of its design specifications.

The ship's electrical power came from two open-mounted auxiliary generators sitting on opposite sides of the penetrating mast. These were also upgrades to the boat's equipment, the added runs of open Romex wiring stapled to overhead beams and deck supports.

I flinched as my bare feet scraped across the raised heads of sheet metal screws used to secure steel plates over the original plank decking. The work had been done fast and cheap, the inexpensive fasteners a poor substitute for recessed marine hardware.

I was thankful the engine wasn't running. While it would have provided some heat, the few minutes I'd been pummeled by its noise and vibration had been unbearable, and the likelihood of it being restarted made me want to leave the area for a less threatening space.

With drops of water clinging to my skin, I began to shiver. I had to risk it. "What about some clothes or a blanket?"

Butch didn't answer. I took a deep breath and turned around. He was giving me the once over, making no attempt to disguise his blatant manner.

Then it hit me. Since regaining consciousness, I'd been struggling against the rope and chain that held me captive. Now I was facing a new threat.

I glared back at him, not out of challenge, but to be able to identify him later, along with the other members of the crew when I filed charges against them.

"Did you hear me? I need a blanket," I repeated. "I'm cold." My impulsive boldness surprised me, and I immediately regretted it.

"That's right," Butch snarled. "It's cold down here. Not warm like it is topside." The corners of his mouth turned upward in a haughty grin. He was enjoying this, keeping me miserable—exerting his control over me.

"Where are we headed, the destination I mean?" I ignored his warning about asking questions.

"Right here. This is as far as you go."

"No, I mean this boat. Where is it going?"

"Where you'll bring the most money."

"What does that mean? You can't just put me to work. I'm not a whore."

"Not yet," he said with a sly grin. "There's no telling how you'll wind up. But it don't matter who buys you, you'll be a prize alright, whether they turn you out or keep you for their own."

"Buys me? Who says I'm for sale?"

"The captain. That is, after he gets you all nice and pretty, teaches you a few things to make you more valuable."

I let it sink in. My understanding of Carl's negotiations with the captain was painfully simple—my husband's wager would be paid in sexual servitude. It had nothing to do with selling me.

"What gives him the right to do that?"

Butch rattled the chain. "What did I tell you about asking questions?"

The threat was clear.

I changed the subject. "You said something about food."

"Yeah, you need to be fed. Let me show you what's on the menu." Butch unzipped his pants and pulled out his cock. "Get on your knees."

I ached to shut it out, to convince myself none of it was real. The stinging bite of my splintered fingernails penetrating the quick of my palm told me otherwise.

I wanted to yell for help, to let others know what this son-of-bitch wanted me to do. But believing there was someone onboard masquerading as my rescuer was a naive delusion. My chances of finding a protector were about as slim as Carl winning that fateful hand of poker.

Butch was acting on the opportunity afforded to all jailors—to abuse and mistreat a prisoner for his own selfish pleasure. Maybe he had the consent of the captain, acting on orders steeped in privilege—a reward for loyal and faithful service.

He began coiling the chain around his arm, taking up the slack. I could either hobble toward him or he would drag me closer. I felt like a fish being reeled into the net.

I'd been stretched out naked in freezing water, my limbs shackled and stressed to the point of agony. Yet none of that mattered—at least not to this man. In spite of what I'd already been through, he was demanding I take his dick into my mouth. And while I hated him for it, his grasp of reality was undeniable: He wanted it. He controlled me. I would have to obey.

I wasn't comfortable with the notion of having sex with near-strangers. Before marrying Carl, I'd had plenty of one-night stands, usually to put an end to a forgettable date. Back then, it often came down to a choice between sex or a lengthy explanation of why I would rather go home alone. Agreeing to have sex was generally easier. Even so, I believed I was exercising a choice—and the choice was mine.

This was different.

I made a decision. If I was going to survive another day, I had to separate from my surroundings, not let my feelings affect me one way or the other. Maybe that was the key—to feel nothing. I held onto the idea as if I were learning a new culture, one in which I was expected to respond as a native. And yet of all the times I would service men in the future, of all the disgusting acts I would perform in front of a faceless crowd, this was the one I would remember—and despise—the most.

"If I feel as much as a nip of your teeth, I'll hang you up by this chain 'til morning. Understand?"

I nodded slowly, realizing my assurance to handle his cock with caution was also conveying my agreement to service him without argument. I dropped to my knees, feeling the bite of cold steel against my shins.

He brought his half-erection to full size with a few strokes. He was uncircumcised, with steely sprigs of pubic hair covering the base of his shaft and sac. The acrid odor of trapped sweat nearly made me gag.

I closed my eyes. It would become my way of getting through the next few days—not seeing, doing it all by touch. Blocking it out made it less real, as if a benevolent stranger were inside me, taking my hands and placing them where they needed to go, whispering in my ear to coax me through the difficult parts.

He pressed his dick against my lips. "Time to earn your keep."

I opened my mouth, letting him slide his cock inside.

"Suck it good, honey. Let me know you care."

I squeezed my eyes tighter, trying to shut it out.

How long is this going to take?

With Carl, prolonging the moment was the goal, wanting him to enjoy it as much as I did, keeping him on edge until he couldn't hold back any longer.

This situation couldn't compare. I wanted *this* repulsive nightmare over with as soon as possible.

Raising my bound hands, I found his balls and cupped them. Even though restricted by the cuffs, I managed to keep one hand clenched around his testicles while bringing the fingers of my other hand to the base of his shaft. I quickly established a rhythm.

Let it go, you bastard. Quit holding back.

I hated the thought of taking his load down my throat, but I was sure it was what he expected. Staying focused on speed and pressure, I tried to think of myself as a clinical practitioner performing a procedure. I felt nothing—no humiliation, no self-pity. I was executing a series of synchronized movements, intended to produce a result.

His torso stiffened.

"Yeah, that's it," he said. "Mmmmm yeah, just like that."

The sudden swell of his shaft was followed by a spurt of cum against the back of my throat. His hot liquid streamed into my mouth.

In moments, it was over.

"Not bad, cupcake. You took it right down." Butch swiped his still-hard penis against the side of my face, leaving a sticky string of cum on my cheek. "You're gonna do fine."

I'd swallowed quickly to diminish the residual taste of his rancid cock. I'd done it for me, not him, regardless of what he thought.

"You know, if you keep this up," Butch added, "you might be allowed topside." He tugged at his zipper, finally using both hands to secure it.

I dabbed at my mouth with my forearm. "Can I go now?"

"Not up to me. Captain decides. He'll want to see how you do." Butch took a step back, giving me enough room to rise to my feet. "But don't worry, the time will pass quick enough. There are plenty of men on the boat. You're going to be . . . busy."

The fact that the rest of the crew would also demand servicing didn't come as a surprise. Butch had been the first, and he surely wouldn't be the last. My value—as far as the men were concerned—was not in selfish exclusivity. It was more a factor of controlled distribution.

"What kind of boat is this?" I hoped the question sounded innocent. I was fishing for its range, it's vulnerabilities and weaknesses—all of which could increase my odds of escape.

"Why? You thinking of startin' a mutiny?" His lips parted in a grotesque smile, revealing dark, decaying teeth along with several obvious vacancies. He stared at me for the longest time and I knew he was weighing the risk of telling me. Finally he said, "She's a motor sailor, 265 feet."

"What about some food? I'm hungry."

"One of the crew will bring it down. And you'll have to pay for it. Nothing's free on this boat."

"I don't have any mon—" I stopped, still unaccustomed to the idea of using sex for currency.

"That's right." Butch said. "No credit. You'll pay as you go." He began wrapping the loose end of the chain around a vertical steel post, securing it with the same padlock that had kept me imprisoned in the cargo hold. "I'll give you enough slack to walk a foot or two in either direction. That's all you get for now."

"You're going to leave me here, in the engine room?" I was frantic, remembering the hammering throb of the machinery.

"Unless you'd rather be back in the hold."

The thought of spending another night lying in the freezing water put me on the verge of panic. "No, that's not what I meant. I'm talking about the engine, it makes a god-awful racket."

"That it will, if the captain has to use it. As far as I know, the winds are good for at least another day. Shouldn't have to run it for long . . . if we need it at all."

His assurance over the unlikely probability of running the engine gave me little comfort.

I looked at the chain, estimating the limits of my freedom.

Freedom. It was an odd word, especially in this place, shackled like an animal. I grabbed a handful of links and yanked.

"It's always the same with you older ones, testing the steel to see if it'll hold." Butch chuckled, revealing his perverse brand of humor. "Go ahead, knock yourself out. You'll dislocate a finger or separate a joint before you stretch another millimeter out of that chain."

I glanced down. There was nothing to sit on or insulate me from the cold steel. "Where am I supposed to sleep?"

"Right where you're standing, missy. That is, unless you turn chatty again or start making trouble. Then you're back in the hold."

"I'll stay quiet. You won't even know I'm here."

"Tonight you'll get a blanket," Butch added. "Maybe an air mattress."

"And the man who brings it . . . let me guess . . . I'll need to pay him for his kindness, right?"

"You catch on real fast," he said.

He stepped toward me. I instinctively flinched, not wanting him to touch me.

"You're not thinkin', bitch," he growled. "Not learning. Now spread 'em."

I looked back at the bulkhead and beyond, into the hold where I'd been shackled on my back in that wet basin. For all I knew, he had the authority to leave me in there for the duration of the trip. I held my breath and widened my legs. He shoved his rough calloused hand between them, raking over my pussy. Digging in with his middle finger, he pushed his way inside.

"Oww!" I winced.

"Quit complaining. By the time the captain's done, it won't make any difference who does what to you." He withdrew his finger and twisted my lower lips until they burned.

I let out a whimper.

"That's right. Today it's pain. Tomorrow it could be pleasure. It's all up to you."

I felt violated. I'd been determined to hide my emotions, keep them inside. I bit my lip, trying to regain control as I swiped at a single tear running down my cheek.

Butch's voice was low and stern. "If you're smart, you'll learn to turn off the waterworks. You'll find no pity on this boat."

I lifted my head, forcing myself to stare directly into his eyes. My words came on a flash of anger. "Don't worry. You'll never see it again."

He could have taken it as a challenge, a reason to drop me to the deck or drag me back to the watery pit.

He let it go with a warning. "First thing you'll have to do is get rid of that attitude. Personally, I could give a shit. But if you mouth off in front of the captain, your lessons will come hard."

Butch turned and began to trudge up a set of narrow metal stairs. Pausing on the landing, he leaned over the railing and looked down. Snapping the lights off and on, he said, "Remember, you can spend the rest of the trip in the dark or you can have some light. It's up to you."

He pulled the hatch closed behind him, cursing as he fumbled with the deadbolt, the warped strike finally seating into the hasp with a loud clang.

Chapter Three

The idea of being sold into the sex trade hadn't registered. Living in Sri Lanka, I'd heard the stories—mostly from sailors with first-hand experience—about young girls who were put to work as prostitutes. Indentured by constantly increasing debt, these victimized girls were treated like cattle, their value calculated by the number of johns they could service in a single night.

If that's what the captain had planned for me, I would have to make my escape before reaching port. Once sold into the trade, I would become a regular part of the traffic, making it impossible to avoid the brutality and virtual imprisonment commonly imposed by club and brothel owners.

Compared to the cargo hold, my new accommodations were an improvement—with one exception. The engine was a few feet away, ready to wake the dead with its booming clatter. My earlier exposure to the noisy diesel had been at a much greater distance—at least twenty-five feet away. Now that I was *inside* the equipment room, the iron monster was a looming threat.

What if the wind died or the captain needed to navigate a narrow channel? I might as well be in a cage with a sleeping dragon, knowing at any time it could awaken and devour me.

The stagnant air reeked of oil and diesel fumes. I worried the mere act of breathing would soon have me sprawled on the floor, dizzy and nauseated.

Finding a comfortable position was impossible. Sitting on the steel deck was bad enough, but the continuous pitch and roll of the boat kept me fighting for balance. With the vertical support my only option for a backrest, I had to change positions every few minutes to relieve the gnawing ache between my shoulders.

I estimated about two hours had passed when the snap of the hatch lock and metallic scrape of the deadbolt announced another visitor.

Another man to service. The next one in line.

How civilized, I thought. *Taking turns with the new whore.*

I tried to prepare myself, shutting down my senses, knowing there was nothing I could do but get it over with.

With a shaft of sunlight behind the approaching figure, I couldn't determine anything more than height and size. I was relieved to see it wasn't Butch—and surprised when the backlight revealed the softer curves and slighter physique of a woman.

Emerging from silhouette, she appeared to be about my age, maybe older. Dressed in denim shorts and a gray cropped pullover, her body was lean and tight, the muscles in her thighs and stomach revealing smooth definition as she walked. Although her skin was beginning to show the early signs of exposure to sun and weather, her short brown hair framed her pretty face in a boyish bob-cut. Even in the harsh shadowed-streaked light, I could see how attractive she was.

"My name's Annie," she said. "I brought you something to eat."

"You're the cook?"

"I'm the cook, maid, and I do the laundry, too. I can also chart and track a course without GPS. But nobody knows that." She was holding a tray. "You hungry?"

Seeing a woman come down the stairs was so unexpected I'd forgotten about food. "Yeah, I could eat."

"At least he left your hands loose so you can use them. He kept the last one chained up in here like an animal, until she . . ." Her voice trailed off as she realized what she was saying. "Here, take this," she added quickly. "A plastic spoon is all the captain would let me bring, so I figured a bowl of chili would be easy to get down."

The twelve-inch length of chain between the cuffs gave me enough leeway to feed myself. I held the bowl, savoring the heat, then brought it close before tasting it.

"He'll keep you naked the first day or two. Tonight you'll probably get some bedding, maybe a blow-up." She seemed to anticipate my questions, as if she'd answered them before. "And the man who brings it . . ." She paused. Apparently this part of the conversation had never gotten any easier no matter how many times she'd repeated it. "The man who brings it, he'll expect you to thank him."

My throat clenched mid-swallow and I forced the sudden surge of fear down with the food.

I noticed she was staring at the bruises on my calves and ankles. Self-conscious, I tucked my legs in tight.

"You don't need to hide what they've done to you," she said. "Not from me." She reached out, gently caressing the mottled skin. "I'll try to sneak in an ice pack to bring the swelling down."

I placed the empty bowl on the tray and brought a plastic cup of water to my mouth.

"You'll get through this," she said softly. "Just do what they tell you. Don't think about it. Just do it. The ones who think too much . . . they end up regretting it."

"Did the captain tell you to say that?"

I expected a quick denial, assuring me she wasn't the captain's mouthpiece or an outright spy. She looked directly into my eyes with unmistakable resignation. "I'll try to come back later, after I'm done with my work." She brought her hand to the side of my face. It surprised me, and I drew back.

Annie shook her head. I wasn't sure if it was her way of telling me I had nothing to fear or she was expressing the kind of compassion some people feel for a lame horse on borrowed time.

"What's your name?" she whispered.

"Jewel."

I saw a hint of a smile. She leaned in and gave me an awkward hug. But this time I didn't move. It was the first gesture of kindness I'd received since being hauled from my house and brutalized in the back of our panel truck. I let it in, stopping just short of allowing it to influence my opinion of her. I couldn't forget that she worked for the captain, and I had no idea what kind of relationship she had with her master. Until I knew more—until I could trust her—I would treat her actions with a healthy dose of suspicion.

Chapter Four

The dreary light from the overhead fixture had been constant, yet I was sure the night had come and gone. The incessant cycling of the circulating pumps had been joined by the rough and muffled chugging of the auxiliary generators. Started automatically, they handled the additional electrical demand from kitchen appliances and the ship's water-maker, as well as charging the batteries that ran the winches and electronics.

My neck and shoulders ached from sleeping on the hard deck. The continuous rise and fall of the boat and the putrid air had left me nauseous.

After Annie left, there had been no more visits from the crew, leaving the promise of a blanket and air mattress unfulfilled. Yet the misery of the hard steel was a petty complaint compared to the unrelenting cold. The few times I'd dozed off, I woke myself up shivering. As the temperature continued to drop with each passing hour, I'd curled up in a fetal position to retain body heat. But without some form of insulation from the deck, the chill went right through me.

Finally, I'd had enough.

I tried to imagine what it would be like—trading the use of my body for something warm. Could I actually make the offer and carry through with it . . . willingly? I'd accommodated Butch under duress, without choice or consent. But this time I would be initiating the activity, providing sex on demand in exchange for something I needed. I would become a . . .

I couldn't bring myself to complete the thought. From now on, I would shun the word *whore* from my vocabulary. It was a derogatory term that carried judgment, without room for mercy or compassion.

The next wave of shivering had been so intense, I'd felt tinges of pain from my fatigued and abused muscles. I might regret my decision later, but right now, I was cold and tired. And I needed that to change. If spending ten revolting minutes with a crewman would bring me some comfort and a few hours of sleep, it would be a reasonable exchange.

Saying the words was harder than I thought. I started a dozen times, clearing my throat, opening my mouth. But nothing came out.

Why was it so difficult? I knew who the enemy was. And it was time to give up a little ground to make sure I would have the strength and stamina when I needed it—when I had a way off this boat.

"I could really use that blanket." I called out through chattering teeth. "And I'm willing to pay for it."

The minutes ticked by with no response. I thought it strange that none of the men were willing to take me up on my offer. After a few more attempts at bartering for warmth, I realized it wasn't going to happen. The crew's silence was intentional—all part of the captain's agenda to reprogram me. No doubt he hoped to weaken my resistance with deprivation, motivating me to initiate an offer, strike a price, and close the deal.

As much as I hated to admit it, his plan was working. A warm blanket in exchange for a brief sexual favor now seemed like a relative bargain. In just a day, his actions—or lack of them—had made me willing to offer my body in trade for what I needed.

It was exactly what he'd intended to accomplish.

And it made me furious.

From that moment on, I swore every concession I made would be done with purpose, every compromise offered with the sole intention of escaping from this nightmare.

The scrape of the ill-fitting deadbolt barely penetrated the steady drone of the generators, the sound reaching my ears as little more than a faint background noise. It set me on edge, not knowing who—or what—to expect.

Emerging from the glaring light, Annie's shape was unmistakable. A wave of relief washed over me. She was carrying something . . . a blanket. My teeth chattering from the cold, I didn't try to speak.

She dropped to her knees and draped the fabric around me, bringing the edges together behind my shoulders. "I tried to come back last night," she said. "I even waited until I was sure the captain had gone to bed. But one of the men on watch saw me walking in this direction. So I made up an excuse, told him I was having trouble sleeping. I couldn't risk being caught a second time. The guy would have turned me in, or more likely, wanted a bribe to keep his mouth shut."

She began tucking the loose edges of the blanket around my hips. "We need to get this under your bottom to insulate you from the deck."

I leaned forward and heard my knees pop. Immediately, Annie sat behind me, straddling me with her legs. She wrapped her arms around my waist to calm my shivering. While I welcomed her touch, I still questioned her motives.

I felt her warm breath on my ear. "Where are you from?" she whispered. "How did you end up here?"

"The captain didn't tell you?"

"He doesn't share many details with the crew. I guess he figures the less they know, the less they can tell the authorities."

She straightened her back and I felt the rush of cold air between us, the separation unleashing a rippling chill that shook me to the core.

"Here, this will help." Without hesitating, Annie unbuttoned her shirt and pressed her bare flesh against my back, transferring more than body heat.

I should have had more questions—about our destination, the ports of call along the way, when I would gain topside privileges—knowledge that might increase the possibility of escape. But I said nothing. I closed my eyes, lost in the sanctuary of her touch, soft and warm against my back.

"My hands are freezing," I said. "I can't even feel my fingers."

"Put them on my legs," Annie instructed.

I shifted my shackled hands to her right thigh, lightly grazing her skin.

"Go ahead," she assured me. "It will help to warm you up." She squeezed me tighter, as if confirming her consent.

The velvety smoothness of her skin was in raw contrast to the hard steel I'd shared the night with, and as I shed the cold, I found not only warmth, but welcome comfort in the snug, easy fit of her body against mine.

Sitting in silence, lost in the shelter of her concern, I began to let go of the fear. With her arms cradling me, I thought nothing of her face nestling against mine, her lips tracing my neck with gentle kisses. In different circumstances, in another time and place, I would have treated her advances with caution, dreading the moment when I would have to say no. But I sensed no threat in her actions and I leaned back, welcoming the unexpected affection.

Another minute passed.

Her hands that first surrounded me in a motherly embrace now lightly caressed my breasts. Interpreting my lack of objection as consent, her lips wandered across my shoulders, tasting my skin, sweeping over me as if she were reuniting with an absent lover.

I didn't stop her.

Annie's right hand drifted lower, exploring my stomach, finally settling below my navel.

Drawing lazy circles with her fingers, I realized she was asking permission. Maybe it was the circumstances of my captivity or the fear and physical discomfort I'd experienced over the last two days. Regardless of the reason, my usual reluctance to the passionate advances of another woman was gone. Parting my thighs a few inches, I invited her touch.

Unlike the rough and invasive thrusting I had received from Butch, Annie's fingers gently caressed me, tenderly covering the area in a tiny hug. She merely wanted another point of contact—a soft and intimate place—to join with me.

And I wanted it too.

It was a saving revelation. Since my abduction, my thoughts were focused on survival and escape—savage, instinctive responses, not unlike those of any cornered prey. Annie's unexpected compassion gave me hope. It meant I was still human, able to respond to another's kindness.

"Annie . . . what's going to happen to me?"

She held me tighter. "Shhh, not now."

"Please, it would help if I knew what to expect."

She hesitated. "I'm not avoiding the question. I just don't know. The captain doesn't talk about his plans."

"The man who was down here before . . . his name was Butch. He told me the captain was going to sell me into the slave market. Was he trying to scare me or is that the truth?"

"Butch is an asshole. He's always shooting off his mouth, thinks he knows everything that's going on."

"So he was lying?"

"He's guessing," Annie said. "He has no idea what the captain plans to do with you."

"But he's done it before? Selling a girl into slavery, I mean."

I felt the reluctant brush of Annie's face against my mine. She was nodding. "The captain buys and sells—"

The screeching hinges of the hatch broke through the generator's low frequency throb. Annie jumped at the sound, quickly sliding away from me.

Her voice fell to a strained whisper. "If someone sees us like this they won't let me come back."

"But I thought—"

"No. And you can't say anything to anyone." She was on her feet, buttoning her shirt, straightening her hair. I could hear the anxious concern in her voice.

I had assumed Annie had the same rights as any other member of the crew, including the captain's permission to take personal liberties with the "cargo." That was clearly not the case. The approach of another crewmember had startled her, not because of her presence in the engine room, but because of our compromising position. It was obvious she had exceeded the extent of her privileges—which apparently included me.

I shielded my eyes against the bright shaft of daylight flooding the room. In the backlit glare, I was uncertain who was making their way down the narrow steps. The resounding hollow thump of heavy footsteps told me it was a big man, someone much larger than Butch.

"So, Jewel, are you ready to spend some time on deck? We have a lot to do in the next couple of days to get you ready." The man was hovering over me, his eyes shifting back and forth between myself and Annie. Finally, his menacing gaze fixed on my face.

There was no mistaking his identity. I could never forget the man who had dragged me yelling and screaming from my own house.

"And girl," the captain added, "one way or another, you *will* be ready."

I gathered the blanket tight around my shoulders and looked up at Annie, wishing she would say something. Only her eyes spoke—sad and resigned, the way a veterinarian looks at an aging and incapacitated dog before injecting the poor thing with a lethal dose of pentobarbital.

I had two choices. I could resist until my stamina and physical endurance were exhausted. Or I could pretend the bastard had broken me, and try to convince him I was ready to cooperate. My decision was simple. Two miserable, grueling nights had been enough. From this point forward, I had to think of myself as a soldier, temporarily abandoning my ethics and moral ideals. I was at war, and my enemy wasn't bound by any so-called *civilized* rules of engagement.

As I considered how much of a shift in attitude and composure the captain would believe without coming suspicious, one question kept eating away at me—*how far would I have to go?* I didn't dare consider the answer—I had no idea what it would take to transform myself into the compliant sex slave he was determined I become.

Chapter Five

Using the chain to keep me in tow, the captain led the way. I did my best to stay with him, hobbling up the metal steps, wincing as the sharply pointed treads threatened to puncture the soles of my feet.

He paused as we reached the landing. "Ready to lose the chain?" he asked.

I nodded slowly. Then realizing I needed to convey a façade of cooperation, I added, "Yes, please."

He pointed to the railing. "Grab on, keep yourself steady." Dropping to one knee, he lifted the ankle restraint, lined up the lock and inserted the key. "The next hour will determine how much freedom you receive for the rest of the trip. And in case you have any ideas about jumping overboard and swimming to shore, forget it. The ocean is cold. You might last an hour before hypothermia sends you to the bottom, and that's if the sharks don't get to you first." His hard expression turned threatening. "And if I have to send a man in after you, I'll lock you in the hold and leave you there until we reach port. Understand?"

"I won't give you any trouble."

"Uh-huh." His voice reeked with doubt. "What do you think, Annie? Can we trust her?"

"She'll behave, Captain. Leash her to me if you want."

"To you?" He seemed genuinely surprised. "That's an unusual request. You must fancy this one."

The lock hasp rattled against the metal landing as it fell from my ankle. I waited to feel some relief. Instead, a stab of pain tore up my leg.

Seeing me wince, the captain grunted in approval. "The circulation's coming back. Walking on it will help take the swelling down."

In a different situation, I would have considered his comment an expression of concern. But I knew he was interpreting my reaction as an indication of how quickly my bruising would heal—enhancing my marketability.

The concept of being a piece of merchandise was slowly sinking in. But I had to keep it in perspective. My captivity was just a circumstance, a situation I could—and would—change. I refused to believe I was condemned to live the life of a back-room prostitute, always a moment away from some pimp beating me because I had displeased a customer.

For now, I would do as I was told, saving my strength until I had learned more about my surroundings, and my best options for escape.

The captain reached for the blanket, removing it my shoulders.

"What about clothes?" I asked.

"Not yet." He pulled a black leather collar from his rear pocket and brought it to my neck, securing it with double buckles. "For the time being, this is all you'll need."

I knew his comment was more than a suggestion of what waited for me outside.

"And don't take it off," he added. "If I see you without it, I'll cinch the next one so tight you won't be able to breathe." He snapped the end-clip of a heavy leather leash into the collar's protruding metal loop. "You don't move unless I do. Understand?"

I forced myself to look directly into his eyes. "I'll do exactly as you say."

I wanted to kick him, send him crashing to the deck. But he weighed well over two hundred pounds and my blows would only irritate him. Besides, I had a plan. It lacked details, and for the most part I was making it up minute-by-minute, but it didn't matter. The fact that I was watching for opportunities told me I was far from beaten.

I followed him through the hatch and felt the heated attack of the sun. While I welcomed the warmth, my eyes narrowed to mere slits in response to its harsh and unfriendly glare.

Stepping onto the deck brought a sense of liberation. It was far from real freedom, but it felt like I was back with the living—as if finally released from a subterranean hell.

The leash tightened, the captain leading me to the left.

Despite the increasing strain on my neck, I hung back. I wanted to look around, to learn as much as possible. Feigning dizziness, I stumbled against a vent tube, holding on in a contrived need for support.

Annie's arm found my waist. "Hold up, captain. She's a bit shaky. Needs a minute to get her sea legs."

"One minute. No more." The leash fell slack. The captain turned to Annie. "You have duties waiting for you in the kitchen."

I searched Annie's face, looking for reassurance. But her expression was guarded and full of caution.

She gave my arm a quick squeeze. "You'll be fine," she said. "Do what the captain says."

Dread . . . anxiety . . . panic. It hit me all at once, causing my hands to shake, assaulting my stomach with pre-faint nausea. I looked into Annie's big brown eyes, unable to hide it.

"You'll get through this," she added. "Just go along with it. Don't fight it."

As she turned away from me, I had the feeling there was more she wanted to say, but was keeping it to herself. I kept my eyes on her until she disappeared inside the large central structure amidships.

I felt an immediate sense of loss, of being completely alone. It was as if Annie represented the last saving thread of human decency, and now, that too was gone. I reminded myself she'd been ordered to leave. There was nothing else she could do.

As the captain waited for my invented dizziness to pass, I cautiously scanned the deck and superstructures, memorizing the boat's profile, looking for marks of identification. Later it would help me provide the authorities with an accurate description of the vessel.

The ship was typical of large schooners built in the fifties and sixties. Once a magnificent showpiece of teak, brass, and mahogany, it had been reconditioned for commerce. With its opulent fittings replaced with more durable fiberglass and stainless steel equivalents, it was obvious that preserving the boat's historical integrity was no longer a priority.

GPS navigation had been added and a radar globe mounted on the main mast. It indicated the capability to sail twenty-four-seven, even with limited visibility. Overhead, the fore and mainsails had been retained, with the gaff topsails and their associated rigging eliminated as ineffective time-wasters. With the oversized diesel engine capable of pushing the ship to the very edge of its structural limits, relying on the wind was a poor choice when time translated directly into money.

Even with haphazard splashes of spar varnish and marine plastic covering the original hand-polished finishes, I could tell the ship had once been someone's pride and joy, perhaps sailing when the pursuit of pleasure was the only reason to lift the sheets.

"What's the boat's name?" I hoped my question sounded innocent, as if extending the courtesy of polite conversation.

"The *Kelsey*," the captain answered.

His lack of hesitation in revealing the name of his ship was a strong show of confidence—he obviously had little to fear from the authorities in this part of the world.

"Did you name her?"

"Name came with the title."

Of course. Changes in ownership were done by simply recording a bill of sale or by using a straw man. Changing the *boat's* name would mean filing new registration documents and the creation of a secondary paper trail.

The captain tugged on the leash. "It's time to meet the crew." He motioned toward the stern.

I felt my throat begin to close, my stomach threatening to heave. I had to find a way to control the fear—and the tears. From the moment I'd dropped to my knees in the engine room to suck off that piece of shit, Butch, I had no doubt about what was in store for me. Yet no matter how much I'd tried to prepare myself, there was no such thing as *being* ready. Perhaps with experience and sheer repetition, I would eventually be rendered numb to the idea of indiscriminately providing a man—any man— with sexual favors. But from where I stood, that state of mind remained a long way off in some distant and unforeseeable future.

Chapter Six

There were five of them. I'd first noticed the men when I emerged from below deck. Assuming they were involved in their normal duties, I'd ignored them. Now I realized they hadn't moved.

They were waiting—for me.

This wasn't the way I'd imagined it. Rather than approaching me one at a time—giving me the opportunity to learn their name, background, or some small quirk that might reveal a thread of latent humanity—they would come at me as a mob of mindless, hormonally-driven brutes, ready to climb on and fuck me.

Turn it off. Don't think. Just get through it.

It was my mantra, and I continued to repeat it as the captain pulled me toward the waiting men.

Oddly, it was the first time I'd thought about modesty. Until stepping out onto the deck, my concern with being naked was motivated by a need for protection against the cold. Now I suspected it was part of the captain's strategy—to desensitize me and effectively remove the word *shy* from my vocabulary. I also reasoned clothing would simply get in the way of my . . . education.

"Men, this is Jewel," the captain announced. "She's our newest asset and ready for training. I trust each one of you will put forth your best efforts in that regard."

The easy smiles from the men told me they had heard the words before, no doubt when the captain had introduced previous girls.

"Jewel, meet five of my best. The tall one over there is Massey."

He was lanky, with red hair and freckles. With one eyebrow higher than the other and a slightly crooked smile, he looked a bit like a cartoon character. I guessed him to be mid-thirties. Upon hearing his name, he tipped his head to the side and stared at me slightly cross-eyed.

"The big boy in need of a haircut," the captain continued, "is Albie, our onboard athletic director."

He looked older than the others, the size of his chest and arms disputing any impotency suggested by his long mane of snow-white hair. He reminded me of a few men I'd dated before Carl. Aging Lotharios, they compensated for their lost youth with inflated doses of testosterone and Viagra. He terrified me.

"Next are Chen and Zeke. They claim to be cousins, but I've never had the heart to hand them a mirror."

Zeke was small in stature with dark skin. He appeared to be of mixed race—part black, part Indian, or maybe Polynesian. He seemed unaffected, even distracted, as if he had other things on his mind and, like me, wanted to get this over with as quickly as possible. For some unexplainable reason, his lack of interest irritated me. It was as if my "training" was undeserving of his full attention, and in a strange turn of irony, he had managed to hurt me with his indifference.

In contrast, Chen—of Asian descent with thick black hair and a large, rounded face— glared at me with calculating scrutiny, as if deciding exactly how he would take me, how long he would wait before he came, and which orifice he would choose to infest me with his semen.

"Rounding out our little group," the captain continued, "is the dapper-looking gent on the end. We call him R.J."

With a slim build and sandy blonde hair, he didn't seem as imposing as the others—or as frightening. There was something familiar about him, but I couldn't place it.

"So much for the formal introductions," the captain said. "I'm sure you'll all get to know each other before the day is over."

With the exception of the way they were dressed—in faded jeans and long-sleeve cotton shirts—they couldn't have been more different. Probably intentional, I reasoned. By requiring me to accommodate a variety of men, there was less likelihood of my developing a preference for race, body type, or age. No discriminating here. I would have to accommodate anyone who asked—like any girl resigned to work the streets.

The fact that Butch wasn't part of the group gave me more respite than relief. Perhaps his training sessions were designed to be of a private nature.

The captain cleared his throat. "Last night, Jewel told me she was disappointed by the lack of activities aboard our ship. She also said she was looking for a way to alleviate the boredom. I told her I would speak to my social directors and get the situation remedied immediately." A slight smirk cracked his steely jawline.

The men began nodding their heads, jabbing each other with their elbows as they exchanged a buzz of crude comments.

"Look at that tiny pussy."

"Don't worry, honey, we'll keep you plenty busy."

"Nice tits on this one, Cap'n. She's gonna bring top dollar."

"Gentlemen," the captain's voice rose to a dramatic conclusion, "I leave her in your capable hands." He tossed the leash at Massey's feet, effectively relinquishing control.

"Wait! Where are you going? What if I need you?" I wasn't sure why I wanted the captain to stay. Maybe I thought the game would be played more fairly if there were a referee to enforce the rules.

The captain stared at me with an intensity that tore right through the sunlight. "You *do* have a lot to learn." He turned to walk away, then paused and glanced toward the men. "Remember . . . leave any marks and it'll cost you a week's pay."

"No worries here, Cap," Massey answered, his freckled face widening with a huge smile as he reached down to pick up the leash. "We'll treat her right." His words were laced with a southern drawl, though he was clearly not a gentleman.

"We'll take good care of her," Albie added, his voice sure and cocky. "Gar . . . un . . . teed," he said, drawing out the word for emphasis.

The men began to talk excitedly in obvious anticipation—fraternal chatter about who would be the first to penetrate me.

Except for R.J.

His smoky gaze was fixed on my face, his attention less offensive than the others, all of whom were scanning me head-to-toe with radar precision. The man struck me with haunting familiarity. With his sun-streaked hair and chiseled features, I would surely remember meeting him. Maybe I was fabricating the feeling, my need for an ally so desperate I was interpreting his less aggressive manner as a bid for friendship.

A tug on my neck triggered an instinctive turn to the right. Massey had handed the leash to Albie, the muscular white-haired man.

Albie immediately acknowledged the hand-off. "That's a pretty name, Jewel. Did your mama give that to you?"

I started to answer, but my churning stomach threatened to bend me double with the dry heaves. I swallowed hard, my lower lip beginning to quiver.

"Now, now, that's okay, sweetheart. It's just a case of the first-time jitters, happens all the time." His concern sounded rehearsed and despicably placating.

I felt the press of hands on my butt. One of the men was cupping my ass, his fingers probing their way between my cheeks, searching for a cavity to accept them. "We don't usually get a high quality product like you onboard."

I recognized Massey's distinctive southern twang. I wondered if he expected me to thank him for the compliment.

Chen stepped forward, facing me.

My chest tightened, my breathing turning short and rapid. Every instinct told me to protect myself by striking out with a pre-emptory blow. Instead, I held my ground, glaring at him, even stiffening my posture to meet his advance. My challenging response seemed to take him off guard. Although he made no attempt to touch me, his lips curled down at the corners, his nostrils flaring in a show of frustrating disappointment. Perhaps he had expected me to cringe and cower like a frightened schoolgirl. While I was quaking inside, I hoped my stance conveyed what I was thinking—*Go to hell, asshole.*

Another yank on the collar switched my attention back to Albie. The snow-haired giant was tightening his grip on the leash. I slowly turned toward him, keeping my eyes centered on the middle of his chest.

In the future, I would always look back, remembering that moment—a split second decision that may have saved my life. While there was no way to prevent these men from carrying out the "training," I refused to let my personal integrity—the core of who I was—define the experience. If I could avoid making judgments about their actions, they couldn't hurt me emotionally. There would be no right or wrong. Without a perpetrator, there could be no victim. I would send my thoughts elsewhere. I would leave the here and now for another place, a hidden refuge somewhere in my mind.

And I would survive.

I began to reframe the situation. I told myself this was not an attack. It was simply their job. They were about to expose me to a world where women were subservient to the desires of men, and indiscriminate sex was an accepted and common way of life. From their standpoint, I was simply another new charge who needed to learn her lessons. I knew it wouldn't be easy, but I swore I would get through it—with my wits intact.

The tension on my collar increased, this time drawing me downward—the big man's way of telling me to bend over. I complied without hesitation.

A flurry of hands groped my breasts, a legion of rough fingers scraping over my skin like sandpaper. Pawing and pinching, they took turns squeezing my nipples, tugging at them until they stung.

The air was filled with a chorus of opening zippers, the harsh metallic sound in shrill contrast to the natural splash of ocean against the ship's hull and the rush of wind filling the sails.

"I'll git 'er from the back." Massey spread my ass-cheeks, finding my pussy, examining every inch of me. He began working a single finger between my lips, pressing it deep. He pumped it a few times before adding a second digit, finger-fucking me with a slow twisting motion. I wasn't ready and the intrusion hurt like hell. I began to squirm, wanting him to stop.

"The bitch is dry. Gimme some of that."

He withdrew, delivering a rush of relief. In seconds he was back, shoving a thick glob of lube deep into my vagina.

"That's better," he said.

Shuffling up behind me, he moved closer, his feet straddling mine. Setting his hands on my hips, he brought the head of his swollen cock to my pussy. But the angle of penetration—his approach being several inches too high—made it difficult to enter. Anxious to fill me, he began increasing the pressure, pushing against the natural shape and contour of my opening.

On the edge of pain, I stood on my toes, compensating for the angle. He seemed to understand what I was doing. Bending slightly at the knees, he met me halfway, aligning himself on a more even plane with my hips. With our difference in height no longer an issue, he set a regular and continuous rhythm, each plunge confirmed by the slap of his upper thighs against my ass.

I'd done it—taken his cock. More than that, I had *accommodated* him, voluntarily changing my position to improve the quality of our coupling— and his pleasure. I waited for the guilt, for the surge of self-pity to release a flood of tears.

I felt nothing. No remorse, no shame, no guilt.

In that moment, I rose above my circumstances. I became tougher, more resilient than *any* of these men—even the Asian, who had been anticipating my withdrawal into fear and panic with cruel delight.

I closed my eyes, shielding myself with a shroud of indifference. There was nothing to see, nothing to remember.

Unfortunately, my defensive strategy was short lived.

The persistent poking at my mouth was like an unwanted visitor who wouldn't go away. Reluctantly, I raised my eyelids to see an engorged cock pushing against my lips, demanding entrance.

They intended to fill me from both ends, reducing me to a receptacle of convenience. With enough repetition, they knew my reluctance to anonymous, on-demand sex would fade. It was as part of the training, I reasoned. Their goal was to replace my hesitation with presumptive permission, to teach me how to accommodate, and even encourage, any man to use me whenever and however they desired.

Without thinking, I brought a hand to my face to shoo away the dick bouncing against my lips.

"Yeah, grab it, wrap your fingers around it and jack me into your mouth." From the dark color of his skin, I knew it was Zeke. He had misinterpreted my actions, believing I was extending my hand in a receptive welcome.

Good or bad, I had given him the impression that I was not only compliant, but cooperative and user-friendly.

In a flash of perverse and twisted logic, I told myself it didn't matter. I had to face the facts about what was happening to me. The sooner this man shot his load, the better. Then I would be done with him and could take the next one, and the next. Right now, sucking another man's dick while being fucked from behind would allow me to finish in half the time.

I reached for Zeke's bobbing shaft. Wrapping my fingers around the base, I began to stroke him.

. . . And when my pussy runs wet with their juices, when I've swallowed all the cum they can feed me, only then will I drop the façade of an accommodating slut and slowly revive my galvanized senses. Not a second before.

It wasn't long before I felt Zeke's tattletale contractions—he would make no attempt to hold back.

I took him deep into my mouth, holding him there until he was completely drained. The first spurt was quickly followed by the next. Without forcing the swallow, I let it collect, mixing with my saliva. Finally, I sent it down naturally, instinctively.

Massey, fucking me from behind, began rocking back and forth, directing my body in opposing sync to his. The other men noticed and added their encouragement with supportive machismo.

"Ram it home, Massey. Give it to her good, so she remembers."

"Making memories now, ain't we, sweetcakes?"

Seeing me swallow Zeke's cum had excited them, winning me a kind of perverse admiration. For a moment, I sensed their approval—but not their respect.

"Let's see what she can do with this."

I glanced up. It was Albie, the white-haired brute with muscular arms. He had a cock to match.

"Ready for another load?" he asked. He began stroking his dick within an inch of my face.

I darted my tongue in and out, then licked my lips. It was a feigned invitation to accelerate the process.

"Yeah, fill her up," Massey added, his words delivered in modulated sync to his rhythmic gyrations.

At first I thought his comment was directed at Albie, encouraging him to add his load to the one I'd just swallowed. It wasn't. He was talking to Chen, the black-haired Asian who had done his best to intimidate me. From my disadvantaged position, I hadn't seen Chen step behind me and take a position next to Massey.

I felt the cold ooze of slick gel between my butt-cheeks. Chen's finger began circling my asshole, testing the opening, working a single digit inside.

Feeling the sensation through the membrane wall was exactly what Massey needed, and he moaned as he began filling me with his hot liquid. He finished with a few ramming lunges, his last thrust tipping me off-balance and pushing into Albie's stroking hand.

"Ouch!" I took the blow directly on the nose.

"Massey, not so hard! She might bruise." Concerned about the consequences of manhandling the merchandise, Albie knew the captain wouldn't be happy if required to offer a discount for wear and tear.

As Massey separated from me, I felt Chen's finger rotate and withdraw. But it was only to add a second digit. I whimpered as he pressed deep, twisting and turning, stretching me for what I was sure would be a much larger appendage.

"Like that, don't you?"

His flippant comment showed his lack of regard for my feelings. I said nothing, refusing to acknowledge him.

Instead of rejection, he interpreted my silence as agreement. "Good," he said. "Then let's continue."

He removed his fingers and aligned them with a third, preparing to thrust all three deep into my ass.

I tried to relax, to free the tension from my hips.

It was impossible.

Searing heat tore through my bottom. "Wait! You're hurting me. Give me time to stretch."

I had been determined to distance myself, to play a role, to simply submit to their demands without resisting. Then, when it was over, I would tell myself it hadn't really happened—that it was someone else on that deck having sex with five strangers. But I had verbally communicated with one of the men—engaging him. It was far more than my involuntary response to being popped on the nose. And now the situation was all too real.

"Relax, honey. We won't be using that hole today," Massey said. He was standing to the side, watching. His assurances irritated me. As far as I was concerned, sticking three fingers in my ass was putting it to *extreme* use, a full-force invasion that left me sore and throbbing. "The boys are just getting you used to the idea," he added. "So you'll be ready from head-to-toe."

Massey had been monitoring the activities of the other men. Maybe he served as the captain's eyes and ears during the training sessions and would provide him with a report after each encounter. I wondered if resisting a full ass-stretching had prevented me from receiving an "A" in his evaluation. If so, I had no doubt there would be another opportunity to improve my grade.

Although Chen had retracted his third finger upon hearing my outcry, he'd continued to explore my smallest hole with two, occasionally re-introducing the tip of the extra digit. Each time, he inserted it a little deeper, letting me take my time in accommodating the additional intrusion.

While Massey had assured me I would not be subjected to an ass-fucking, the feel of Chen's rock-hard cock pressing against my thigh made Massey's words seem as reliable as a politician's promise.

Chen began shifting his torso, placing himself in direct alignment with me. Removing his fingers, he grabbed my hips and pulled me tight. Certain he would make a liar out of Massey and push his throbbing organ into my asshole, I braced myself, clasping my thighs, hoping to relax the muscles in my butt.

Apparently sensing my apprehension, Chen betrayed his previous hostile veneer and offered some impromptu advice. "It'll be easier if you learn to relax, no matter what's happening to you."

I wondered if he was repeating a line from the captain's manual of slut training.

Massey's word was good, at least when it came to ass-fucking. As Chen's engorged cock found its way inside my pussy, I released the breath I was holding.

Chen quickly established a rhythm so consistent, I was sure he was silently counting the strokes—five short ones, then three longs, and always slamming the entire length of his cock deep into my vagina for each thrust of the trifecta. Whether he had a greater need to achieve orgasm or he simply didn't have the kind of staying power Massey had demonstrated, in less than a minute he exploded deep inside my belly, adding his semen to the mix.

Another one down.

Albie had continued working his rod in front of my face, his pleasured groans indicating he was more than ready. So far he hadn't tried to push his way into my mouth. Suddenly he leaned in, bouncing his cock off my lips.

"You're not to spill a drop, understand?"

"Give it to me." I said it without thinking, without considering how it would sound, then realized it didn't make any difference—not to the men, and oddly, not to me, either.

I opened my mouth as wide as I could, tasting the salty head of his dick as he slid it onto my tongue. Covering his shaft with my lips set his leg muscles quivering. I reached for his balls, squeezing them as I pulled on the sac. He came in seconds, filling my mouth as each contraction provided an equally huge serving.

His left hand shifted to the back of my head in a characteristically male move. But as it slid to my neck, I wondered if I'd misjudged his intent. I froze as his fingers found my throat. Was he about to choke me, enhancing his orgasm by restricting my breathing?

My fear was unfounded. Instead of abusing me, he simply wanted to feel the sensation of my tongue and throat muscles contracting as I swallowed his cum, working to get it down.

Completely drained, he retreated in shuddering detachment.

Dropping my head to relieve the strain, I felt the unexpected press and release of gentle pressure on my shoulders. Albie was revealing another side—one that suggested a vague sense of compassion.

Whether it was my quick and unintentional shiver in response to his touch or he was concerned his actions could be interpreted as affection or even gratitude, he quickly drew back, the awkward snap of his hand a sure indication he knew he shouldn't have done it.

"Your turn," Albie said, as he wiped his cock with the back of his sleeve.

I didn't have to look up to know who he was talking to. Only one man remained. With his sandy-blonde hair and piercing green eyes, R.J. had waited quietly, adding nothing to the conversation—or the activities.

At first, I had intentionally avoided keeping track of the men, preferring to remain disinterested, choosing not to remember the roughness of their hands or the way they groped me. Now I *wanted* to know. Not necessarily to keep them separate; it just seemed more civilized that way, adding a bit of propriety to being fucked by five strangers. Like it or not, I was acclimating to my situation.

No, it was more than that.

I was adapting—to survive.

"She's swallowed enough cum on an empty stomach," R.J. said. "I'll take her from the back."

Stepping behind me, he nestled close and slowly traced my spine with his fingers. Unlike Albie, he showed no signs of a conflicted conscience, no personal struggles with discipline as he continued touching me in an oddly gentle, almost affectionate manner.

It didn't feel good or bad, just distracting, as if he was trying—and failing—to calm me. I wondered if R.J. was preparing me for his own special brand of deviant sex-play. If true, it would contradict my first impression of him—quiet, even detached during the frequent exchanges of male swagger and bluster. While the others had taken their turn, he had simply watched, content to wait in silence.

I felt his cock nudge against my dripping pussy. Keeping his torso tightly pressed to mine, he began flexing his hips, sliding his dick between my lips. I kept waiting for him to penetrate, but as he continued his abbreviated grinding, I realized what he was doing.

He was *pretending* to fuck me.

Why?

Did the overflow of cum from my pussy make the idea of joining the mix uninviting or disagreeable?

111

That made no sense. He was a crewman on a sex slave ship. He'd been assigned—perhaps even earned—the privilege of participating in the sexual training of young girls. The physical circumstances common to a gang-bang would not prevent him from enjoying himself.

His right hand slipped underneath, as if adding support. It was a strange, *confusing* kind of connection. I interpreted it as his way of asking me to conceal what he was—or wasn't—doing.

His intentions a mystery, the situation turned even more bizarre when he began tapping on my stomach. It wasn't a nervous reaction—it was definite and measured. I counted seven taps, then a pause, then the same seven taps.

He was sending me some kind of code.

I could only work with what I knew for sure. This guy was faking it, and not because he had to. His cock was rock hard; he could have easily slid inside me. He was depriving himself for a reason. So what did he have to gain?

Maybe it was his personal strategy, an attempt to set himself apart from the others. But in a world where sex was equivalent to the prevailing currency, selfish schemes and personal agendas would be a threat to the captain's authority.

I even considered the remote possibility he was attempting to show me some degree of compassion. But that seemed as unlikely as him not wanting to deal with the previous deposits of the other men.

Without an obvious reason to explain his reluctance to fuck me, I was left with the only other motive I could think of—he wanted to form a secret alliance. It was a long shot, but if I were right, there could be an advantage in going along with his charade. Perhaps he could convince the captain to give me more freedom to roam about the ship, increasing my odds of escape.

I decided to treat his performance no differently than the others.

I felt his muscles stiffen as he held me tight against his crotch. Gripping my hips, he launched a deep growl from his throat, ending his mini-thrusts with one final shudder. While I couldn't see him, I could tell from the other men's reactions he'd been convincing.

Did he expect me to confirm his orgasm, to validate a virtual deposit of semen? I hadn't commented on the other men's performances, singling him out might sound suspect. I would keep my mouth shut.

"A little she-devil, this one." Massey's accent had become irritating.

"Yep, she's been a real surprise," Albie agreed, then added, "Come on, Chen, you can't tell me you didn't enjoy this one."

The air was filled with locker-room bravado, the men disclosing their personal experience of having shared the same woman. I almost expected them to break out with a bawdy drinking song followed by a few sad remembrances of all the girls they'd left behind.

The men's raw conversation made me question my original assumptions about the so-called "training." I had rationalized their indiscriminate and insensitive efforts to penetrate me by associating their actions with some greater objective—an organized attempt to desensitize me, the first step in enhancing my value as a sex slave.

I silently berated myself for excusing their behavior as serving some vile purpose. While the captain might have a larger agenda, these men had taken advantage of my misfortune because they could—fucking me as if they were a pack of junkyard dogs because I was here, available, compliant. From their perspective, every inch of me represented an opportunity for pleasure.

"Did everyone enjoy themselves?"

I hadn't seen or heard the captain's approach. I straightened up and turned in his direction. Annie was standing beside him.

"Aye Cap'n, she's a sweet piece of ass, this one."

"She did fine," Albie added. "Better than most for a first time."

I wondered how long they'd been watching. I didn't care so much about the captain, but I hoped Annie had missed my performance. I wanted her to see my good side, the one that was civilized and honorable. Knowing she'd seen even a few minutes of the training made me feel embarrassed, as if I should apologize or explain myself. Her opinion was important. In fact, it was the only one that mattered. Even if it turned out she'd been playing a part scripted by the captain, I didn't want her to think of me as another lost girl who'd merely submitted to the demands of her captors. I was better than that—and I wanted her to know it.

"And you, Jewel, did *you* enjoy yourself?"

Enjoy myself? He couldn't be serious. But from his earnest tone, I realized what I said next would matter. I also knew the captain would immediately recognize a lie. I had to appear authentic—keep my emotions in check.

I began slowly, doing my best to sound sincere. "I've never had sex with more than one person at the same time. And I think I learned how to go from one man to the next, without over-thinking the situation or letting stray thoughts get in the way."

Massey and Albie raised their eyebrows, indicating their surprise—and approval. But they weren't the ones I had to convince. I could feel the captain's intense scrutiny. He was searching my face, looking for a tattletale twitch or involuntary tic.

"Do you have any questions?" he asked.

While his interrogation seemed to be for my benefit, perhaps to give me a voice in the situation, his clinical manner seemed patently rehearsed. I would later learn he was using a powerful psychological technique designed to wring the emotional trauma from the experience, to remove the notion of having been abused or victimized.

I paused, not wanting to answer too soon. "No, nothing comes to mind right now."

"Is there anything you want to say to the men?"

What the hell did he want me to say? Encourage them to come back soon? Or maybe evaluate their performance and rate their proficiency?

As I glanced between the captain and the group, I noticed Annie had taken a step back, her expression straight-faced and serious. Her eyes were shifting side-to-side. She was sending me a signal. Or a warning.

"Nothing I can think of," I said. "Unless the men have something to say, I'll leave the experience right here on the deck."

The captain offered a slight nod. His response was limited, but the relief on Annie's face was clear, her validating smile letting me know I'd met his expectations.

"Annie, take Jewel to your cabin and clean her up."

She reached for the collar and began unbuckling the strap. "I'll take care of her. Okay if I leave this with you?"

I didn't see the captain's response, but as Annie removed the leather choker from my neck, I assumed he'd agreed.

As I fell in line behind her, the men were quick to speak. Instead of jeers, taunts, or catcalls, they offered simple comments of closure.

"Good job, Jewel."

"Well done, sweetheart."

"You did fine, girl."

I wanted to flip them off, spit in their faces. Instead, I offered a half-wave with the back of my hand. It was a counterfeit play, and the pretense infuriated me. But despite my feelings, I had accomplished what I'd set out to do. My performance had been convincing enough for the captain to turn me over to Annie.

The captain's precise focus on *my* thoughts and feelings made me realize my assessment of the training as a chaotic, testosterone-driven fuck-fest had been wrong. This had not been a spontaneous gang-bang. These men knew exactly what they were doing. Each one had a lesson to impart. Chen had driven three fingers in my ass to elicit a response, to break down the wall I had so carefully constructed. I was sure if I'd taken the third finger without a word, he would have added a fourth, continuing to stretch me until I reacted.

And while I'd done my best to avoid showing fear or resistance—knowing neither would serve me in the long-term—my decision to grant them the unchallenged use of my body had not been enough. They had wanted me to interact with them, to learn to separate the simple physicality of sex from the contrived schoolgirl fantasies of romance, soft whispers, and a dozen roses the day after.

The so-called "training" wasn't about enhancing my ability to provide pleasure. It was designed to weaken and ultimately eliminate the conservative belief that sex was only practiced behind closed doors, between consenting partners, out of view of both friend and stranger. With enough practice, they hoped I would eventually accept a sexual advance as naturally as I would a handshake. A blowjob would be as commonplace as exchanging a hug or a kiss on the cheek. And the first step was to coerce me into dialogue while being fully engaged in an overwhelming cluster-fuck.

Realizing their treatment of me was prescribed—their actions dictated by methodology rather than wild instinct—helped to counter the lingering traces of anxiety that had nearly taken me to my knees when the captain first offered me to the men. Though not a guarantee, I was fairly certain none of them would intentionally inflict harm or subject me to the truly bizarre solely to prove his alpha status to the rest of the pack.

Annie continued to walk ahead, leading me forward amidships and finally, through a short passageway providing access to the lower deck stairway. When she was sure we were out of sight and beyond earshot, she reached back and took my hand.

"You must be ready to explode, or cry, or scream," she whispered. "But right now, you need to keep it in, don't let them hear it. You got through it and that's all that matters."

I knew Annie's words were intended to soothe me, yet for some reason, I didn't feel anything. I briefly considered the possibility of having retreated into the refuge of shock. But my thoughts seemed rational, without the mind-numbing effects of sensory overwhelm. So why didn't I feel violated? For reasons I couldn't explain, I'd moved on, and as I'd told the captain, I actually *had* left the experience—and the men—on deck. If anything, I felt a twinge of guilt over my indifference.

We descended the flight of stairs and walked a few steps into the narrow hallway. "I wish I'd been able to handle myself that well," Annie said, "especially the first time."

Still holding her hand, I pulled back. "*You* were a captive, too?"

"We're all captives, in one way or another."

She was being cryptic. I wanted details. "How did you end up here? Were you sold to pay off a debt?" It sounded raw and primitive, as if we were living in some bleak dystopian future where rates of exchange were calculated in measures of personal service, right along with gold and silver.

Annie nodded. "In my case, I was able to convert my debt into time and serve it out another way. It's taken longer than I'd hoped, but I'm less than a year away from getting my freedom."

I took a deep breath. "Do you think I'll ever get *my* freedom?"

She stepped closer. "I saw you working the men. It was only the last few minutes, but I could see it in their faces. You made them feel important, strong. A man will do nearly anything a woman asks when she has that kind of power."

She *had* seen it. But there was no pity in her voice. Not even a touch of sympathy. Instead, she conveyed a sense of appreciation, even though I didn't understand her comment about having sexual power over the men.

We stopped at the second door. "This is it," she said. "The crew calls it the bridal suite, probably 'cause I have my own shower. Sometimes I have to give it up when the captain has a visitor onboard."

She opened the slatted door and let me walk in first.

Unlike the utility refurbishment so prevalent throughout the working portions of the boat,

Annie's stateroom had retained most of its original appointments. I was drawn to the single fixed porthole that hovered over an endless stretch of blue water. No more than a foot in diameter, it delivered light to every corner of the small cabin. After sunset, the room's illumination would depend on two electric fixtures protruding from the mahogany-lined walls, their compact bulbs capable of little more than preventing a stumble in the dark. A double bed took up a third of the floor space. Unaware the mattress was a flexible foam pad, I wondered how it had fit through the narrow hallway and around the cabin door. Opposite the bed, a built-in vanity and mirror provided a dressing table. Flanked by two sets of drawers, the additional storage was no doubt considered a luxury at the time the boat was constructed. An oddly placed opening in the corner of the room led to the bath, the privacy door removed as an unnecessary indulgence. A quick peek inside revealed an electric marine toilet, a single sink, and a compartment shower. Curious, I drew back the plastic shower curtain to find the original tile surfaces had been replaced with a narrow one-piece fiberglass enclosure.

Annie reached around me and turned on the valve. "There should be some hot water left. You don't want to get caught covered in soap when the temperature changes, so rinse as you go. The water will turn *really* cold."

The shower nozzle was attached to a flexible hose with a trigger release. It looked exactly like the one on my kitchen sink.

"Okay, it's warm. Jump in." Annie flattened against the wall, giving me room to step inside the enclosure.

I hadn't expected her to stay while I showered, yet I didn't want her to leave. She handled me the soap, and then held the narrow white plastic curtain in front of her as she sprayed me from top to bottom.

"How many men are onboard?" I asked.

"Twelve, plus me and the captain," she answered without hesitation.

"Have long have you worked on the *Kelsey*?"

What I really wanted to know was how she ended up on a slave ship—if she'd been shanghaied, betrayed by a disgruntled lover, or sold by a conman looking to make a quick buck.

"Just over two years. Another ten months and I'm done." She took the soap from my hand.

I waited, assuming the unspoken part of my question was too obvious to ignore. She remained quiet, absorbed in gently soaping my back.

I tried again. "Were you . . . I mean, how did you get here?"

"I'd been in Bangkok a couple of months," she said, releasing the curtain to spray my legs. "I was working in one of the nightclubs. Like a lot of girls, I'd answered an ad promising big money for entertainers. It sounded legit, all handled through a professional booking company. They even sent a contract, guaranteeing the money."

"You were a singer?"

She shook her head. "Dancer."

"So what happened?"

"When I started, the club owner put me on a stage where the men could look, but not touch. I did two shows a night. After a couple of weeks, I'd made about six hundred dollars. I complained about the money, and that's when he told me I could make a lot more working the floor, receiving tips."

"Working the floor?"

"Serving drinks. At night, the place filled up with businessmen, all wearing expensive suits, flashing a lot of cash. So I thought, why not?"

"Was it better? The money I mean."

She grimaced. "I didn't realize most club owners shake the girls down for ninety percent of their tips. They keep them broke, pushing them into the back rooms, telling them that's where the real money is."

Annie stopped, letting out a deep breath, a look of resignation sweeping over her face. Maybe the anguish of those memories had subsided, but the regret would linger forever.

"The owners usually own a house or two," she said, "or have an arrangement with a cheap hotel. Right up front, they tell the girls the job includes room and board and the cost will be taken out of their pay. Then the bastards charge rent at triple the normal rate. Meals are also added to the bill, and after a couple of months, a girl usually owes the club owner more than a year's income. That's when the owner sets the hook."

I could sense her building anger as she remembered the men who set her up to take advantage in the worst possible way. It took less than a second to realize my situation wasn't all that different.

"So what happens to them?" I asked. "The girls I mean."

"Those who refuse to provide sex to the customers are usually sold to traders like the captain. He pays off their debt and then re-sells them for a profit at the auction."

"There's an auction? Where they sell people?"

Annie grimaced. "Yeah, you can't imagine."

"So how did you wind up here, on this boat?"

"After a month in the club working as a server, the owner said I owed him four thousand dollars and I'd have to work it off in the back rooms. When I told him to go to hell, he said he would give me a week to change my mind. At that point, I became a prisoner. I couldn't leave the club. I slept on the floor and ate kitchen scraps. That prick didn't care if I danced anymore or not. His objective was to break me, to force me into having sex with the customers."

"Weren't you afraid he'd get violent?"

"Club owners have to be careful. If they get a reputation for beating their girls or using brutality to get their way, the word gets around and they can't get new girls to work for them. So they pass the *problem* girls off to someone else, and make plenty of money in the process."

I had to ask. "During that last week, did you ever think about changing your mind?"

"I didn't get the chance. I guess he could tell I wasn't going to budge. Three days later, he drugged my coffee. The next morning, I woke up here, on the *Kelsey*. That's when I found out he'd sold me to the captain."

"But he treats you like part of the crew."

"Not at first. About ten days after I was brought onboard, the cook got sick. Burst appendix. That's when I lied and told the captain I'd worked as a chef in the states. The crew finally convinced him they needed to eat more than he needed the money I would bring from an outright sale, so we struck a deal. I agreed to work on the *Kelsey* for three years to earn back my freedom."

"Three years to pay off four grand?"

"The value isn't based on the original debt or what a trader has to pay to acquire us. It's how much we would bring on the open market if he'd sold me as a sex slave."

I took a deep breath, stunned over this new form of economics. It gave barbaric purpose and meaning to the despicable practice of selling human beings.

"So you've been working on this boat for over two years," I said. "And the crew leaves you alone?"

"They do now. Wasn't always that way, though. That first week, before I made the deal with the captain, I spent plenty of time in the hold and on deck in his so-called training program. I finally did exactly what you did. I went along with it, giving the men what they wanted rather than spending every night cold and hungry."

"But that stopped after you began your job as a cook, right?"

"Not right away. Even after I went to work in the kitchen, the men expected me to service them. Not because it was part of the arrangement, but because I was here and available. A couple of them even told me they were sure I'd eventually come around to their way of thinking, get selective, and want to have sex with my favorites."

"Favorites?"

I couldn't imagine having a relationship with any of the men on this boat. I had to believe Annie felt the same.

"It's the way men think . . . at least *these* men. Looking back, I might have been given more privileges a lot sooner if I'd let them continue to fuck me. But I've held out for over two years, and I've never had a reason to change my mind."

"Two years?" I blurted out. "You know, since you've . . ." I didn't finish the question, and in the following few seconds of silence, I began to regret asking it.

128

"Yeah," Annie said, wrinkling her nose. "Oh, I've thought about it. And there have been plenty of nights when I wanted someone next to me." She hesitated, as if unsure how to continue. "But I manage," she added. She cocked her head slightly and, for the first time, I saw a genuine smile.

"I like that." I pointed to her mouth, almost touching it. "This . . . the smile." I dropped my voice to a sympathetic whisper. "I guess there hasn't been much to smile about since . . ."

I realized she was looking at me, taking in every detail.

Pushing the curtain open, she reached out and took my hand, bringing my finger to lips. Leaving it with a light kiss, her expression softened. Drawing me in, she placed her lips on mine.

I wasn't expecting her advance. It took me a second to respond, telling myself it was okay. The softness of her lips was warm and welcome, so unlike the experience I'd had with the men on deck.

She began to laugh. "Your mouth tastes like cum."

"I can't imagine what my pussy tastes like," I blurted out.

Her eyes brightened. She gave the area a few playful squirts with the hose.

I hadn't shaved in several days. Carl always insisted I keep myself completely free of hair and shaving had become a regular part of my daily routine. Now I felt the rough stubble of new growth.

"Do you have a razor?" It seemed silly to be concerned over such a minor point in my grooming, but the idea of doing something normal was appealing.

Annie opened a wall-mounted cabinet and handed me a disposable Gillette. "I've used it once. Should be okay."

She continued warming me with an occasional shot of water from the spray nozzle as I removed every trace of hair, including a quick touch-up on my legs.

I wanted to hear more of her story, how she'd controlled the men after making her deal with the captain.

"So after you started working in the kitchen, what happened between you and the crew? How did you get them to leave you alone?"

Her mouth turned down in a scowl. "It wasn't easy. Telling them *no* didn't work. In fact, I think it made it that much more exciting for them. They kept ambushing me, grabbing my tits and butt. Occasionally, one of them would press me up against the wall and man-handle me. I finally figured out the only way to end their advances would be to make the prospect of fucking me so unpleasant they would give up on the whole idea."

"Like how?" I began to imagine Annie smearing herself with kerosene or some other foul-smelling substance.

"Every time one of them climbed on top of me or stuck their dick in my face, I would ask him how the food tasted the night before, if he liked the *special* ingredient I'd put in the soup or the gravy."

"You put something in the food?"

"No. Not really. But when they asked me what it was, I told them I'd had such a hard time deciding between engine grease and the long piece of shit I'd strained out the toilet, I'd used both."

"And they believed you?"

"They didn't know what to believe, not at first. But I kept at it, showing them all sorts of crap I pulled out of the bilge. One night, I set a separate plate of mold scrapings on the table. I told them it was leftover seasonings from their lunch and they should count on finding similar ingredients in every meal as long as they continued trying to force-fuck me."

I caught myself grinning. I could almost see them, a group of rugged men assembled around the dinner table, grumbling about the food and whining about the "unfair" treatment.

"And you were never tempted to drop even a small piece of garbage in the food?" I asked.

"As it turned out, the threat was enough. They ate dry cereal for a couple days. Then I made my pitch. I let them know I was planning to fix an untainted meal that night, *if* they left me alone. And the food would continue to stay clean as long as they kept their hands to themselves. It was a kind of 'fuck me at your own risk' policy. From that point on, they left me alone."

"They didn't complain to the captain?"

"All day long, from morning 'til night. But he didn't interfere. He told me he wasn't going to be a watchdog and I'd have to make my own arrangements with the crew. 'Course, the captain continued to get his regular meals. A couple of times I caught him hiding a smile as he watched them choke down dry corn flakes."

My impression of Annie was changing. I had assumed she'd resigned herself to a life of servitude—following orders because she'd lost her will to resist. But she was a fighter. And like me, she was waiting until she could walk—or in my case, run—away from this nightmare.

She and I were going to be friends.

Annie turned off the valve and handed me a towel. I hadn't been clean since being abducted, and the shower had done more than wash away the dirt. The tiny compartment felt like a temporary refuge, a place where, for a few minutes, I was safe. It was nothing more than a fantasy, but having Annie close, touching me, *protecting* me, helped to ease the memory of that first night in the hold.

I sat on the bed and dried my hair, rubbing the worn cotton all the way into my scalp.

"We're nearly the same size." Annie said. "Except for the obvious," she added, staring at my naked breasts.

I smiled. It was the first time since being dragged from my house that I'd felt comfortable hearing a compliment about my appearance.

Kneeling next to her dressing table, she began shuffling through a drawer. She held up a pair of shorts. "These will work. Now we have to figure out a way to handle those boobs. I usually wear a sports bra on deck when the weather's good. But my stuff is too small for you." She thought for a moment, then opened a second drawer. "Try one of these." She tossed a couple of tops on the bunk. "If they're too tight to button, tie them off at the bottom."

I picked up a light green blouse and held it against me for size. I was hesitating, not sure if I should ask the question. Finally, I said, "Annie?"

She turned, and in the muted light from the porthole, I saw a much younger, more innocent face.

"I understand the agreement you have with the captain. But the debt is illegal. You don't owe him anything. What keeps you here? Why don't you leave, run away at the next port?"

Annie's expression dropped. "If I run," she said, "he'll put a bounty on my head. In this part of the world, it's pretty much a guaranteed way to get your property back. And after tracking me down, he would sell me for sure."

"But once you were off the boat, you could go to the authorities and tell them what happened."

"I don't have my passport. Without identification, the police are useless. They turn deaf and dumb to anyone who can't prove their identity. I'd end up back in the captain's hands. He'd send me to the auction or sell me straight out to a street pimp. There's a good chance I wouldn't survive the traffic. The crazies on the street—sometimes taking a beating is part of the service. It's safer to stay here, wait out my time, and then—"

She stopped, both of us realizing she had just described my future. And it didn't sound like the odds were in my favor.

Annie sprang to her feet and joined me on the bed. "You're going to be okay," she said, putting her arm around my shoulder. "You're so much prettier than me, with a better body. And in this business, that's what counts. It makes you valuable, keeps you safe. I'd wind up with a bunch of drunks and addicts—anyone with the price of a couple of drinks. You're different. Your looks alone will keep you out of the bars and back rooms. I'm sure the captain will set a high reserve price at the auction. You might wind up with a wealthy businessman, somebody who won't shop you out. Maybe even royalty or an oil sheik who'll wrap you in diamonds and show you off to his friends."

The fear was back and I didn't try to hide it. I swallowed the lump in my throat and took a deep breath to ease my twisting stomach.

"Annie," I whispered, "I don't think I can do this . . ."

We slid together in a simultaneous embrace—she offering comfort and I desperately needing to receive it.

"I'll do everything I can to prepare you so you'll know what to expect." Annie's fingertips glided gently over my bare shoulders. "The best way to fight these bastards is to use the circumstances to your own advantage." Her hand found the small of my back. "I'll make sure you know what to look for, when to push and be aggressive, and when to pull back and let the men have their way." She reached lower, gently caressing my bottom.

Without hesitating, I buried my face in Annie's neck, streaking her skin with my tongue, the sweet tang in sharp contrast to the dull, residual taste of cum remaining from the loads of semen I'd swallowed an hour before.

I had shared kisses with one other woman. A year ago, our friends Mark and Tammy had stayed with us while visiting from the States. On the last night of their visit, the men suggested the women put on a show for them. After a couple rounds of margaritas, it sounded like fun.

Tammy and I left the room to change into lingerie and, in the process, hatched a scheme to drive our men nuts. She suggested we start with a few light kisses, then as the men became more excited, we'd drop a few hints about how much more motivated we would be if rewarded for our efforts. We knew they'd want us to continue, so we prepared to bargain with them.

"Shoes!" Tammy said. "We'll make them promise to buy us shoes."

"Two pair," I'd added. "If they really want us to put on a show, it'll take two pair."

Looking back, we'd done a convincing job. And while the caresses Tammy and I exchanged were certainly pleasant, they were scripted, meant to excite and tantalize our men and nothing more.

But now there was no audience, no one watching—no motivation other than my own desire to be embraced by someone who understood what I was going through.

Annie had been waiting, needing some sign I would welcome her affection. Her hands swept my body in a reckless embrace, tracing every curve and crevice. Cupping my breasts, she brought her face close, the touch of her lips warm and moist against my skin.

For a moment, I tried to think of a reason to stop her. But as I raked my fingers through her thick, soft hair, the scent of warm coffee and almonds filled my nostrils. The idea of resisting her advances completely vanished as she covered my right nipple with her mouth, her suckling releasing a rush of desire that sparked a tingle much lower.

I refused to question what was happening between Annie and me. As genuine as it was intense, there was no reason to believe my actions were driven by anything other than my own need.

I wanted this. No . . . I wanted Annie.

Pulling me flat on the bed, Annie covered me in a fury of wet kisses, exploring my naked form with determined hunger, tasting every inch of me. Overwhelmed by passion, her urgency was unsettling. And yet, anything less would have left me disappointed.

My own urge to respond, to give her the same pleasure, was more than I could bear. Bringing my hands to her breasts, I brushed her soft skin with my lips, letting my tongue swirl over her hardening nipples. I slid lower, resting my face in the perfect cove of her belly. Delighting in the soft contour of her stomach, I wandered over the area like a lost child, feeling my heart race as I traced the moist triangle below her navel.

Patient with my exploration, Annie let me take my time, allowing me to touch, taste, savor. It was an ache we both shared, our growing anticipation quickly becoming an unspoken promise of fulfillment. Nuzzling between her legs, I covered her wet pussy with gentle kisses, lingering in the exquisite pleasure of being so close to another woman. Extending my tongue, I found her swollen clit and drew it between my lips, my caress causing her thighs to quiver.

I blindly reached for her breasts, unwilling to break our connection for even a moment, wanting to join with her in every way.

Reveling in the tender affections that can only be shared with another women, I delighted in the smallest shift of her leg, the tender trace of her fingertips on the back of my neck. Every shiver, every tremble was shared—our individual pleasure impossible to separate.

Even after Annie shook in orgasmic surrender, after she cried out in ecstasy, I could not part from her. And in that quiet interlude of contented exhaustion, I stayed close, as if she were a living refuge, a place where I could find safety and hope.

I felt Annie's hands encouraging me to move and face her in a lover's embrace. Sliding higher, I joined her in a perfect union, her mouth finding mine, both of us eager to share the remaining traces of our passion.

As we lie together on the bed, I basked in the unanticipated bond forming between us. I briefly thought of rationalizing my actions with excuses, even speculating that my attraction to Annie had been motivated by vulnerability and fear, that her invitation was an opportunity to offset the cold detachment I'd assumed while the men mechanically used me for their own pleasure.

But there was no point in lying to myself. I had simply not expected to find such comfort, such satisfying abandon in the arms of another woman.

"Any chance the captain will let me stay here with you?"

"I don't know. I'm hoping he gets distracted with business and asks me to keep an eye on you."

"Even at night?"

"Especially at night."

I nestled closer, bringing my hand to her left breast.

Annie sighed. "But I'm guessing he'll want you at dinner tonight, with him and the other men."

"Will I be expected to . . . entertain them?"

"Before the night is over, he'll want you to show him want what you've learned. And remember, he's testing you, watching your reaction. He'll notice everything, so don't turn away or hide your face. And whatever you do, don't show any fear or anger. Anger is the worst."

Annie was making it clear that attempting to lie to the captain was useless. And since that's what I'd been doing all along, did he already know my actions were a sham? If so, he could be plotting something even more demanding than this morning's session. The prospect scared me.

"Is there any way to beat the captain's built-in lie detector?" I asked.

"Turn off your emotions. Convince yourself it doesn't matter to you one way or the other. When you talk about sex, joke about it. You could even compliment the men on their performances this morning. Say you could have used a bit more, that it ended too soon."

"You're kidding, right?"

"It's what the captain wants to hear. If he suspects you've got some fight left in you, he'll spread you out on the table and let the men have another go at you."

"He wants to see me jump up and down and beg for it, like a kid in a candy store?"

Annie thought for a moment. "Not exactly. I think he looks for a pattern, an attitude. He wants to see you enjoying the sex, no matter who you're with. You have to convince him that you

141

don't care where it comes from, you like it because it feels good and that's why you do it."

Everything Annie said made me want to scream. "How the hell am I supposed to convince him I'm getting pleasure out of this?"

After this morning's gang-bang, I couldn't imagine how any woman could derive the slightest degree of satisfaction from being passed around like a bottle of cheap wine.

Annie shrugged. "Look at it this way. He wants you to think of sex as being no different than having your shoulders rubbed. You're receptive to it because it feels good. He wants you to become selfish about your own pleasure, even a little demanding about it."

Annie must have seen the confusion on my face because she answered my question before I could ask.

"Yeah, I know, it sounds strange, but from a man's point of view, a woman who is focused on her own pleasure is the perfect challenge. I know there's that old world concept of the woman always being subservient, you know, walking three steps behind the man, only speaking when spoken to, all that crap. Now, there's lots of men, especially the ones with money, who want to show off their sexual skills by satisfying a woman who has demanding requirements. They want to demonstrate their world-class technique." She snickered, shaking her head at the testosterone-impaired logic.

Annie was spouting psycho-babble, and I had no idea how any of it applied to me. I needed to know how to act, what to say—anything to help get me through the next few hours.

I went right to the bottom line.

"I know you're trying to help, but I don't understand how any of this is going to . . ." I hesitated, my voice breaking. It took another few seconds before I could add, "Annie, I don't know what I'm supposed to do."

She brought a hand to my cheek and gently kissed me. "It's all about the money. In this business, the big bucks go to girls who generate repeat customers, men who can be manipulated into believing they have a relationship with the girl—that she's more than just somebody to fuck. The girls who stay a bit detached and make the guys work for it are the ones who bring in the most income, and receive the most respect."

Respect. That seemed like an odd word to use.

"How long has the captain been doing this? Selling girls, I mean."

"I've never heard him say. From what I've picked up listening to the crew, he's been transporting girls for several years. Maybe longer."

"And no one's ever tried to stop him? Parents, family, nobody?"

Annie's eyes locked on mine. "Do you think someone is coming after you?"

My heart dropped. "I . . . had a husband." There was a part of me that continued to hold out hope, believing Carl would realize what he'd done and mount a recovery effort.

Annie looked surprised. "You were married?"

"I thought so. Apparently, he didn't feel the same way."

"And the captain knew that when he took you?"

"Of course he did."

"That's unusual. As far as I know, he's only bought and sold girls who were single, with no ties to anyone."

"The captain knew all right," I bristled. "He met my husband first . . . before he met me." I paused, my voice filling with emotion. "A few hours later, I had a price on my head."

"I don't understand."

It was all I could do to push the words out on a whisper. "He used me for collateral, for a poker bet. And then he lost me."

144

Annie fell quiet, no doubt thinking how pitiful my marriage must have been.

Finally she asked, "Any chance your husband works for the government or has political connections? Is that why you were living in Sri Lanka?"

I knew where she was going with her questions—being married might improve my odds of rescue, the existence of a stray legal record helping to prove my identity to the authorities.

"No, nothing like that. Carl and I were on an adventure, to see the world. We'd stopped in Sri Lanka to take a break and figure out where we wanted to go next."

"What about your family?"

"I was an only child. My parents died when I was in my teens."

I waited, dreading the question that always followed—*how did they die?* I had learned to explain their deaths in generic terms, to describe their demise as an unfortunate car accident so I didn't have to go into the details of how a freak tire blow-out had caused their car to roll a half-dozen times, rupturing the gas tank, and enveloping the car in flames.

Annie must have sensed my discomfort. Unlike most, she didn't pursue it.

"I'm curious what made you choose Sri Lanka?" she asked.

"It wasn't so much a choice as it was circumstances. We'd been traveling for months and were ready for a break. We'd originally planned to stay a few weeks, a month at the most. Then Carl saw an ad for a boat mechanic. It was an opportunity to replenish our savings. The job turned out to be something he enjoyed, and then we found this great house, and—"

I stopped. I was rambling on about how much I had enjoyed our life on the island—a life I would never see again.

Annie seemed confused. "But something must have happened, between you and your husband, I mean. Weren't you getting along?"

I understood her question. How could any husband bet their wife in a poker game, especially one who supposedly loved her?

"I don't know," I began. "Maybe we'd started to take our relationship for granted. Apparently, he took it one step further, making it disposable."

The sudden change on Annie's face told me she knew.

"He's not coming after you, is he?"

The truth was obvious, even to her. And no matter how much it hurt, it was time I admitted it

146

to myself. I'd been bought and paid for. I was a possession—something less than human—owned by a man who planned on selling me to anyone who would pay the price. In this world without love, my value would be decided at auction, where the ruthless elite would evaluate me as they would any other asset. The fact that I was human—born with a need for compassion and freedom—was a minor inconvenience.

I shook my head, feeling the tears zigzag down my cheeks. "No. I doubt he's even looking for me." I remembered the look on Carl's face, the way he turned his back on me as the captain carried me off. "He's done with me," I added.

Annie snuggled closer.

"I must seem pretty pathetic," I said, "thinking he might still care about me."

"We all want to believe there's someone who cares about us. I believed it too, a long time ago."

"Was that before you went to Bangkok?"

Annie paused, as if retrieving a deeply buried memory. "There was a man," she said. "It was over four years ago, when I was in my early twenties. We lived together, even talked about getting married. Turned out, that's all it was . . . talk. To him, a wife and family were always in the future, something he would think about after he'd made his fortune, become famous, or

147

fulfilled some other fantasy that conveniently kept him from making a commitment. We were two years into the relationship, and I still didn't know how he really felt about me. I got tired of waiting, not knowing if he was serious. I finally told him I would stay one more year, but only if we began planning a future together. He accused me of pressuring him, attempting to mold him into a middle-class zombie. A week later he told me we should spent some time apart so he could figure out what he wanted to do. As far as I was concerned, that was his answer. The next day I moved out. I wanted to get as far away from him as possible. And that's when I saw the ad for entertainers in Bangkok. It sounded like a chance to make some fast money and enjoy a change of scenery."

"I've looked back at that decision a thousand times," Annie continued. "There were so many other things I could have done, other places I could've gone. And the sad part is, I have no one to blame but myself. That first week at the club, I sensed something was wrong. I should've packed my stuff and gotten out. But I kept waiting for things to get better. I believed a lie, let my guard down, and I ended up here, doing time on this fucking slave boat."

Annie's story was heartbreaking, and yet, from what she'd told me about the business, she'd been one of the lucky ones. Most of the girls who ended up on this boat were unwilling passengers on their way to the auction and an uncertain future—like me.

"Selling women . . . that's the captain's only business?" I asked.

"Sometimes he delivers a shipment of guns or other contraband. But not often. Most of his money comes from buying and selling girls, picking them up wherever he can find them and rolling them over to club owners and pimps after they've been *trained*, and are ready to go to work. If they're pretty and light-skinned, he takes them to auction where there's a lot more money.

I was becoming keenly aware that it was more than my body that would be offered for sale. It was my entire life. Perhaps it was macabre curiosity, but I had to know what I was worth. "How much are we talking about?"

"Are you asking if you can buy your way out?"

"Is that possible?"

"It would have already happened. You can bet the captain talked to your husband before we left port to see if he wanted to buy you back. He probably had some computer geek hack your social, run your credit, and do a background check to see if you're related to a wealthy family. He's in it for the money, and he doesn't care where it comes from."

"So what *am* I worth?"

"When a girl is sold at auction, the final price depends on how much the buyers are willing to pay. If the high-rollers show up, a young, pretty girl can easily bring fifty grand. If she's white, drug free, and cooperative, she can bring up to a hundred thousand."

I felt my stomach turn sour as the blood left my brain. I imagined some girls—those not fully understanding the kind of future that waited for them—would be impressed, even flattered that a potential buyer would put such a high price on their body. I knew what it really meant—I was never getting out on my own. Even the lesser amount was far beyond what I could ever work off, borrow, or steal.

Annie gave me a squeeze. "I know it sounds hopeless, but I've heard stories about girls who beat the system. They become the favorite of a wealthy man, and then use their influence to gain the man's trust and eventually, with a little manipulation, their freedom."

The favorite. Compared to how many others?

Maybe it was naïve to believe, but I had to ask. "Do any of the guys ever wind up falling for the girls they buy? Do any of them ever get married?"

Annie shook her head. "It doesn't work that way. Not here. In this part of the world, a relationship with a working girl is always temporary, never permanent. They're considered playthings, toys for the rich. They have no place on the social scale, and they're never acknowledged by other women who come from good families. Once a girl steps foot inside one of those clubs, she becomes invisible. Nobody helps her. Nobody cares. Not even the men who pay to ride her night after night."

"What about the cops?"

"Most of 'em get to fuck the girls for free, especially if they're connected. A high-ranking official can do the weirdest shit you can imagine, and nobody says anything."

I caught Annie's scent, the musty aroma mixing with my own. I brought my hand to the inside of her leg and then higher, resting it between her thighs.

"I can't stay," she said. "I have to get back to the kitchen and do the prep work for dinner. And I need to do some laundry."

"Can I help?"

151

"It's best if the captain doesn't see us together while I'm working. I don't want him getting suspicious and think we're plotting something."

"But he made you responsible for me. You're supposed to make sure I don't wander off the ship and fall into the ocean."

She smiled. "Turning you over to me was a token gesture. He expects me to convince you to go along with the program, to make sure you don't get any ideas about jumping overboard or looking for a place to hide. He'll also want to know if I think you can be trusted with free run of the ship."

"And . . . can I?"

"I'll find him when I leave here, let him know you're a safe bet. Give me ten minutes, and then you should get out and walk around. It will help clear your head."

The idea of roaming around the boat by myself made me shudder. "What about the men?"

"They won't touch you unless the captain gives them permission. As far as I know, he hasn't given any of them a green light to go beyond this morning's session."

"What if you're wrong? What if they're waiting for me to show up on deck so they can have another party?"

"I've never seen it work that way. The captain likes to keep things organized. And he doesn't allow any of the men to act on their own initiative during the training period."

"But you had to fight them off, even threaten to poison them before they would leave you alone."

"That was after the training, when I was on an equal footing with the men. The captain knew I had to prove myself, make them respect me. So he let the situation run its course."

"So I can roam around the ship? Go anywhere I want?"

"Yeah, and there's something else." She paused. "This is important. When you run into the crew, act as if what happened this morning was no big deal. Above all, never show fear. Never turn around and walk in the opposite direction. If you try to avoid them, and the captain hears about it, he'll set up another gang-bang. He's always watching, listening, and he'll be asking the men how you react when you're around them."

I let out a heavy sigh. "I'm not sure how to handle this. Give me an example."

"If some of the men bring it up or make jokes about the training, talk to them openly, without emotion. Treat it like an afterthought. You can't let the sex mean anything."

I had done everything I could to push the morning's activities out of my mind. The idea that I might have to revisit the details, talk about it with the same men who had bent me over and filled me at both ends was revolting. "I don't think I can do that."

Annie bristled. "Remember what I told you? About making them respect you?"

"What the hell am I supposed to say? That it was great? That I really enjoyed being cluster-fucked by a bunch of filthy assholes?"

She must have seen it in my face—the absolute misery and heartbreaking grief of losing both a husband and my freedom in the same short span of a few days. Since waking up in the hold, I'd told myself I had to stay strong, hide the despair and hopelessness of my situation. But Annie had given me a glimpse of my future, and it was one that was twisted and depraved, controlled by people who would think nothing of keeping me a prisoner for the rest of my life.

I laid my head on her shoulder and let the tears come, exhausting the pent-up emotion I'd been holding for hours.

Taking my face in her hands, Annie kissed my forehead, then said, "I know this is hard. Think of it as a game, and you're learning the rules so you can play to win."

"Tell me what I should say to the men . . . exactly." My voice was breaking.

"Ask them if they enjoyed themselves, if there was anything more you could have done. Make them believe you're someone they can talk to, have a conversation with."

"Really? That's what they want to hear?"

"It's exactly what they want to hear. And you've got to convince them you mean it."

I supposed in the juvenile and often perverse workings of the male ego, what Annie was telling me made sense. A girl that retreated into her shell, afraid and withdrawn, left the men feeling rejected. As a result, their treatment of her was impersonal, detached, and prescribed. But a *fuck-buddy* would give them someone to talk to, someone they could form an emotional bond with, no matter how informal or short-lived. It reminded me of the tomboys with the cute haircuts and overly-muscled thighs, the girls-next-door who were always up for a last-minute date that was sure to end with a Coke and a blow-job.

Annie was right. Call it respect, camaraderie, or a brotherhood of bastards, a girl who knew how to man-talk was always treated differently than the prissy debutante—or the cowering fraidy-cat.

Somehow I had to learn to play the part of this stronger-than-steel girl Annie was describing. And I would have to do it without a rehearsal, learning my lines as I went along, playing off the words and actions of the other actors—because to me, that's all they were.

Chapter Seven

The keel of the ship cut the surface of the unsettled ocean with straining uncertainty. I felt the rise and fall of every wave, the ominous shuddering of the hull an intimidating reminder of the power of the elements. I knew the captain and crew welcomed the stiff breeze, the boat's resistive tremors nothing more than minor complaints in comparison to the advantages of increased speed and reduced time to reach the next port. But I could sense the ship's struggle to please its master.

There was a lot of the *Kelsey* I hadn't seen—another half-deck forward of Annie's cabin and, above that, the bridge. The more I learned about the ship's layout, the greater the likelihood of discovering its weaknesses. I might even find a temporary hiding place I could use during an escape.

I pulled on the shorts and shirt Annie had left for me and tied my hair back in a ponytail. Looking at myself in the mirror, I noticed the marks around my mouth from resisting the gag-ball were nearly gone, and a slight shadow of discoloration on the upper part of my arm was all

157

that remained from being thrown against the spare tire in the back of the van.

My battle scars—at least the visible ones—were fading. The memory of how they were acquired would last a lifetime.

I sat at Annie's dressing table and picked up one of her lipsticks. Twisting the base to expose the color, I felt my stomach turn. The idea of intentionally making myself attractive was revolting. Painting my lips, making them more noticeable, would suggest the pleasure they could provide when sliding over a fully erect cock.

I might as well write the words *fuck me* across my forehead.

I set the tube back on the table and picked up the bottle of sunscreen, slathering it on my arms and legs.

. . . *The captain wants to see a change in your mindset, a transition to being outright selfish about your own pleasure, maybe even a little demanding about it.*

Annie's words haunted me.

Was this what she was talking about? While the absence of makeup and lipstick would probably go unnoticed, its presence could work to my advantage. According to Annie, I had to show the captain I was becoming cooperative, even eager to please. Maybe my efforts to be more appealing and desirable could actually help convince him I was ready to play the game. Based on her logic, if I no longer behaved like a captive, he would stop treating me like one.

It was the complete opposite of how I felt.

I applied the light pink gloss, smacked my lips, and ran a Kleenex over my teeth. I prayed Annie was right.

Topside, the men were busy at their stations, watching the horizon for other ships, performing maintenance on idle winches, and replacing worn line and pulley-blocks. Acknowledging me with an occasional smile or nod, they paid little attention to my presence on deck.

I found the main salon and went below to search the galley, expecting to find Annie preparing the crew's dinner. I was disappointed to find the kitchen empty. I decided to poke around.

Equipped with two ovens, a five-burner stovetop, and a large refrigerator, I was amazed at how it all fit in the tiny space. One of the walls had been reframed to accommodate two microwaves and a large metal storage cabinet. Inside, I found a coffee maker, two serving pots, a four-slice toaster, a blender, and a mean-looking can opener. The only thing missing was Annie.

I remembered she needed to do some laundry. The most likely place for a washer and dryer was below deck in the hold or engine room. I would look for her later. I wasn't comfortable returning to either place.

Returning topside, I walked forward as far as I could. Noticing a vent stack a few feet behind the pulpit, I sat and leaned back against the base, wondering if it would be safe to shut my eyes. It wasn't sleep I craved, but distraction. I wanted the rush of the ocean and the feel of the wet breeze on my face to relax me—give me a few moments of peace. But after a few minutes, the usual sense of calm and tranquility didn't come, and I realized the diversion offered by the elements could not penetrate the virtual bars of my floating prison. Instead of inspiring me with hope, the influences of nature were a dismal reminder of my captivity.

Refusing to give up, I concentrated on the wind, sensing its changing direction, trying to imagine where it might take me. Pretending it possessed the power to lift me off the ship and carry me up into the sky, I focused all my energy into believing it was true. With each new gust, I kept waiting to feel the rush of air underneath my legs, the sudden chill from my moist skin confirming my weightless ascent from the deck.

If it would blow strong enough, I could travel to...

The truth was devastating. I couldn't think of a single destination that offered a sense of refuge—no place where family or friends were waiting for me. When my parents were alive, I'd received the selfish privileges afforded to an only child. Now, with them gone, my lack of siblings was a massive liability. There was no one to look for me, no one to miss me. And that included my bastard of a husband, who was probably already hustling the bars, searching for another pretty cherry—someone young, ripe, and ready.

"Hi, Jewel. Remember me?"

It wasn't the captain's voice—I would have recognized it immediately. I turned to face the approaching crewman. It was R.J., the one who had pretended to penetrate me during this morning's fuck-fest.

I'm trying to forget you, asshole. The words were on the tip of my tongue. I stopped myself. For some reason, R.J. had trusted me to keep his secret. I had no idea why he had chosen to simulate sex with me, and frankly, I didn't care. I would treat him as I would any stranger—especially one who had exhibited the courtesy of not shoving his cock inside me before introducing himself.

"Yeah, I remember you . . . from this morning. You were the last man in line."

"No, before that."

I shook my head.

"We met in your house," he said. "At the card game. The captain introduced me as Roy, but the men usually call me R.J. You probably don't recognize me because I had a full beard and much longer hair. Before we left port, I cut it, shaved everything off. I wanted a clean start."

I shut my eyes, desperate to block it out, or at least keep it under control. But there was no way to hide the contempt I felt for the four men who had abducted me. It was a volatile combination—fear and hate—and whether conveyed in my expression or the way I shifted away from him, he must have noticed, because he jumped right in.

"I don't blame you for being upset. You were sold down the river. You didn't even know what was going on until it was too late. That's why I didn't—"

"Fuck me?" I finished his sentence, the disgust in my voice painting my words a livid red.

His eyes dropped to the deck, but not in the same distracted manner I'd seen this morning, when he'd seemed disconnected from the rest of the group. His mouth was tense, his lips pressed thin. He was irritated. Maybe he didn't appreciate being interrupted or didn't see himself as the deserving target of my resentment. Either way, he was getting pissed.

I felt the slow creep of uneasy concern spreading from the center of my gut. My short taste of freedom had made me testy, ready to pick a fight. What if he fought back? While he might not use direct force, he could no doubt make my life a lot more miserable. I remembered what Annie told me: *Temper your attitude, remain neutral.* If she was right—and I had no reason to think otherwise—I had to get my emotions under control.

I filled the silence with a question. "So what's going on?"

R.J. looked up. Not at me, but higher, into the rigging and beyond. "Just wanted to see how you were doing. That's all."

"Did the captain send you?"

"Nope. He doesn't use messengers. If he wants to talk to you, he'll do it face-to-face."

I didn't believe him. And I certainly wasn't ready to trust him.

"You've known him a long time? The captain, I mean."

"Long enough. Out here time isn't measured the same way. Life moves much faster. More bang for your buck."

I changed the subject. "You'd been to Sri Lanka before? I mean before the other night, when you met my husband." It was all I could think of.

"Many times." His eyes relaxed. "I was born in the States, but I grew up in Venezuela, raised by my grandparents in Puerto Cabello. I started working the docks as a teenager."

The idea of having a normal conversation with a man who regularly participated in the training of sex slaves seemed as rational as dancing through a minefield. And yet, I wanted to know the reason he'd approached me. Even though he denied being the captain's puppet, his tactics had all the earmarks of a test, to see how I would interact with a member of the crew. If it was, I had just stepped on stage, the curtain was going up, and it was time for my opening line.

"I'm originally from California," I began. "Born and raised. My husband and I came to Sri Lanka about a year and a half ago. For the adventure, I guess."

"I'm sure you never expected it to turn out like this." The underlying tone in his voice, the hint of pity—it almost sounded apologetic.

"How *will* it turn out?" Maybe R.J. knew what was going to happen to me, maybe not. Either way, I wanted to hear his answer—even though I had no way of knowing if he would tell me the truth.

He was quiet for a moment, as if sizing me up, deciding if I could handle it.

"I've heard the stories," he began, "and that includes everything from the garbage that happens on the street to the auctions where girls are sold at high prices."

"Any of them have a happy ending?"

He hesitated, as if searching for the right words. "It's not about being happy, at least not in this part of the world. You do what's necessary to survive."

There was something in the way he said it, inferring an undeniable reference to himself. If this was part of the training, he was quickly falling out of character. It was a good time to ask about his earlier deception, why he pretended to fuck me in front of the other men.

"I'm curious about this morning, when you put on a show for the others. What was that about?"

His voice fell to a whisper, barely discernible above the sound of the boat's hull cutting through the water. "Have you kept it to yourself?"

"Yes."

"Even from Annie?"

"Would it make a difference?"

My question seemed to throw him, and it took a moment for him to answer. "I know this is going to sound strange, but I've never been comfortable with the training, the way it's done."

I didn't attempt to hide my astonishment. "*You're* not comfortable? Did you ever think about me, or any of the other girls?"

"That's what I mean. It's mechanical, the repetition designed to break down your resistance."

Despite his fairly convincing display of sincerity, I wasn't ready to believe him. "So you never join in?"

"Just the opposite. Most of the time, I do it without a second thought. But I don't like it."

"So why did you make an exception with me?"

"Every once in a while, we get a girl onboard who reminds me of someone I once knew. And it makes me realize what I gave up, the life I could've had." His expression had fallen, casting the unmistakable shadow of sad resignation.

"And that's what stopped you? I reminded you of someone else?"

R.J. leaned against the cabin structure. "Yeah. Not that you look exactly like her, but the blonde hair, the shape of your body, it was enough to take me back a few years. That's usually how it happens, when there's something familiar in one of the girls we're delivering . . . gets me thinking about second chances. So sometimes I hold back on the sex, thinking that after she gets to know me, maybe she'll *want* to be with me, instead of just going through the motions."

"And that's what happened this morning?"

"Yeah, seeing you, the way you walked up to us. It all came back to me."

His act was well-rehearsed. I wondered how many times he'd repeated it—and how many trusting innocents had believed him. He was attempting to convince me he was an anomaly, an albino of the species, a hopeless romantic who possessed the conscience of a saint. In other words, total bullshit. Only freaks and monsters belonged in the skin trade. Possessing even a sliver of decency would make him a misfit, a maverick who couldn't be counted on when the situation called for a ruthless response.

As I'd listened to R.J. spin his yarn, I wasn't sure what angered me more—his blatant assumption that I would take the bait or that his performance was an attempt to test my gullibility. Later I would learn that naïve young girls were in great demand, sought after by the most despicable in the trade. More easily persuaded with promises of a privileged lifestyle or an early release from enslavement, an inexperienced girl—one quick to believe whatever she was told—made the ideal candidate for buyers who engaged in deviant and perverse alternatives to traditional sexual practices. These girls were the pearls of the business, with fiendish Svengalis finding them much easier to brainwash, before suspicion had replaced rainbows and unicorns.

I wondered if R.J. were about to suggest I dress up in a Catholic schoolgirl uniform and prance around the deck sucking my thumb.

Any lingering doubt about his claims of heartfelt compassion vanished as I looked up and noticed the captain watching us through the heavy plate windows of the pilot house. Shifting his attention from the sea, he'd lowered his binoculars to monitor the interchange between us. I doubted he could hear our conversation, but he could definitely see us. And I knew he was evaluating my behavior—my gestures and expressions.

Knowing R.J. was testing my gullibility made me want to rip him a new one. But I held my tongue. If I expressed curiosity instead of rejection, it might reduce the amount of additional training I would have to tolerate. I would play R.J. like the idiot that he was.

"Would it have been better if I had *offered* myself to you?" I asked.

"You mean this morning?"

"Yes . . . would it have made a difference if you thought I wanted you inside me?"

The change in his expression was immediate. He hadn't expected me to be so responsive—and it threw him.

Now I understood what Annie was talking about. I *could* take control. He was only one man, but it was a victory nonetheless.

"I . . . think so," he stammered. "And after you've left the boat, I know I'll regret it—not having been with you."

There it was. In total contrast to the decidedly more virtuous image he'd portrayed a few minutes ago, it was definitely an invitation. In the language of hardened sailors working the sex trade, his words were mere suggestion, innuendo at best. Yet he was dangling the bait.

And if I went for it, initiated some kind of sexual overture, it would prove to him—and the captain, watching from above—that my conversion to a willing and responsive sex slave was well under way.

I had to convince both men I was ready to accept the unseemly future that waited for me. And that meant building their trust, earning their confidence, and then, when the time was right—in a moment of distraction—I would escape.

I spoke with as much sincerity as I could muster. "I want you to have the memory."

Rising to my knees, I reached out, beckoning to him with my fingers. He tried to suppress the smile forming at the corners of his mouth, no doubt pleased with my invitation. As he approached, I slid my hand between his legs and gripped the back of his thigh. He hesitated at my touch, perhaps thinking I was preparing to slam my fist into his crotch.

"It's okay," I added. "I want to do this."

"You don't have to," he said. "That's not why I came over. I just wanted to talk."

It was a ploy to give me an easy way out. I had to give him credit. Even with the promise of my consenting touch, he was going to play his part to the very end.

I brought a finger to my lips. "Shhh. Enjoy it."

I began shutting down. No more deliberation or considering the alternatives. The captain's eyes were on me, and how I handled myself in the next few minutes could make an impact on how he treated me. My logic was simple: If I could convince the captain I was ready to cooperate and make the best of my circumstances, it might increase the amount of freedom I received for the rest of the trip.

I opened the fly of R.J.'s jeans and found his swelling cock. Freeing it from the confines of the fabric, I brought both hands to the task, to make fast work of it.

Moving slightly to the right, I feigned the need to get more comfortable. In reality, I was giving the captain a better view. I didn't want him to miss a single moment of my performance.

Although R.J. seemed a bit wary, his full erection told me his concern was quickly being replaced with eager anticipation. No doubt he'd harbored some level of expectation when approaching me, but he couldn't have assumed I would be this receptive.

Ignoring the trace odor of sweat, I brought my lips close, brushing them against his shaft. I felt his hands against the back of my head, pulling me in. He wanted more.

Don't resist. Go with it. Get it over with.

Closing my eyes, I swirled my tongue over the tip of his dick, jacking him with my right hand. Keeping his cock slick with saliva, I heard him gasp as I began working my mouth and hand in concert, stroking him with a constant, unbroken rhythm.

Groaning with pleasure, he grabbed my ponytail as I took his dick further down my throat. I felt his ragged nails catching loose strands of hair. I fought the distraction, determined to keep a steady pace.

Carefully cupping his balls with my left hand, I tested his reaction to a squeeze and release.

A low grunt erupted from his throat. "Mmmmm . . . yeah, that's good."

I pushed my thumb between his testicles, applying enough pressure to maintain that fine line between pain and pleasure.

In less than a minute, his legs began to tremble. He was ready.

Feeling the contractions at the base of his cock, I clamped down with my fingers, not letting the ejaculate enter his shaft. I would let the pressure build until he was on the verge of exploding.

"Oh god! Let go! You've got to let go." He was twisting his torso back and forth, begging for release.

I held on for a count of three before letting his cum flood my mouth. Tightening my lips around his foreskin, I let it collect, holding it in my mouth as I jacked the last of it from his system. It would have been easier to let it spill to the deck. But the captain was watching.

Completely spent, R.J. backed away.

I increased the suction, making sure I didn't lose any as he withdrew. I swallowed, his thick load traveling halfway down my throat. Bringing a hand to my neck, I pretended to work it down as I gulped again. Finally, I opened wide, letting him see my empty mouth.

I remembered Annie's advice.

"Was it alright?" I purred. "Did I do okay?"

His nod was barely discernable.

Rising to my feet, I instinctively reached out, needing a handhold to offset the pitch and roll of the sea. R.J. grabbed my wrist and pulled, the momentum sending me into his arms. His quick step back told me it wasn't intentional. The implication was clear: He was done with me.

"I have to get back to work," he said. "I've already been gone too long."

I glanced up at the wheelhouse, expecting to confirm the captain's continued scrutiny. A lone crewmember stood behind the controls. He offered an approving nod.

When had the captain left? Had he missed the show I'd so meticulously staged for his benefit?

R.J. had turned and was already walking toward the passage leading to the main salon. From my earlier exploration, I knew the same entrance provided access to the crew quarters. I assumed he was headed below deck to clean up . . . and no doubt brag about his conquest. The thought that he might encourage the other men to take a turn made me shudder.

I couldn't let it get to me. I'd deal with it when—if—it happened. Right now, I wanted to enjoy my moment of victory. I'd won another small battle, and even if the captain had missed my grand finale, at least one member of the bridge crew had seen it. I had voluntarily provided sexual favors, and certainly, the ship's master would hear about my willingness to provide sex on demand. With any luck, it would be enough to convince the captain that no further group training was necessary.

Luck . . . and manipulation. They were my most powerful weapons. If I could keep my wits intact and my eyes open, the right opportunity would present itself. No matter what it took, I would find a way off this boat.

Chapter Eight

Seeking a break from the hot sun, I made my way to the stern. The few crewmembers I passed were friendly, but not aggressive.

"Hi, Jewel. Do you need anything?"

"Can I help you find your way?"

Annie had assured me the men wouldn't bother me unless given permission by the captain. Even so, I was relieved to find their attitude tempered, almost restrained in comparison to the uninhibited aggression I'd experienced this morning.

Not ready to return to Annie's cabin, I kept walking until I reached the stern of the boat. Grateful for the shade cast from an overhead canvas awning, I stretched out on one of the built-in benches and closed my eyes. I wanted a cool place to rest while I mulled over every detail from the last two days—everything I could remember. There might be something the captain overlooked, a dropped clue that would raise questions about my disappearance. While Carl would try to explain my absence with a fabricated excuse about personal or family matters requiring my return to the states, there would be a few people who knew me well enough to doubt his story. If they took their concerns to the authorities, I might end up on the international watch list, and Carl would have a lot of explaining to do.

I must have dozed off. When I opened my eyes, the captain was standing over me.

Startled, I tried to recover. "Were you looking for me?"

He ignored my question. "You'll be joining me for dinner tonight. There will be five at the table. My second and two senior crew members."

"Will Annie be there, too?"

He studied my face. I let the question stand.

"She's always there, serving. It's part of her duties."

"What I meant was, will she be sitting at the table, with us?"

"As I said, she has duties to attend to." He wouldn't budge.

I wasn't ready to give up, not yet. I had to show him I wasn't afraid to ask for what I wanted, and that I could be confident as well as compliant. "Could one of the crew take over, just for tonight?"

"You seem to like Annie," he said.

"Don't you?"

His expression grew stern, the lines in his forehead contracting into bumpy ridges. I was pushing it, but I was counting on him to interpret my boldness as spirited mischief.

"I don't want you getting chummy with anyone on the boat, and that goes for Annie, too. If I have to, I'll keep you separated." He said it matter-of-fact, without raising his voice. It didn't sound as much a threat as it did a rule.

I had underestimated the importance of recognizing his dominion. On *his* ship, he demanded absolute submission to his authority. I needed to give him a reason to consider my request. Otherwise he might keep Annie and me apart simply to exert his power over me.

"I thought it would be nice to have another girl at the table, that's all." I could see by his unchanged expression, it wasn't enough. "But it's your decision," I added. "You're the captain."

The change was barely perceptible, a slight twitching of the muscles around his eyes.

He cleared his throat. "Getting one of the men to take over in the kitchen is inviting disaster. I suppose if Annie did most of the cooking, I might trust one of them to serve." He cocked his head. "I'll have to promise him something. You still want Annie at the table?"

Another test, to see if I would exchange sexual favors for something I wanted.

"Of course." I offered an inviting smile.

The corners of his mouth lifted slightly. He seemed pleased, not only with my answer, but with my quick response. He was master of the boat, yet he was just another man, subject to the same weaknesses from which all men suffered.

"Dinner's at seven. But first, we have some work to do. I want you to go to Annie's cabin. Use her makeup, do your hair. Then come to my quarters." He looked at his watch. "It's five o'clock. You have thirty minutes, no more."

I felt my face falling, my breathing turning short, labored. *He mustn't see it. Block it out.* I tightened the muscles in my forehead and lifted my chin. "A private party?"

"Call it whatever you like. I need some pictures. I have buyers who want an advance look."

I let out the breath I was holding. "What should I wear?"

"Nothing."

Chapter Nine

The captain's cabin had been the ship's master stateroom. Saturated with the smell of wood polish and sweet-oil varnish, the room exhibited a museum-like quality, a place arrested in time. Much of the original woodwork and finishes remained, and the décor resembled the interior of an early twentieth-century posh hotel room. If I hadn't already seen the rest of the boat, it would be easy to assume I was traveling on a luxury liner from sixty years ago.

Furnished with period pieces, the bed was topped with two thread-worn throw pillows and a faded burgundy spread. A loveseat was tucked against the far wall, and on either side, a pair of claw-foot end tables supported electric chimney lamps, their bases bolted to the surface to prevent movement. On opposite end-walls, a built-in mahogany dresser and matching armoire completed the decor.

The captain had answered my knock with a single-word command—*Come*. Arriving naked, I'd closed the door behind me and waited for instructions. As much as I wanted to throw something around me, I didn't dare. I saw it as an opportunity to show him unflinching cooperation, to do as I was told without bitching or whining—a trait I hoped he would remember when I asked for more privileges.

I found him hunched over a foldout desk with a laptop computer and large notepad. I recognized the screen display as a familiar e-mail program. Without looking up, he said, "Make yourself comfortable. I'll be ready in a minute."

I estimated his cabin at no more than 250 square feet, and from where I stood, I could see everything except the bath. Not knowing what else to do, I walked to the opposite end of the room and peeked inside the head.

Like Annie's, the space was a hodge-podge of old and new. The original marble vanity had withstood a half-century of use, even though it had faded to pale yellow from long-term exposure to the salt air. The toilet had been replaced by a marine electric, and yet, the bathtub—an absolute luxury aboard a ship of this size—remained in place, offering enough room for one.

"We do the pictures first." The captain was on his feet and pointing to the bed. "Then we can change things around for the video," he added.

A part of me was thankful there was no one else in the cabin. While I wasn't sure what the captain's "customers" expected to see in the pictures—perhaps a demonstration of acrobatic skill or an expression of feigned delight in spreading my legs for the camera—I was relieved the poses would not require the crew's assistance. Even so, I was certain the captain would be watching my reactions, evaluating me to determine if more training would be required before I was put on the market.

"On my back or stomach?" I waited for him to direct me. The more specific he was in his instructions, the more effort I could make in demonstrating my cooperation.

"Sit with your legs apart, facing me, and turn your head slightly to the right."

As I went through the motions, I thought about how many times I'd wanted to have a boudoir session with a professional photographer, thinking how much fun it would be, even blushing as I imagined pushing the boundaries of "artistic expression" to produce one or two pictures my husband would have enjoyed. Now the very thought of doing something special for Carl turned my stomach.

With each change of pose and position, the captain reminded me to keep my legs wide, exposing every detail. I thought about the men who would be looking at the pictures, and the criteria they would use to evaluate me.

"Now turn around and bend over."

I did as he asked.

"Spread your cheeks with both hands. I need a close-up," he added.

The captain made an adjustment on the camera and fiddled with the lens. "Relax your grip. You're distorting things."

He took half a dozen shots, but I could tell he wasn't satisfied.

"You're not wet enough. I need to see your lips glisten. The shinier the better."

He may as well have asked me to spontaneously grow wings and fly. Somehow I had to figure out how to give him what he wanted. "Do you have any lotion?"

He shook his head. "Doesn't work. Never looks like the real thing. And if a customer spots a fake, he'll question what else is being misrepresented."

"Can you use the shots you've taken?"

"I'd rather not. Wet brings more dollars—higher bids, more profit."

It sounded like another test. I slowly began to nod. "I understand . . . give me a minute."

I stuck a finger in my mouth, coated it with spit, and worked it between the lips of my vagina.

Normally, I flowed with the least bit of arousal. But this situation was too clinical, too calculated. I needed more stimulation. I needed . . . Annie.

Lying back on the bed, I concentrated on her image, her smile and sparkling eyes, the gentle fingers that had touched me like a soft evening breeze. I thought back to a few hours before, when her mouth had been so inviting, her tongue playfully jousting with mine. I remembered how she had slowly worked her way down my stomach, then lower to my clit, taking it gently between her lips. I brought my free hand to my abdomen, pretending to caress the back of her absent head, letting my fingers roam through her soft, silky hair.

Perched on the bottom of the bed, the captain had changed to a digital video camera to record my efforts to masturbate. Rather than issue verbal commands, he kept silent, perhaps realizing it would be to his advantage to let my hands—and mind—wander without direction.

Back to shooting stills, the captain crawled around the bed, using several angles. I tried to ignore him, keeping my focus, letting both shutter and flash dissipate into a background of creaking timbers and rushing wave-wash.

"Okay, that's enough. Move your hand so I can see it."

My juices were running freely, so much so I was sure I was soaking the bedspread. From the repeated strobe-flash that followed, it must have been exactly what he was waiting for.

He switched back to video. "Put your fingers in your mouth."

I did as he asked, remembering how Annie had tasted, imagining my coated fingers had come from her pussy instead of mine.

"Good," he snapped.

Maybe it was meant as praise, but his static tone and inflection reminded me of the reflex response expressed by a dinner guest who'd been passed a saltshaker. He returned to his computer and connected one of the cameras, preparing to download the images. "You can stay here or go back to Annie's cabin. Dinner's in an hour."

I didn't want to stay a second longer than necessary. "I need to borrow something from Annie's closet, and I'll like to fix my makeup."

He nodded without speaking. Apparently we were done.

As I stepped into the hall and shut the door behind me, I should have felt a sense of relief. The refuge of Annie's cabin was waiting for me, yet I was hesitating, as if the choice between staying with the captain or returning to Annie was an oddly difficult decision.

Then I realized the problem . . . I didn't want to do either.

I wanted to go home.

Chapter Ten

I was becoming accustomed to walking around naked. Even the increased sense of vulnerability I'd initially experienced was beginning to fade. And from what I was learning about the sex business, clothing was another tool of the trade, used to tease and titillate, to exploit the body to best advantage.

Annie's cabin was the only place on the boat offering any sense of safety, and yet I'd been standing in the hallway for the longest time, staring at the half-inch mahogany door, unable to bring myself to open it.

I knew Annie was working in the galley—her room would be empty and bleak.

For the first time since being abducted, loneliness had overtaken fear. I missed my house, with its covered front porch, clapboard siding, and the gingerbread trim that hung from the front eaves. I missed its compact kitchen with the bay window over the sink, where I'd watched the clouds build over the Knuckles mountain range, wondering if the next flash of lightning would release a curtain of sheeting rain.

And for an instant, before the reality of what my husband had done to me shattered my daydream, I missed Carl. In all my fantasies about our often predictable, sometimes too comfortable relationship, 1 never imagined him selling me like a worn sofa, trading me to a stranger to settle a gambling debt. Maybe he'd been afraid of the beating he would have taken if he'd tried to fight for me. Even the possibility of using our .38 police special to equalize the odds had not been enough to overcome his reluctance to defend me. Fear was a powerful motivator. In the last two days, it had convinced me to do things I never would have considered. *My* reasons were easy to rationalize—I had done it to survive. Maybe the same thoughts had gone through Carl's mind as he'd watched the captain sling me over his shoulder and carry me screaming out of the house. Maybe at the time, that was all he could think about—*his* survival.

The abrupt *clomp-clomp* of footsteps descending the stairs from the main deck startled me and I grabbed at the door handle.

Bullshit! I was done with hiding. It made no difference on which side of the door I stood. If someone was coming for me, they would find me, despite my attempts to be inconspicuous.

It was Massey.

I felt my stomach tighten, the muscles in my legs and shoulders turning me to stone.

"How are you making out, Jewel?"

I continued to face the door, my back to the hallway, determined not to show any fear. "Okay, I guess."

His hands were suddenly around my waist. My breath caught in my chest.

"If you need something, let one of us know."

With that, he slipped past me, his touch nothing more than a polite buffer in the tight hallway.

I waited for that sense of relief that comes after the threat passes, when you realize all the apprehension and worry was unnecessary. But the deep sigh that emptied my lungs left me feeling alone and abandoned.

I was a prisoner in a place where justice and mercy had no meaning, and unless I found a way out, I could easily spend the rest of my life condemned to serving the fantasies of those who were willing to pay the price.

Chapter Eleven

The main salon was the largest interior space on the *Kelsey*. Serving as both dining room and general gathering space for the crew, most of its original opulence and splendor were gone. The elaborate mahogany moldings, oak chair rails, and wainscoted walls were covered with white-wash, eliminating the more labor-intensive maintenance required by exposed wood accents. It was the same for the stamped tin ceiling, the once impressive pressed-metal tiles now buried under several coats of beige paint.

Annie had returned to her cabin for a quick shower and change of clothes before escorting me to dinner. After asking to borrow one of the three dresses I'd seen in her closet, she'd convinced me to stay with shorts and a top—the same way she was dressed. 'You don't want to appear overdressed,' she'd cautioned. 'The captain might interpret it as a statement of status, that you're suggesting you're better than your situation. He could tell you to take everything off and eat naked—he's done it before. And remember, as far as the crew is concerned, it's just another meal. You want to blend in, let them see you as just having shown up to eat . . . nothing more, nothing less.'

As I looked around the room, I could see she was right. It was obvious most of the men had showered and a few had even shaved. They wore clean versions of the same unofficial uniform—denim jeans and loosely-woven cotton shirts.

I had no idea what was expected of me, and Annie had seemed intentionally vague, assuring me 'it was better to play it by ear.' Her comment had left me tense and apprehensive. But I didn't press her. Maybe she didn't know, or if she did, she thought it best not to tell me. Either way, our exchange of hugs and kisses before leaving the cabin made me trust her even more.

Four tables for six provided extra seating capacity for guests and visitors while in port. The captain's table was designated by its position—at a slight distance from the others. He was seated with his two senior crewmembers. The two men rose and stepped away from the table as Annie and I approached, giving us our choice of seats.

Annie sat first, next to the captain on his left. I pulled out the chair next to her, but the captain stopped me. "No, Jewel, sit here." He pointed to his right.

He wanted Annie and I sitting directly across from each other, with him at the head of the table.

"You ladies are looking very nice this evening." Annie introduced him as Mario, the chief mate, a gruff-looking sort with beady eyes. Completely bald, he sported a skullcap of sun-damaged skin that snaked down his back and shoulders, the splotchy-pattern suggesting his genetics had been influenced by a maternal encounter with alien DNA. Even the edges of his ears—reduced to a dark, paper-thin crust from exposure to the sun—implied extraterrestrial origin. He seemed anxious to make sure I understood his privileged rank and authority.

Annie's dismissive glance told me his comment was hollow and insincere. Probably something she'd heard before, when other girls sat in the same chair.

Sitting next to me was Carlos, the second mate. A middle-aged Latino of average height and build, he was strangely unremarkable—the kind of man who could move invisibly through a crowd and then suddenly pop up as if out of nowhere. His sullen expression seldom changed, and when the captain introduced him, he offered a slight nod. Whether he knew it was pointless to compete with Mario's free-wheeling rhetoric or was quiet by nature, he kept his thoughts to himself.

I leaned in and whispered to the captain. "Thank you for letting Annie join us."

"Don't forget. There's the matter of compensating the men who took over Annie's duties." He motioned toward two crewmembers who were busy setting salads on the table. I didn't recognize them from this morning, and judging from the taunting exchanges between them, they were looking forward to experiencing what I was sure had been described in exacting detail by the five I had already serviced.

Two men.

I let it go unchallenged. Expecting any exchange to be fair—especially one negotiated by the captain—was foolish.

"So, Annie," the captain began, his eyes shifting around the room as if monitoring the crew's behavior, "how do you like having a night off from the kitchen?"

"From the way you're asking, it sounds like I'd better not get used to it."

He raised his eyebrows, not expecting to be challenged at his own dinner table.

"You have our guest to thank." His voice was condescending, like a parent admonishing a child to mind their manners.

Annie ignored him, directing a quick smile at me, conveying a sympathetic kinship. It was all she could do above the table. Underneath, I felt her foot rubbing softly against my leg. She had slipped off her sneaker and was flexing her toes against my shin.

"In the morning," the captain said, "we'll begin the final leg of our trip, a sail around the tip of Burma, then north into Yangon. We should be at anchor by this time tomorrow."

The review of the itinerary was for my benefit. I was sure the rest of the crew had made the run dozens, perhaps hundreds of times. I hoped his decision to share the details of the route was a show of camaraderie, in recognition of my apparent cooperation.

"Normally the sea is calm this time of year," he continued. "But there's a front moving in from the west. It'll bring some large swells. Wind too. By early morning, we may run into rough ocean." He looked directly at me. "You may want to spend the night in my cabin. The bigger bed will be more comfortable if we get a lot of roll from the waves."

Annie lowered her foot. I felt like I'd been cut loose, my lifeline to sanity unexpectedly terminated.

"Tomorrow," he continued, "I'll tell you more about the auction, what you can expect to see and hear. Also a few suggestions about what to say to the buyers before the bidding starts."

"And during," Mario interjected.

"And during," the captain repeated.

"It's all about how you respond," Mario continued. "You want to encourage the buyers, push the interest level up to get their last nickel. 'Course, I've seen girls do the opposite. They bring the price down with a smart mouth or say they're going to run first chance they get."

The captain's number two seemed anxious to demonstrate his personal knowledge of the process. And from the captain's sudden change of expression, I could tell it wasn't appreciated.

"Do a lot of girls do that? Run, I mean, after they're sold?" I cringed as I heard the expectation in my voice.

"A few," the captain replied. "But most of them regret it. We'll talk about it tomorrow."

"I don't understand. What happens to them?"

Annie's foot was back at my leg, this time flailing with desperation. She was warning me, urging me to drop it, change the subject. The captain scooted back slightly in his chair, his towering presence seeming to darken the entire table.

"If you run," he said, the threat in his voice sure and certain, "then I'll have to—"

"Then the captain has to call out the gremlins to bring you back," Annie chimed in. She was trying to defuse the tension. "The girls sold at auction have to be transferred to their new owner before the sale is considered final," she added. "If a girl runs before being delivered to the buyer, the seller has to find her and bring her back, or there's no deal."

The captain took a deep breath. "No more talk about this until tomorrow," his irritation obvious. He picked up a fork and stabbed a piece of tomato.

Anxious to reduce his suspicions, I said, "Well, I've got nothing to run back to, except to castrate that son-of-a-bitch I used to call my husband."

The captain glanced up from his salad.

"Besides," I continued, "I could end up with a whole new life, even a better one. That happens, doesn't it?" I stared directly into the captain's eyes.

"I don't keep tabs on the girls I sell." His face turned sullen again, almost stern.

"I thought—"

"Maybe the boys would like to watch us dance." Annie cut me off again.

This time I understood. The captain was strictly business. And it was *his* business, not to be discussed at the dinner table. The only thing I learned for sure is that he had no interest in what happened to the girls after he sold them. As far as he was concerned, I was a piece of merchandise.

The captain turned to Mario. "Put on some music." He motioned to Annie and pointed to a center space between the tables. Apparently, this was to be a command performance.

Annie rose and walked around the table. Reaching out, she hoisted me from the chair. "Step between my legs and stay tight," she said. "If we give them the kind of show they want, they won't try to cut in or separate us."

I brought my head next to hers. "How far do we take this?"

"The captain wants the men entertained. And he'll be watching to see how you perform in front of them. Unless he stops us, plan to go down on me."

"Another test?"

Before she could answer, the wall-mounted speakers exploded with a Latin Salsa. She dropped her hand to my butt and pulled me tight.

The men's reaction was nearly as loud as the blaring music.

Annie's hips began to sway.

I felt awkward, my movements stiff, out of time with the beat of the music.

She brought her lips to my ear. "Slide up and down, and stay close. Don't be afraid to come from behind and use your hands."

I did as she suggested, grinding my crotch on her thigh.

Annie's talent as a dancer was immediately evident. Curling around me like a slithering python, I caught myself shivering as she left traces of her tongue against my skin.

At first, I avoided making eye contact with the men. I didn't want any of them interpreting a fleeting look as an invitation to join in. But an occasional glance over Annie's shoulder reminded me I might not have a choice in the situation. They appeared captivated by our every move, as if hypnotized by an irresistible siren song.

Weaving her fingers into my hair, Annie pressed her lips to mine. The men roared, edging us on with their crude remarks.

"That's right, Annie. Tongue that bitch. Fuck the little princess, fuck her good."

"Hey, Annie, that's my cum you're tasting. Plenty more where that came from."

Our lips separated. "Rip my top off," Annie commanded.

I began to unbutton her blouse.

"No, tear it off. Go after me like you did this afternoon when we were alone."

I looked into her eyes, searching for the same passion I'd seen earlier when we were in the seclusion of her cabin. I saw something, but it was different—manufactured, missing that wild trace of soaring abandon.

Grabbing her top, I yanked it open. Buttons flew across the room, the men diving to the floor to snatch them as if they were treasure coins from a Spanish galleon.

Annie whispered in my ear. "Suck my tits."

Even though I knew it was staged—an act to entertain and distract—I welcomed the warmth of Annie's breasts, the soft contact providing a welcome separation from the catcalls being thrown from a few feet away.

As my mouth found her right nipple, I felt her hand slide between us. Popping the snap on her waistband, she lowered the zipper. A few exaggerated gyrations of her hips brought the shorts to her ankles, exposing bare skin.

The men shouted their approval.

"There's the Annie I remember!"

"Been a long time since we've seen that fine piece of tail."

Annie lifted my face to hers. "Grab my butt," she ordered.

My hands fell to her bottom, my fingers tracking the crevice of her ass, the smooth canyon drawing me to the moisture between her legs.

I noticed several men opening their zippers, pulling out their cocks.

"Move your hand to the front and put your fingers inside me . . . now!" Annie commanded.

I knew what she was doing. By convincing the men we were about to fuck each other, they wouldn't dare interrupt us. Their reaction—most of them already beginning to stroke themselves—was exactly what she'd hoped for. They would empty their own cocks, sparing me from having to do it later.

I felt the slick wetness of her soft passage as it opened to my probing fingers. Despite being simply a performance, it was a connection I didn't want to break.

I was counting on Annie. She was the strong one, keeping me focused on improvising a convincing display. But as spasms of pleasure began to course through her legs, I worried she would lose her concentration.

I should have known better.

"We need to crank it up a notch," she said. "Let's change the position. This time, come at me from the back . . . and stand to the side so they can see."

It wasn't her raw direction that surprised me, it was her voice, filled with breathless anticipation. In spite of the crude remarks, the men's explicit response, and the less-than-intimate setting, she was deriving an erotic high from the experience. Perhaps it was something left over from her days as a dancer, when she relished in the voyeuristic sensuality of being watched, even admired as she captivated an audience. Part of me wished I could share the same feelings. But I was too distracted by what was going on around me.

I slowly withdrew, my fingers coated with a glistening mixture of sweat and her juices.

"Wait!" Annie whispered. "Bring them to your mouth first. And make sure they're watching. Look into their faces as you suck them."

She was scripting our actions in the spur of the moment. But I had to trust her. She'd been through this before. She knew the men, and their expectations. This was not the time to challenge her logic.

I did exactly as she instructed, making eye contact with as many as I could. A few appeared on the edge of orgasm, their expressions of total intoxication in perfect harmony with the increased speed of their stroking.

The taste of Annie's fluid was as liberating as the most potent liquor, the sudden rush of my own desire helping to lower my inhibitions. Maybe it came from Annie's precise direction, knowing she was there to help me, or maybe I'd reached my limit of how long I would allow fear to persecute me. But in that moment, I felt a sense of reckless release, my defensive anxiety falling away like the spent leaves of autumn. The men no longer mattered, their insensitive taunts bouncing off me as easily as a chorus of whistles from a construction crew.

Let the disgusting pigs watch, I thought.

I placed my hand on her backside. Annie bent over, grabbing her thighs for balance as she pointed her bottom toward the bellowing crowd.

Starting with a single wet finger, I began gently, slowly.

"More," she commanded. "Two fingers, in and out. Make sure they can see it."

I added a second finger. The additional girth brought a squeeze from her pussy and a muted whimper from her throat.

"Is that okay?" I was afraid I'd hurt her.

"God yes," she panted. "It's what they want to see."

I understood. Just as I'd been using her body to detach myself from the attention of the men, she was using mine to isolate herself from their perverse suggestions.

Some of the men began to moan, their voices confirming the pleasure so clearly demonstrated on their contorted faces. It gave me an odd, unexpected sense of satisfaction; we were providing them with such a stimulating display they were content to masturbate rather than break us apart.

As the room filled with grunts of carnal pleasure, I leaned over and caught the sweet smell of Annie's hair, the scent washing over me like a wave of new hope.

A rough pair of hands came from behind, gripping my waist, then sliding lower, cupping and kneading my ass.

I was more dumbfounded than startled. *What the hell does he think he's doing?*

My mind raced with objections.

His hot breath scorched my shoulder, his rock-hard cock pressing against my butt.

This man wanted more than self-gratification, and he was making it clear he intended to plant his seed deep.

"Annie can go or stay," he said. "It's up to her."

It was R.J.

I wasn't surprised by his desire to fuck me. But it angered me. Earlier, he'd tried to pass himself off as the sensitive caring type—that he was somehow better than the rest. Now, apparently, there was no advantage in continuing his ruse. Whatever his game had been, he was done pretending.

My fingers slipped from Annie's pussy.

She turned. "What's going on? Do you need to—"

Annie's eyes locked on R.J.

Her hands clasped my face, our noses nearly touching. More than offering reassurance, she wanted my attention, saying something, mouthing the words.

Finally, I got it—*the captain is watching.*

I saw him over her shoulder. Standing about ten feet away, his expression was intense, as if analyzing every detail—and my reaction to it.

Somehow, I'd known the captain would want to test me in another encounter with the men. I didn't know when or where, but I knew it was inevitable. He would want to evaluate my reaction and compare it to my earlier response on deck. *Had I learned anything? Was I more compliant?* Now he was ready to make whatever sick and bizarre observations he felt necessary.

With Annie's eyes straight-lining into mine, she offered a smile meant only for me. "I won't leave you," she whispered.

I reached for her, but she was already sliding behind me, unbuttoning my top, giving R.J. access to my breasts.

Her lips against my ear, she concealed her instructions with an overt display of tongue. "It will look better if you take the bottoms off yourself."

Showtime.

I didn't hesitate. My actions—or lack of them—could easily make the difference between the captain believing my sudden transformation to willing harlot was real or a ploy to gain his trust.

Popping the snap on my shorts, I let them fall to my ankles. R.J.'s hands skimmed over my bare ass, acquainting himself with every nook and cranny. Abandoning all former pretense, his invented reluctance was gone, and so was any simulated consideration for my feelings.

He began fondling my pussy, pushing a finger deep inside.

I clenched.

Relax. Turn it off. Don't let it get to you.

Using his other hand, he began relentlessly kneading my right breast. He reminded me of a persistent child tugging at his mother's apron strings, determined to capture my attention.

"Reach out, grab his cock," Annie said.

I followed her instructions without question. I knew she was doing more than just help me deal with R.J. She was preparing me for what was about to happen. But I refused to think about what this could ultimately lead to. I had to stay in the moment, keep fear from getting a foothold.

The restriction of the shorts around my ankles made my stance awkward. Afraid I might trip over them, I stepped free of the fabric.

"Let's get you more comfortable," Annie said. "Follow me and stay close."

With R.J. in tow, she guided me to an empty tabletop. Taking the lead, she plopped her bare bottom onto the smooth Formica surface and scooted back, ready to cradle me. I leaned back into her arms and spread my legs, giving R.J. full access.

I was trembling, as nervous as I was afraid. I wondered if Annie could feel it.

In seconds I had my answer. She tapped my shoulders, warning me not to show it.

Struggling between panic and resigned acceptance, I closed my eyes.

"No," she whispered. "Open them. Let the men see you watching."

It ran counter to every instinct—to the overwhelming need to protect myself. And yet I did as she insisted, letting it all in.

Hoping to inject a ring of confidence in my voice, I spoke with as much courage as I could muster. "I guess you didn't get enough this afternoon. Tell me how you want it."

Again, Annie leaned in. "Talk with your body, not your voice."

R.J. stepped between my legs, his stiff, protruding cock bouncing in eager anticipation. He was quickly joined by two men—Carlos, the second mate, and Butch, the first man to demand and receive my favors. The thought of Butch touching me made me cringe.

Don't let it show.

The decision to choose or exclude any man was no longer mine.

As if on cue, the anxious pair grabbed my ankles and lifted my legs, keeping them spread wide as they propped them on their shoulders. I felt a confusing rush of hands groping me, squeezing my breasts, pawing at my thighs.

The added frenzy of racing fingers . . . R.J.'s pulsing cock pressing hard against my pussy . . . the shrieking music piercing my ears. It was too much. I couldn't stop the quick *yelp* that released an uncontrollable tremor.

"Hey girl," Carlos said. "You need to calm down."

I'd blown it. Unable to keep it inside, the men had seen a glimpse of the real me, and it had betrayed the role I was attempting to play.

"She *can't* relax," Annie shouted over the stereo. "That's a muscle spasm. She's in a strain."

Annie was covering for me and, giving me time to redirect my focus and get the suffocating stranglehold of panic under control.

"Push her toward me," Annie said. "I'll give her more support." Annie slid back a bit more, giving me enough space to lie flat with my head in her lap. For a moment, our eyes locked. I half-expected to see sorrow or pity. Instead, I saw the fire of grit and determination. She would be my anchor. She would get me through this.

She bent low, her voice cutting through the raucous music. "I don't know if the captain saw it or not. But don't worry about it. If a dick comes within reach, start stroking it."

In every way that counted, Annie was there, ready to direct me. Although I had momentarily slipped out of character—allowing myself to feel, to think, to be that young woman who spent her afternoons lost in the pages of a romance novel and dreaming about some future time when Carl and I would settle down in our perfect-forever-place—I had a job to do. My performance was being evaluated on the spot, and I might not get a second chance.

The rest of the men had left their chairs, gathering around us to watch. Behind them, I caught another glimpse of the captain. He'd stepped closer, to better his vantage point.

It irritated me—his cold detachment as he silently directed the crew. He was the consummate puppet-master, pulling the strings of his single-minded minions as they shared the spoils of conquest.

I felt the last traces of fear melting away, replaced with the kind of resolve borne from the fury of revenge. Anger was quickly becoming my new ally. I would use it, channeling it for my benefit.

In an intentionally dramatic move, I pointed directly at the captain. Beckoning to him with a wave of rippling fingers, I saw the mask of command leave his face. Whether confused or curious, it was obvious I had broken through his façade of authority. He took a step toward me, then another. R.J. noticed his approach and shifted to the side, relinquishing his position.

Annie pinched at my ear. It was the only signal she could give without being obvious. I had no idea if she was urging me to continue or break it off. I had to go with my intuition. My come-hither signal had worked, and now I had to make the best of it.

I reached out and took his hand. It was like grabbing a snake, encouraging the slithering, slimy reptile to explore my orifices.

He couldn't hide his conflicted uncertainty. He was always in control, the one to initiate physical interaction, to say when, where, and how much. Now he was on the receiving end.

I guided his fingers to my mouth, running my tongue up and down the full length of each one, pausing at the webbed spaces between.

His eyes softened, maybe in appreciation of something new, something he might have taken for granted. No longer needing my suggestive teasing, his free hand began to roam my stomach, then higher, to my breasts. Cupping one then the other, he rolled each erect nipple between his fingers, as if assessing their size and elasticity.

There was no point in holding back. My behavior—here and now—could make or break my chances of negotiating a better future. I reached down, searching for his cock. More than the indiscriminate play I was offering to the other men, I would leave no question that my actions toward *him* were intentional.

The deep lines in his brow began to relax and, for a moment, I saw the hint of a much younger man beginning to emerge.

It lasted mere seconds.

In the time it takes to flip a light switch, he shut me out. Backing away, his near-instantaneous transition was complete—he had reassumed the hard, dismissive stance of captain, his familiar veneer of protective indifference confirming his status of ship's commander.

Glaring at me with fierce disapproval, his grim expression made it clear I had crossed the line.

This would be my first lesson in the hierarchy of command. Joining with his men in any common activity—especially one of pleasure—would reduce him to their equal, just another member of the pack. The captain couldn't allow any of the crew to see him in such a vulnerable state. He had to distance himself—and quickly.

For a few moments, I'd broken through the wall that separated his emotions from cold hard logic. I knew it, and so did he. And if necessary, I could do it again.

R.J. had delayed his penetration in deference to the captain and was anxious to pick up where he'd left off. He wanted his dick inside me, and this time, it wouldn't be a simulation.

As he spread the lips of my pussy, my leg muscles tensed, my body resisting his dry entry.

Annie felt it.

"Wait a minute," she said. "Let me help." She brought two fingers to her mouth, coating them with saliva. Nudging his eager cock to the side, she gently placed them inside, drawing on my natural juices.

R.J. waited, watching Annie, apparently convinced she was working in our mutual best interests.

"Now try it," she said.

As R.J. slid inside, Annie encircled the base of his shaft with her thumb and forefinger. I knew what she was doing—the extra pressure would help speed his orgasm. Yet to me, it was much more than that. She had joined with me, becoming an equal part of the experience. Each thrust from R.J. was buffered by Annie's touch, reassuring me, bolstering my courage and calming my fears. I had become a target for the sexual cravings of strangers, and Annie was teaching me how to separate myself from the cold, calculating intensity of their desire.

The captain continued keeping a watchful eye. I was sure he was waiting for that nearly imperceptible twitch of my forehead or a quiver in the corner of my mouth. His ability to detect and interpret facial movements was a skill he'd developed out of necessity, to deal with those whose intentions were laced with deception. It not only gave him a negotiating advantage, it also provided him with a built-in lie detector. On the boat, I'd seen him deduce a crewman's answer to a question before he could finish asking it. If I wasn't careful, his keen eye would quickly see through my guise of a cooperative participant in what was quickly shaping up to be another chaotic gang-bang.

With too much at stake to let an unconscious tic disrupt my strategy, I could think of no better way to stay focused than to distract myself with the activity around me. It seemed like a contradiction, yet it made perfect sense. Losing myself in my newly invented persona of a willing and eager sex kitten would make it far more difficult for the captain to discern my real objective.

Instinctively, I reached up and brushed the side of Annie's face. She didn't hesitate. Bending to reach me, her lips covered mine, her open mouth inviting our tongues to mingle. As her free hand swept my chest, I immediately discerned her touch from the others. Challenging those already playing, she began to fondle my breasts, switching from one to the other, massaging them with unhurried attention. Unwilling to share, she protectively covered my right nipple, wanting it exclusively for herself.

I'd been tolerating R.J.'s cock in an attempt to convince the captain of my receptivity to random sex, but Annie's touch had set my clit on fire, my pussy to flow.

I wasn't the only one to notice it.

"My god, you're so wet." R.J.'s rhythmic thrusting was increasing in speed to match his contorted expression. Now jack-hammer-quick, I knew his release was seconds away.

Annie's words echoed in my brain: *There are a lot of men who want to prove they can satisfy a woman with demanding requirements. They want to be one of the few who can please her.* If that were true—if it was about my pleasure as well as his—

I had to convince R.J. I was actually enjoying our coupling.

I looked straight into his eyes. "Don't stop. I want to feel you come inside me."

Trembling, he lifted his head and dug his fingers into my butt cheeks, his juices mixing with mine, filling me until I overflowed onto the table.

"About time, R.J. Others are waiting."

I glanced around the room. Several of the men were blatantly stroking their dicks, preparing for their turn.

I closed my eyes and swallowed hard.

I would have to take them all.

I waited for the rush of fear to overtake me, for the paralyzing apprehension of being subjected to another fuck-fest.

I felt nothing.

I wondered if seeing the men eager to fuck me—again—had rendered me numb, and as soon as the initial shock gave way to the reality of cocks and cum and foraging hands, I would feel the wretched sadness, the crushing misery of despair common to all who are stripped of their freedom.

Maybe that would be waiting for me later, when the truth of what I'd done became all too real. But right now, I didn't feel deprived, or in distress, or even particularly unhappy.

Had I crossed the line between make-believe and reality? Had I subconsciously—out of necessity—become the character I had invented? The idea terrified me. The very essence of who I was seemed to be in flux and, if I weren't careful, about to be changed forever.

In the most intimate, meaningful way I knew how, I reconfirmed my identity—if only to myself. I was still in control—still Jewel—with choices and a sovereign future where I would regain dominion over my body and soul.

Something touched my forehead, distracting me. Even as I looked up into Annie's face, I couldn't be sure what it was—until I saw a second tear rolling off her cheek.

I didn't understand. Annie was much stronger than I was. Maybe she was feeling sorry for me, concerned I was about to be overwhelmed with a sea of cocks, all ready to penetrate me. I started to tell her it was okay, that I was going to make it through this.

But I didn't get the chance.

Annie began sliding out from under me, changing her position to lie beside me. She brought her lips to my ear. "I'm not going to let you do this alone," she whispered. "We'll take them together." Leaving a light kiss on my lips, she added, "It will be over much sooner this way."

I had misread Annie's tears. Her pain did not originate from pity or sympathy. Her grief was the unmistakable sign of a lover's sacrifice. She'd surely remembered a time when she had been on that same table, resigned to service a hoard of rowdy men, simply to survive. And now, the thought of watching me go through it alone was more than she could bear.

From the very beginning of her enslavement, Annie had fought for the right to be left alone, and through her own persistence, had found a way to keep the men at bay. Only after intimidating the crew into compliance had she been able to make a successful transition from sex slave to cook.

Now she was about to throw it all away . . . for me.

She scooted tight against me, preventing anyone from squeezing between us. Poking Butch with her foot, Annie's intentions became immediately clear as her voice broke through the men's tribal song of mumbled expectation. "Jewel's not going to have all the fun," she scolded. "I want some of this, too."

Her words hung in the dank air. If there was any hint of a victim's surrender in her voice, Annie had masked it completely. She gave every impression of *wanting* to join in, of being eager to participate.

I laid my arm across her, my hand drifting down her belly, then lower, to her swollen clit. Gently taking it between my fingers, I felt her legs quiver.

Even surrounded by a pack of sex-hungry men, the passion between Annie and I could not be suppressed. As my own desire continued to build, I became less and less concerned about the random hands that groped me or the field of erect cocks poised to fill me. Regardless of the way it began or the captain's intentions as it progressed, as far as I was concerned, it was only Annie and me. The thought was a powerful one, and as it settled comfortably within my brain, it ignited the most primal of instincts, my own clit now screaming for attention.

As if able to read my mind, Annie's fingers plunged into the flowing river of cum left by R.J.

Grunts of approval filled the room. It gave me an uneasy sense of encouragement, and I accepted it for what it was—perverse anticipation.

Annie began massaging my swollen button of skin, the initial tingle of pleasure shooting to my toes. Carlos and Butch were the first to notice, their eyes showing surprise as they felt my leg muscles quivering in response.

"Annie, you luscious piece of ass! See what a fine influence you've had on this one."

"We should ask the captain to keep Jewel onboard. She could help with *all* the chores."

"He'd certainly never have to worry about a mutiny, aye, boys?"

More comments filled the room, some in admiration, others offering suggestions.

"Excellent show here, Captain."

"R.J. left her sloppy. I'm sure Annie will take care of that, make her squeaky clean."

Our efforts at mutual masturbation provided only a momentary distraction, and now our obligation to satisfy the men's needs was unavoidable.

In moments, Albie stepped in, bringing his engorged cock to my pussy.

With Annie guiding his penis inside me, he began vigorously thrusting, the repeated smack of wet skin and moist, sticky suction easily heard over the men's continuing crude encouragement.

With both of us spread out in front of him, Albie couldn't contain himself. In less than a minute, he began filling me, the sensation between us diminishing with the additional lubrication. Separating from me, his warm liquid followed, running down my crack and over my smallest hole.

I hated myself for thinking it, but I couldn't deny it—it felt good. Maybe it was having Annie next to me or the men vying for position in a confused, randomized cue, ready to fuck us. The reason didn't matter. It was as satisfying as it was depraved—this incongruous sense of power, having such raw and commanding influence over them. We were the center of attention, both of us desired by every man in the room.

Overwhelmed by the unexpected good fortune of having two girls to enjoy, the men became momentarily frustrated. "Which one? I want them both."

Mario immediately offered a suggestion. "I'm going for Annie. Haven't had that pussy in far too long. Then I'll finish up with Jewel."

What I did next was as unthinkable as it was outrageous—I smiled at them. Not at any particular man, but all of them. They were no different than little boys excited over new toys, wanting to play with everything at once.

The men's seemingly disorganized approach quickly took on a systematic and methodical process. Starting between Annie's legs, each man took a minute or two to fuck her. Then, like moving down a buffet line, they shifted to me, filling my pussy, coating their cocks with a mixture of our juices. Having aroused their appetites, they leaned over the table toward our mouths, their glistening cocks bobbing inches from our lips. Without hesitation, we turned our heads to meet their glossy manhood.

I'd held onto Annie as long as I could. I needed my hands elsewhere. Turning slightly to the side, I took each one in turn, stroking his shaft while working the ball sac. I knew from experience it was the most effective—and fastest—way to jack-off a man.

One after another they came to us. Most lasted long enough to make the full circuit, their spurting loads of cum flowing like a thick, hot river down our throats. Once, between men, Annie tapped my shoulder, a dribble slipping from the corner of her mouth. I stretched to meet her, my lips covering hers to form a tight seal. The load passed between us several times before we swallowed our equal share.

Two days ago I would have been terrified. Yet in a very short time, I had learned to survive the most despicable of circumstances. I had taken control of my thoughts and emotions—even as a dozen men ravaged every inch of me. I was discovering how to read them, picking up cues from each man, identifying his preferences from moment to moment. My reactions and expressions were quickly becoming calculated gestures, displayed to produce a desired response and, if necessary, make any one of them believe the most useful lie.

As they reveled in my eager submission, I realized they were undeniably susceptible to my influence. I could convince a man he was providing me with pleasure beyond anything I had ever experienced or I could show disappointment and crush his ego, cutting him deeper than the sharpest blade.

I compared facial expressions, looking for similarities. It was almost too easy. Wide eyes, dilated pupils, taut jawlines, furrowed creases across their brow and, just before orgasm, a slight lift of the chin revealing strained, corded muscles in the throat.

I was learning a new language, one never taught in school. And from the collective focus of their attention, combined with the grinning aftermath of those having spent their load, I had become an excellent student.

Even though the circumstances of my captivity were abhorrent and the probability of my future as a sex slave all but certain, in some ways I had been fortunate. I had discovered the key to my survival, intangible benefits that could translate directly into power—power over men, and surely over a few women as well. Although my current situation didn't grant me the kind of sovereignty that offered the prerogative of choosing whether to stay or go, it was no less real. When required to service a man, I had the choice of being merely compliant—lying there like a mannequin—or I could grant him the favor of an enjoyable, even memorable, experience.

Was this what the captain had wanted me to learn?

The captain! I quickly scanned the room. His wasn't there. Perhaps he'd seen enough. It brought an odd sense of disappointment.

A sudden string of cum laced over my nose, the warm load leaving a sticky ribbon across my cheek. Another burst of hot semen came from another direction, coating my chin and throat. Several in the group had grown impatient and were huddled around my head, stroking in unison as if playing to an unseen conductor.

No longer recognizing the distinct touch of any individual man, their multiple appendages converged with a solitary purpose, transporting me to a greater sense of what it meant to be truly fucked. The sheer number no longer mattered. I would remain connected to the beast until it was over.

I'd shut my eyes to protect them from the streams of flying jism. The gentle touch of Annie's fingers on my face startled me. She was wiping at my cheeks and forehead, removing the crusting gel.

Annie.

She had offered herself to these brutes even though she was not the one under scrutiny. There had been no reason for her to try to improve her situation in a world where a subtle wink could mean the difference between working in a dirty backstreet bar or servicing the highest stations of royalty.

She had done it for *me.*

Annie gave me a sly smile and rolled on top of me, her warm lips nibbling at my ear. "We're done," she whispered.

The tension in my limbs began to dissipate. "You sure? There's nobody left?"

"I'm sure," she said "You are so fucking sticky," she added, her grin wide enough for me to feel the stretch in her cheek against my face.

"You think if we stayed this way for a few minutes we'd end up glued together?" I asked.

Annie sighed. "I'd like that. Nothing else between us. Forever."

For the first time since meeting Annie, I felt a pang of guilt. Her inference told me she was moving forward much faster than I. Her words were all encompassing, her suggestion of commitment describing the alpha and omega of love. While my feelings for Annie were strong, I was discovering the nuances and subtleties of sharing a romantic experience with another woman. I cared deeply for Annie, but I hadn't thought about a future together.

The men were cleaning themselves with towels and napkins. Some made a quick run to the head to wash their hands. The tables were beginning to fill with food when Annie helped me to my feet.

"You hungry?" she asked.

"A little, but . . . "

"I know. I can't eat in here either. I'll fix us something later, after the crew is done."

Without hesitating or a second look at any of the crew, we left the main salon and headed to Annie's cabin.

Chapter Twelve

We walked the entire distance in silence. Expressing my gratitude was impossible. I longed to tell her how I felt, but mere words were so inadequate, so trifling in their ability to convey how much her sacrifice meant to me. It seemed more significant, more meaningful to simply cling to her as we walked side-by-side.

Closing the door behind us, Annie finally spoke. "I think the captain was pleased. Sometimes it's hard to know what he's thinking. But from the expression on his face, I think our show made an impression."

"A believable one?"

A small frown tugged at the corners of her mouth. "Even if he suspects it was an act, the fact that you could pull it off in front of the men means you could do it again in front of a buyer. In his world, sincerity doesn't have any influence on setting a price. It's mostly about how others perceive you."

Annie guided me toward the shower, drew back the curtain, and adjusted the temperature valve. Designed to accommodate one person at a time, we both squeezed into the tiny compartment.

For the first minute we let the water run down our skins, giving us time to mentally separate from the barrage of groping hands, nameless cocks, and probing fingers.

I sighed as she brought the soap to my breasts. Working her fingers under the folds, she removed every trace of man.

I lowered my head, resting it on her shoulder. I couldn't hold it in any longer. I had to tell her how much her surrender to the men meant to me. I knew how much she had given away, and how difficult her life might be tomorrow with the assumptions they would make.

"I couldn't have done it alone." I whispered.

"Of course you could," Annie said. "But there was no reason for you to try." She paused for a moment, then added, "I want you to realize how strong you are, not to give up on yourself, that you can handle anything that happens to you. It's not who you've become, it's who you've always been."

I knew it was more than an offhand comment. It was a blueprint for survival—take it as it comes, fight when you know you can win, bend when you know you can't.

"What happens tomorrow?" I asked. "Now that the men have had a taste of you, they're going to want more."

"Shhhhhh," she said. "No more talk about them. This time is for us."

For the next few minutes, we took turns soaping and rinsing every inch of each other, adding the occasional lick for good measure. Scouring her mouth with my tongue, the hint of semen was strong, but it didn't matter. We continued to share it, dilute it, until I recognized the distinctive and natural taste of Annie's mouth.

We were date-night clean, yet in no hurry to finish. Our wet bodies slid against each other in absolute abandon, the on-demand spray-head dripping in the background as the shower echoed with the sounds of our breathing.

It was a far cry from the life I was living a week ago. While I'd never thought of my life as boring, I'd occasionally had to remind myself I was living in paradise, leading a privileged life. I had time to read, take long walks on the beach, and think about what I wanted to do with the rest of my life. Never in my wildest fantasies had I imagined a future when I would be passionately embracing a beautiful woman within the confines of a tiny shower aboard a slave ship.

"Jewel, I need you to come to my cabin." The captain's voice shattered our warm cocoon like a well-placed rock against a brittle sheet of glass.

"Nice of you to knock," Annie shot back sarcastically.

The shower curtain parted in a flash of white plastic, the captain's huge form filling the narrow entrance. "What's nice," he said, his voice rising, "is I'm allowing you to enjoy your new playmate. If you keep forgetting whose boat you're on, this will be the last time you touch her."

"I was just kidding," Annie said quickly.

"Really, captain," I added, "Annie was telling me how fair you've been about the arrangement, and how you were willing to work something out with her."

Annie pinched my bottom. I'd said too much. The captain's scowl confirmed it.

"She needs to keep her mouth shut." The captain glared at Annie as if she were a wayward child on the verge of being punished. "Both of you get out of there and dry off. And Annie, I want you to fix Jewel's hair and do her makeup."

"More pictures?" I asked.

"Yes." His eyes searched my body from top to bottom as if assessing my breasts, hips, and legs for some feature he'd overlooked in the previous photo session.

"Be ready in twenty minutes," he commanded. "And come naked, like before." He jerked the shower curtain closed. A few seconds later, the snap of the cabin door confirmed he had left.

I blew out the breath I was holding. We both broke into hushed giggles. We were wrapped around each other like a pretzel, no doubt looking like a couple of scared nine-year-olds who'd been caught pilfering the cookie jar.

"What else could he want?" I asked, draping a towel around Annie's back. "He took every pose you can imagine."

"Sometimes a buyer will request specific shots. Close-ups of the face or back of the neck. You'd be surprised what some of these perverts want to see." Annie smiled in a pathetic, what-else-can-you-do-but-pity-them way. "No, I guess you wouldn't," she added.

Brushing the wet hair from my face, Annie deftly applied eye shadow and mascara, and then dusted my cheeks with blush. Adding a dollop of conditioner to my hair, she combed it through before drying it straight.

Turning my head toward the mirror, she said, "You look great, even after the workout the crew put you through." She patted a few loose hairs into place. "Okay, you're all set. Let's get you there on time. I don't want to piss off the captain any more than I already have."

"How long is this going to take?"

Annie knew what I was really asking. "Don't worry. I got the impression it's strictly pictures. I'll stay if he'll let me."

The captain had instructed me to arrive naked, so I objected when Annie covered my breasts with a white lace camisole. A quick glance in the mirror changed my mind. It was sexy, and would convey my desire to show off my features to advantage—another way to motivate potential buyers.

Annie threw on a short blue robe.

Holding hands as we walked down the narrow hallway, I began to pull back as we approached the captain's cabin.

"What's going on?" Annie asked.

"Why do you think the captain hasn't tried to fuck me?"

"You want him to?" She looked stunned.

"No, of course not. I just thought it was odd, him never taking advantage of the situation."

Annie shrugged. "He might be afraid of you."

"Afraid?" Of all the traits I could have attributed to the captain, fear didn't even make the list.

"Afraid of you getting to him," she explained, "of breaking through that wall he stays behind. He can't afford to develop feelings for anyone. It could lead to guilt or remorse. Selling a human being takes a cold-blooded approach to life. I used to think the people involved in this business were born to it—like a serial killer, having no conscience, no way of telling right from wrong. But I've seen how the money changes people, blinding them to the suffering and misery. Sometimes I think the captain is always riding the edge, a heartbeat away from realizing how cruel it is to abandon a girl he's just sold, without any idea of what will happen to her." She was silent for a moment, then added, "Maybe he's worried you could make him reach inside and rediscover his humanity . . . and *that* would be bad for business."

Annie knocked on the captain's door and received the familiar, no-nonsense, "*Come*." Like before, the captain was working at this desk, typing away on his laptop. Without looking up, he pointed to the bed. Apparently, it would again serve as a posing prop. Annie and I sat on the edge of the mattress, waiting.

"I've received some interest from a buyer," the captain began. "He's responded to the pictures I sent out earlier." He turned toward us, his expression poker-firm. "He's not sure if he's going to be at the auction personally, so he may bid through a representative. He's asked for more photos. Also has a few questions."

"What kind of questions?" I asked.

The captain raised his eyebrows, as if interpreting my curiosity as a challenge.

"I'm just curious," I added quickly. "This is all new to me, remember?"

The furrows in his forehead began to relax. "He wants to know about your personality, your temperament."

At first the idea of having my character analyzed for the purposes of determining my value as a sex slave confused me.

Then it ticked me off.

Who I *really* was would remain a secret. The real Jewel had gone into hiding, off the radar, to be eventually rescued, after which she would resume a normal existence. I would protect *her* with my life.

I did a lousy job at controlling the sarcastic edge in my voice. "And my training? Did he want to know how I handled that?"

Annie jumped in, trying to diffuse the rising tension. "So where do you want to start?"

"Right where you are. Jewel, take off the top and get on your hands and knees. Point your butt toward me."

Annie stood up, took my camisole, and tossed it on a chair.

As I maneuvered into position, he handed a curious piece of metal to Annie. "Put this in . . . a little window dressing."

Annie showed me the stainless steel butt plug. About four inches long, the insertable portion was shaped like a rose bud. Quickly tapering to a slender stem, the inch-and-a-half diameter base was inset with a lavender crystal.

"It won't hurt," she assured me, "This is a small one." She placed the plug between her lips and twirled it in her mouth, coating the surface with saliva. A moment later, I felt the steely tip pressing against my opening.

Feeling the resistance, I flinched. "That's really tight."

"Captain, do you have something we can use for lube?"

"Check the head."

Annie disappeared in the bathroom. I heard her rummaging through drawers and cabinets. She returned with a jar of petroleum jelly.

Scooping a dab on the end of her finger, she separated my cheeks and applied the thick gel, lubricating the point where skin and metal would converge.

"Try to relax," she whispered. "You'll barely feel it once it's in." Adding more jelly to the gleaming metal, she slowly seated the steel plug into place, my sphincter muscle finally pulling it flush to my bottom.

"Perfect," she added.

With the tulip-shaped portion of the plug completely inside, the sting of insertion was quickly replaced by the surprisingly pleasant sensation of fullness.

This would have driven my husband wild. I imagined him parading me around in front of his friends, then bending me over to show off my decorated butt-hole. I could almost hear him— *'This is how I keep her ready and primed for my cock.'*

The fucking bastard.

The captain hadn't expressed any objections to Annie remaining in the cabin. Now I knew why. On his knees, his eye pressed to the camera, he said, "Annie, bring your face in."

I felt her cheek press against my rump. For an instant, the flash from the camera projected her silhouetted profile on the wall in front of me.

"Jewel, roll over on your back and bring your legs up to your chest."

I flipped over and grabbed my knees. "This guy must really be into ass. Do you know him?"

"I've done some business with him."

That seemed to pique Annie's interest. "What's the guy's name? Anybody I'd know?"

"Gregory Housing."

Annie's face fell, the color draining from her cheeks. "Didn't he buy at the last auction?"

I head the quiver in her voice, as if she ready knew the answer.

"Apparently he wants something new—a replacement. The reason's not important. He's got the money . . . that's all that matters."

It was obvious the captain was in no mood to discuss the idiosyncrasies of his customers. I looked at Annie. Her somber expression told me I'd have to wait.

I sensed a sudden and frosty rift forming between Annie and the captain. I wasn't sure what it was about, but I didn't want it to escalate. "Well, from all the pictures you're taking of my butt, we can definitely assume the guy is an ass-man."

I thought it was funny. Neither the captain nor Annie smiled. As I held the new pose, I noticed Annie had fallen quiet, noticeably distracted. Something more than the oaky-pitched scent of the cabin was bothering her.

After snapping a few more pictures, the captain announced, "We're done." Turning back to his laptop, he plugged in the camera and began the download.

I glanced at Annie, hesitating. I was pretty sure he'd given us permission to leave, but if we casually strolled out of his cabin without asking, it might appear presumptive.

I waited, letting the next few seconds pass in silence. I wasn't about to go without knowing I was done for the night. I didn't want him barging in on Annie and me later, insisting I return to his bed.

I spoke up. "I'd like to stay with Annie in her cabin."

He answered without taking his eyes off the screen. "Sleep where you want. You have a busy day tomorrow."

Annie grabbed my hand, picked up the camisole, and headed toward the door, her actions uncharacteristically abrupt. Apparently she wanted out of his cabin as much as I did.

I waited until we were out of earshot. "Something's bothering you. Tell me what's going on."

She looked back over her shoulder, as if a crewmember might be lying camouflaged in the woodwork, ready to eavesdrop on our conversation. "This Gregory Housing guy," she whispered, "the one who asked for the pictures. It's a problem."

"Why? What's wrong?"

"We have to make sure he doesn't buy you."

The alarm in her voice was unmistakable.

"I don't understand. Who is he?"

She shook her head, warning me to wait until she was certain our conversation would remain confidential.

Her cabin door was only a half-inch thick. Punctuated with louvers at the top and bottom, it provided only the illusion of privacy. Yet after closing it behind us, I realized there was another reason she wanted the separation provided by the thin slab of perforated mahogany—she didn't want the crew to see how upset she was.

"Can you give me a minute?" she asked.

Her chest was heaving, her breath coming in short, erratic draws. She headed straight for the bath.

"Take your time," I said "When you're done, I want to get rid of this butt-plug."

Annie stopped. "You go first." She nodded toward the head. "There's antiseptic soap in the medicine cabinet."

I quickly washed the plug in the sink, wrapped it in a washcloth, and tucked it behind the soap dish.

As I scrubbed my hands a second time, I could feel the tension, a cloud of apprehension so thick I could barely draw a full breath. I grabbed a cut-off T-shirt from the towel bar and put it on.

Annie was waiting on the bed, still wearing the short blue robe, the front open and untied. I sat down beside her.

She seemed hesitant, so I jumped right in. "So how do you know this guy? What's his name . . . Gregory?"

She took my hand, her misting brown eyes locked on mine.

"Listen to me," she began. "At the auction, you need to find someone who is buying for themselves, not an agent. Then play up to him, promise anything and everything. Sell yourself as if your life depended on it."

While her words were troubling enough, it was the building emotion in her quaking voice that worried me. She was holding something back.

"Annie, what's going on?"

She turned away, her lower lip beginning to tremble.

"Take your time." I laid my hand over hers. "Whenever you're ready."

She swallowed hard. "I don't know where to begin. Maybe it will make more sense if I tell you the whole story."

She had me on pins and needles, but I was determined to stay calm, to help her get through whatever was upsetting her.

"Gregory comes from money," she began. "His family owns a large shipping company, does business all over the world. They've been big-time for three generations. Gregory was next in line to inherit the company and take over the operation. But he got into trouble in his early twenties. At first, it was minor stuff, things that didn't hurt anyone. But as he got older, his activities became a lot harder to hide. By the time he was thirty, he'd earned a reputation for being the bad boy in the family. So bad, in fact, that even with all his money, his father couldn't protect him, at least not in the States. I suppose if Gregory had restricted his *hobby* to prostitutes and runaways he might have gotten away with it.

But when he started fucking around with the daughters of influential families, his father shipped him overseas to put more distance between his son and the law."

"I don't understand. What was he doing?"

"Normal sex doesn't interest him."

"Define normal."

"He's way beyond the kinky stuff. A couple years ago he got into some real bizarre shit, using electricity to get himself off."

"I've heard of that," I said cautiously.

"Not like this. He ties the girl to a table and shoves an electrode up her ass. Then he puts one up *his* butt. He completes the connection by fucking her. A member of the crew said he actually saw him do it. Gregory kept turning up the power to see who could stay conscious longer. Eventually, he couldn't stay hard or take the pain. So now he only wires up the girl."

It took a few seconds to sink in. As it reached my gut, I laid back on the bed, afraid I would faint. "Jesus, Annie. And this is the same guy who wants to buy me?"

"Yeah, same one." She paused. "There's something else."

I waited, the silence growing tense.

Annie was biting her lip, fighting to hold back the tears.

I reached up and touched her shoulder. It was all I could do. She needed consoling as much as I did, but I was wrestling with my own building fear, and right now, I was empty—and scared.

"I didn't think I'd ever hear his name again," she said, "especially after the last time. I figured he'd gone into hiding or his father had shipped him off to some new shit-hole."

"What happened . . . *the last time*?"

"Remember when the captain was taking pictures of us and I mentioned a girl he'd sold at a previous auction?"

"I remember."

"That was about three months ago—" Annie's voice broke. She cleared her throat, trying to shake it off. But as she wiped her eyes, her trembling hand revealed she was on the edge of losing it.

I'd seen Annie express kindness and affection, both of which could quickly escalate to passion. The other emotions—sadness, resentment, loneliness—she had managed to keep hidden, concealed under a protective shell of apathy. But the anguish from a much-too-recent memory had returned with overwhelming clarity, and apparently, a freak named Gregory Housing had something to do with it.

She tried again. "That same girl was on the *Kelsey* for nearly two weeks before the captain sold her to Gregory." Annie shook her head, unable to continue.

She had known the girl and, from her reaction, it was obvious they had become friends, maybe even lovers.

I forced myself to sit up. Regardless of my own fear, Annie deserved more than a pacifying touch. I wrapped my arms around her, hoping my question wouldn't upset her even more. "What happened to her?"

"After the auction, I heard rumors about the guy who bought her. Several of the crew told me he was some kind of maniac who liked to torture the girls he bought. I didn't connect it with Gregory. Not then. But a few weeks later, Massey ran into a street pimp who said he saw him do it."

She stopped, taking a few sporadic draws of air.

"Do what, Annie? Tell me."

The words burst from her mouth on a flash of anger. "The fucking bastard killed her."

I felt the blood leaving my face, a nauseating wave of dizziness threatening to take me to the floor. My dinner— all the cum I'd swallowed—

was in my throat. I made a dash for Annie's bathroom.

I was hugging the bowl, my stomach threatening to heave when I felt Annie's hand cradle my forehead.

A thousand questions were exploding in my brain. How did the girl die? Is anyone looking for her? Are the authorities searching for Gregory? But first, I needed to know something even more important.

"Her name," I whispered. "What was her name?"

"Her stage name was Lily. She was a dancer, working in Bangkok." I sensed Annie's face softening, remembering. "Her real name was Eve."

"Are you sure the story's true?"

Before Annie could answer, I dry-belched between shallow breaths, then silently scolded myself for letting fear get the best of me. I told myself I would have to be a lot stronger than this.

"I know what you're thinking," Annie said, "a bunch of guys sitting around a table with their brains pickled in beer. Then somebody says something that's total bullshit. A day later, it's being repeated as fact. But Massey told me the pimp had no reason to lie. He said he heard it the guy's voice . . . how disgusted he was, even bitter about it, saying how pretty Eve was, and how somebody should put a bullet in Gregory's head."

The dull queasiness of nausea was keeping me on my knees, but I couldn't wait for it to pass. I had to know how the captain figured in all of this. "You think the captain knows what happened to her?"

"Yeah, I'm sure of it. Remember Albie, you know, the muscle-bound guy with white hair? He overhead the captain talking about it on his cell phone, making sure her death couldn't be traced back to the *Kelsey*."

"So you think the captain knew about Gregory and what he might do to Eve, before he sold her?" I asked.

"At first I wanted to give him the benefit of the doubt, but—" She stopped, releasing a deep sigh. "There's no question about it. The captain knew what Gregory was capable of doing. And if he's willing to sell you to that same asshole, then he's just as guilty." She thought for a moment, then added, "Maybe even more so, since he has the power to prevent it from happening again."

Losing Eve had been a double loss for Annie. Not only had her friend been murdered, it had been a senseless death. And while Eve's legacy was a sad one, Annie had been holding out hope that Eve's murder would have made such an impression on the captain that next time, he'd make sure Gregory—and others like him—would not enjoy the privilege of killing without consequence.

But the truth was a terrifying disappointment. The captain's morality was as subjective as his preferred brand of whiskey. Maybe years ago, his actions were tempered by the normal dose of evil apportioned to every man. But each time he'd sold a girl at auction, he'd traded away another piece of his integrity, ultimately letting the devil take his soul without challenge or regret.

The captain had chosen his master, and it was money.

The nausea was lifting. I sat back and reached for Annie. Part of me wanted to throttle her. More than scare me, she'd turned me into a quivering child. Yet I knew she was trying to save my life. Letting me go blindly into the auction—knowing it might lead to my death—would have been the worst kind of cruelty. It would have made her no better than all the other soulless parasites who made their living selling young girls into slavery.

"Annie, the captain is planning on selling me to a serial killer. What the hell am I supposed to do now?"

She dropped to one knee. "Listen to me. I'm going to make sure Gregory doesn't get his hands on you."

She was doing her best to give me a sliver of hope. But an empty promise didn't make me feel better.

"How?" I whispered.

"After we dock, I normally leave the ship to get supplies. I might be able to sneak my way into the auction, work the crowd, let the big money bidders know how special you are, find someone to outbid that bastard."

"Sounds like suicide," I said. "What if the captain or one of the crew sees you? From what you've told me, you'd be one of the few women on the auction floor who wasn't a captive. You'd stand out. Somebody would get suspicious."

She nodded slightly. "I thought about disguising myself . . . but it doesn't matter now. We've got another problem, something the captain said. I'm not sure he even knows he let it slip out. And it changes everything."

"You mean about Eve?"

"That's part of it." She paused, as if putting the pieces together. "He knows what happened to

Eve, and he knows who killed her. And it doesn't mean anything to him. He doesn't regret what he did because he's willing to do it again. Otherwise he'd never consider selling you to that bastard. And that means—"

She shook her head, then said, "I'm screwed. My deal with him is bullshit."

Now I understood. Annie had carried the captain's lack of integrity to its logical conclusion. She'd realized if the captain would knowingly sell another girl into a situation that would most likely result in her death, he would have no hesitation welching on his agreement with her, even after she'd fulfilled her contract. Annie knew if she had any chance of getting off the *Kelsey*, it would have to be on her terms, not the captain's.

"So now what?" I asked.

"We run."

It really didn't sink in until I saw her face— an expression etched with icy determination.

"*We*? You're coming with me?"

"You'd never make it on your own. The network would find you . . . and take their time in bringing you back."

"What network? What are you taking about?"

"A bunch of goons and street-thugs. They work like bounty hunters, always on the lookout for runaways. They collect a reward for the ones they return."

Bounty hunters, searching for runaway sex slaves.

I had assumed my biggest problem would be finding a way off the boat, and once I'd escaped, the playing field would be neutral. I'd never thought about an organized network of eyes and ears, always on the lookout for runners. I would be easy prey on the street, at the mercy of a web of malicious hoodlums, and from what she was telling me, the word *mercy* wasn't in their vocabulary.

"I've made some contacts," she continued, "and there's a few of them who will hide us . . . for the right price."

I shook my head in frustration. "We don't—at least I don't—have any money."

"You have something better." She patted my bottom. "You've got this. There are plenty of men out there who will trade for what we need."

It sounded desperate—and overwhelming. We would be fugitives on the run, traveling in the shadows.

"Help me up. I'm tired of staring at this toilet."

Annie extended her hand. "You sure your stomach's okay?"

"I'm alright. I just want to sit for a while."

Like a coddling mother, she guided me back to the bed and settled next to me. For several moments, we sat there, waiting for the right words to come.

I tried to imagine what was going through her mind—the heartbreak of losing someone close, wanting to help me escape the same fate, and now having to face the reality of the captain's personal brand of ethics.

I reached back, steadying myself against the roll of the boat. The motion broke Annie's silence.

"I know it was a lot to hit you with all at once. But I couldn't keep it to myself, not after the captain told us Gregory was an interested buyer. You had to know, and there was no easy way to tell you."

"It's not your fault," I said. "It's hard for both of us." I paused. "We need some kind of plan."

"I'm working on an idea, but the timing has to be—"

"What about when the crew is bringing the boat into the harbor?" I interrupted. "We could slip overboard, and if no one sees us, we'd be able to—"

"No." Annie cut me off. "Our best shot will be right after the auction, when the girls are being transferred from the cages. There's always a lot of people standing around, plenty of distractions."

"Escape from the auction? From inside a building?"

"Not from inside. Usually the girls are delivered to their new owners *outside*, by their waiting cars and trucks. There's a span of two or three minutes when the girls are held in the parking lot, while the buyers are completing payment and sellers are transferring clothes and personal items."

"And then what? We just disappear into the crowd?"

"The place is surrounded by a chain-link fence topped with barbed-wire. No way over or under it. I've heard stories about girls who tried, and it didn't end well. The only way in or out of the auction is through the main gate. We'll need a car. Or someone to drive us."

My heart sank. Escape was becoming more complicated by the minute. In fact, it sounded nearly impossible.

"Annie, tell me the truth. This isn't going to work, is it?" My eyes welled up with tears.

She hugged me with one arm. "We'll *make* it work. I know how these bastards think, what makes them tick. There's one guy in particular, he works security in the parking lot. He has a van. All I have to do is promise to spend twenty minutes with him and he'll do anything I ask."

"Okay," I said, "Let's say this guy can get us off the auction grounds. I still have to get away from the captain, or my new owner."

"That's going to be the easy part . . . I hope. After the bidding is over, the captain sends most of the crew back to the ship. He'll leave a single man to guard you. And that's when I can get to you."

"Get to me how?"

"Massey's usually the one who guards the girls. I'll run up to him in a panic, tell him the captain needs him inside the building and I'm supposed to take over, stay with you until the buyer picks you up."

"Won't Massey be suspicious? I mean, with you suddenly showing up at the auction and telling him the captain wants you to take over? He's not stupid."

"I'll make it sound like an emergency. He'll believe me *because* it's so unusual. I'll tell him the captain has a problem with the buyer, the sale's not going through, and he needs his help. What else is he gonna do? He can't ignore me."

"What about cell phones? Couldn't Massey call the captain?"

"The auction doesn't allow cell phones on the property. It's a security risk. They don't want calls made to the outside by anyone for any reason."

"No walkie-talkies either?"

She shook her head. "Same deal."

"So you think he'll just turn me over to you?" I could almost see the two of them arguing in the parking lot . . . Massey finally giving in, partly out of frustration, partly out of loyalty to the captain.

"He'll probably handcuff us together before he goes back inside the building. But that's not a problem. I've got a key to everything on the ship, including all the padlocks and cuffs. Of course, nobody knows that."

"What if the captain leaves more than one man to watch me?"

"He's never done that."

I started to object, to argue that the captain couldn't be depended on to continue the same practice out of habit, but Annie wasn't finished.

"Jewel, listen to me. He won't use an extra man if you're not putting up a fight."

"And you're sure about the rest of the men, they'll already be headed back to the ship?"

"The captain doesn't like the men spending any more time at the auction than necessary. Drugs and handguns are traded in the parking lot, and the captain doesn't want the men messing around with either one."

Annie's plan was risky, but she knew the layout of the property, how to get in and out. If we were going to run, I would have to rely on her every step of the way.

Something else was bothering me. "What if Gregory decides I'm not what he wants, or nobody else bids on me and I don't sell? How do I know for sure I'm going to end up outside in that parking lot?"

For the longest moment, Annie stared at me, her eyes transparent with compassion. I knew what she was thinking—I'd been too sheltered as a child, my naiveté and lack of experience leaving me unprepared for the real world.

When she finally spoke, her voice was calm and matter-of-fact.

"They will *all* want you. The only question is how many will be able to pay the price."

"And this man, Gregory . . . he has enough money to outbid the others?"

"He can't compete with royalty or the oil sheiks, but he can produce a banknote for a hundred grand on the spot." She paused, a hint of frustration creeping into her voice. "I know what you're thinking, that there's the possibility you could be bought by someone who won't abuse you, someone who will take care of you, even treat you well. It could happen, but . . ." Annie glanced at the fading orange light rimming the small porthole, as if the words she needed were about to be delivered on the last rays of sunset. Finally, she said, "It's not likely. If Gregory has already shown this much interest, you can bet he's going to be there. And he'll bring plenty of money . . . so you have to be ready to run."

Annie was my confidante—and now my co-conspirator. She believed the best opportunity for escape would come after the auction, while I was waiting to be transferred to my new owner. Now I had to believe it, too.

It meant I would have to face the auction alone.

Chapter Thirteen

I let it all sink in. Gregory. Eve. The captain.

Annie's revelation had changed everything. Escape had always been in the back of my mind, but now it loomed over me as if I were condemned prisoner waiting on death row, my only hope of survival an ill-advised break for freedom just before being strapped in the gas chamber.

The auction was less than forty-eight hours away and I'd been putting off the question. Now it was imperative—I had to know what to expect.

"What will it be like? The auction, I mean."

Annie's smile thinned, then disappeared. "Tomorrow night before we dock, the captain will lock you in the engine room to make sure you don't try to slip off the boat. The next morning, he and a couple of the crew will drive you to the auction site. While the captain does the paperwork, the men will put you in one of the display rooms. That's what the auction house calls them, but they're cages made from old shipping containers."

"They're going to put me in a box?"

"You've seen a cargo container, right?"

I nodded.

"One of the sides has been cut out and replaced with chain-link fencing. The men will look at you through the wire."

Before Annie laid out our escape, I had planned to work the room, pick out a buyer who held the promise of treating me well, then convince him to bid whatever it would take to buy me. I had no idea I was going to be caged like an animal. Although the strategy had changed, the idea of confinement frightened me.

"I thought the captain expected me to flirt with the men, you know, to bring a higher price and give me a better shot at—" I stopped, realizing the size of the final bid was no longer an indication of how safe I would be. Gregory had been the high bidder for a girl named Eve, and she ended up dead.

"It used to be that way," Annie said. "It was called *parading*. Some of the girls, the ones who had learned to behave, were led around on a leash. You'd also see a few in full body harness, to keep them from bolting for the outside. It was a red flag the girl wasn't fully trained."

"They don't do that anymore?"

"There were clashes between the buyers and the girls, especially the ones who didn't like being manhandled. Most of it was slaps and punches, directed toward the men who couldn't keep their hands to themselves. Then a couple of high-dollar buyers got scratched up. One lost an eye. Now the girls have to stay in a cage."

"But doesn't that reduce the number of buyers who can see me?"

"The containers are big enough to walk around in. You'll be able to attract the bidders, talk to them if you want. Some of the girls press themselves against the wire and let the men touch."

"But I won't have to do that, will I?" I imagined the men lining up, anxious to push a couple of dirty fingers into my pussy or ass—or both.

Annie shrugged her shoulders. "It depends. If you don't cooperate, the men may complain to the captain. A buyer who's willing to pay top dollar can insist on a personal inspection. Think of it this way. It's better to keep them on the outside of the container—with the wire between you and the men—than having the captain let a few of them inside so they can take their time with you."

"So I just let all of them finger-fuck me?" It was an absurd paradox—the metal cage I initially thought would be confining might actually serve as a protective enclosure, preventing the perverts from getting too close.

"You can tell the crewmen to fuck off. You'll be able to recognize them by the condition of their hands. A buyer ready to spend fifty grand or more won't have the callouses you'll see on a typical deckhand."

I remembered the moment Butch revealed the captain's plan to sell me. The idea terrified me. Since then, I'd told myself I would get through it by taking things a day at a time, and when I was finally put in front of buyers, I would somehow be ready, prepared to handle whatever the crazy bastards threw at me. But I'd made the assumption I'd be treated like a human being.

That had been a mistake.

Every new revelation about the business of sex trafficking confirmed its practitioners to be humanity's outcasts, merciless monsters that looked for any opportunity to profit, regardless of the suffering it brought others. And yet, I'd spent the last two days convincing myself to make the transition from housewife to harlot, reasoning it was for my own survival, eventually putting me in a better position to negotiate my freedom.

Now I wasn't so sure. In fact, I was beginning to question if my decision to placate the beast didn't also color me a bit insane.

"I know it's a lot to take in," Annie added. "We'll talk more about it later."

"No! I want to hear it now. I have to know what to expect, how to prepare myself."

She was taken back by my insistence, but I couldn't see any reason to put it off. I waited in silence, anxious about how bad it might be.

"You sure that's what you want?"

I took a deep breath. "Let's hear it."

"Just because we've got an escape plan doesn't mean you can act any differently during the auction. You need to keep up the act, continue giving every indication to the captain you're co-operative. Otherwise, he'll get suspicious, change the way he does things, warn the men to watch you like a hawk. He might even restrict me to the ship to make sure I don't try anything. He obviously knows I care about you."

"That makes sense." I felt like I was on auto-pilot, responding mechanically so she knew I was paying attention. I would work through the disgusting parts later.

"Let's concentrate on the things that are most important," she continued. "First, you can't make assumptions. Just because a buyer wants to prod or poke at the girls, it's not necessarily an indication of how he will treat her after he gets her home. He may be testing the girl to find out how submissive she is. It's part of the process."

"So I should expect my cage to be surrounded by men who want to grope me."

Her nod was reluctant, but her answer was clear.

"What about competition from the other girls?" I asked.

"If it's a typical auction, there won't be much. Not for you. You're white and blonde. You'll stand out and draw the most attention. You'll also bring the highest bids."

"How long do I have to stay in the cage?"

"Depends on how many girls are being sold . . . could be an hour, maybe two. The captain draws a number when he brings you in. It determines the order of sale, but not the delivery. Once in a while, they make an exception and let the buyer take a girl right after making payment. But transferring a girl during the auction process can be a distraction to the other bidders, so the auction boss normally makes the new owners wait until the end before taking delivery."

Annie saw my hands trembling. She reached out and covered them with her own. "You want me to go on?"

"Yes."

"The bidding takes place in English, with everything repeated in French and Spanish, so you'll have the advantage of knowing what's going on. You'll see lots of girls who won't. A couple of years ago, they began bringing girls in from Russia and the Ukraine. They didn't know the language, had no idea what was happening to them. Some of them fought back. The sellers decided the best way to handle them was with a cattle prod."

Annie sighed. "Of course, there are plenty of buyers looking for that, too. You'd think for as long as I've been in this part of the world, nothing would surprise me. But it breaks my heart every time the crew tells me about a girl they've seen struggling, out of control." She paused, her face flushing with hot, angry color. "But that's not the worst part."

I grimaced. "Which is?"

"The buyers who are ready to break them, and take pleasure in doing it."

I couldn't hide the quick shiver that came from a jolt of gut-wrenching fear. The only auctions I'd seen were on television, where expensive merchandise was displayed in front of a large group of civilized bidders raising a numbered paddle to indicate their willingness to pay a higher price. But selling humans was anything but civilized. The merchandise was young girls, their value enhanced by the erotic and sick fantasies their new owners planned to inflict on them.

Chapter Fourteen

Receiving the captain's consent to spend the night with Annie had given me a brief reprieve from the exhausting stress of my captivity. For a while, anticipating the comfort of lying next to her had kept me calm.

But now, all I could think of was the auction, a place where I would be put on public display, where being groped and even penetrated was an accepted practice. Worse, I knew there was one man in particular who would be waiting for me. A man who had requested my pictures and would be ready to examine me in scrutinizing detail . . . his sole agenda to determine if my physical specifications made me a desirable candidate to become his next victim.

My only chance of preventing Gregory—or anyone else—from carrying me off and making me their permanent sex slave was riding on Annie. She had to leave the boat, secretly make her way to the auction, and then convince one of the local men to drive us off the grounds. And she'd made one thing very clear—timing was critical. There would only be a two or three minute window of opportunity to convince Massey to turn me over to her.

Our plan went no further than that. Not because leaving the auction grounds would put us out of danger, but rather, I suspected Annie had serious doubts we would make it that far.

"Want something from the kitchen?" Annie asked. "I could run and grab something."

I shook my head. "I'm not hungry. You?"

"Maybe later."

I felt my stomach rise and fall, this time from the pitch of the boat. For a moment we seemed to hang in the air before plunging headlong back into the sea, the slam of water against the hull knocking several plastic bottles off the bathroom counter.

"I guess we weren't able to outrun the weather," Annie said. "It's going to be a rough night. I need to put the loose stuff away."

I helped her gather the containers of shampoo and skin lotion rolling across the floor. She tucked them behind the railed shelves of the medicine cabinet and twisted the door latch.

Outside the wind was picking up, the occasional howling gusts setting my nerves on edge. "I hate the wind. I don't mind the rain, but wind makes me—"

A cobalt-white flash pulsed against the porthole, preserving the interior of the cabin in an eerie freeze-frame. Although still in the distance, a low rumble answered slightly out of sync.

"Thunder?"

It seemed unlikely. Ten minutes ago, the ocean's surface was an unsettled lather of whitecaps, its irritation seeming to come from beneath, not above. But now, the continuous shifting of the cabin hinted at a turbulent front, gathering strength and momentum.

"It's coming in fast," Annie said. "Maybe it will blow through and leave some decent weather behind."

Peering through the porthole didn't make Annie's hopeful forecast any easier to believe. The throbbing twilight revealed a desperately troubled ocean, its foam-frosted swells smacking against the ship as if warning the helmsman to change course.

Outside, a dark, boiling cloudbank mustered directly overhead. A minute later, it announced its presence with a sudden downpour, setting a thousand tiny hammers drumming furiously against the hull.

"Hold on," Annie warned. "Feels like it could be a big one." She grabbed me in a bear-hug as the boat lifted to meet the next breaker then dropped into the trough of the swell, the falling wave pounding the deck with an angry fist of water.

"I'll never get used to this," she added. "It's going to be a real roller-coaster. Let's ride it out in bed."

"Whoops!" I locked my knees against the intense pitch and roll of the boat as it left the top of the wave and dropped into the next.

We began inching across the floor, keeping our arms around the other's waist.

"There's a tie-down I can pull across us after we're on the mattress," Annie said. "It's a bit confining, but it will keep us from being thrown around."

"You ever hear the story of Hafgufa? I asked.

Annie smiled. "I think he just woke up."

I'd heard the legend repeated many times by aging sailors, about a gigantic one-eyed creature that rose from the depths every hundred years to sweep the surface of the sea, removing trespassers and intruders from his kingdom. With the ocean's escalating assault, it was easy to imagine the monster having awakened after a century of sleep, his massive arms stirring the water in a prelude to rising to the surface.

"Maybe he'll take pity on a couple of girls who are passing through," I added.

I waited for Annie's reply, expecting it to be equally flippant, perhaps suggesting we might have to offer ourselves to one of Poseidon's henchmen in exchange for safe passage. But maintaining our balance was becoming more difficult and she was focusing her attention on getting us to the relative safety of the bunk.

We took two short steps and stopped.

"Wait," she cautioned. "We need to let this one pass." Reaching out for the wall, we rode the rise of the next swell, then leaned against the angle of the plunging boat as the pull of gravity threatened to take us off our feet.

I felt my heart thrumming in my chest. The *Kelsey* suddenly felt puny and frail, the adequacy of its steel-braced hull offering a questionable defense against the brute force of nature.

"Annie, is this normal?" She'd undoubtedly been through many storms, and I needed her assurance this one would eventually blow over, leaving us unharmed.

"There's no such thing as *normal* during heavy weather. I've ridden out plenty of squalls before and each time it's different. Usually the captain heads for the back side of an island or a protected harbor. I'm surprised he's taking this one head-on. It came on quick, so it's going to be strong . . . and probably give us one hell of a ride."

Wind-driven sheets of rain raked across the porthole, reminding me of the signature scene from one too many horror movies. My imagination easily provided the shadowy image of a crazed serial killer staring through the lightning-fired window, the shrill squeaks from the tip of his glistening, razor-sharp knife making his intentions terrifyingly obvious.

We were less than five feet from the bed. A couple of quick strides and we could strap ourselves in. I stepped forward, but Annie pulled me back. "We'll jump for it right after we clear this wave."

I was tired of fighting the storm on my feet. "Come on, Annie, we're only a few—" I stopped. She'd tilted her head as if listening to a distant whisper, her confident expression turning anxious.

"What's going on?" I asked. "What do you hear?"

"We're in a slosh pit. The prop's lost its bite."

She had picked it up in the background, the unfamiliar noise indicating an unusual change in the operation of the boat.

"Is that bad?"

"The edge of a wave carries a lot of air. As we pass through it, there's nothing for the prop to grab. The captain can't control the boat until it settles."

The only words I heard were *'The captain can't control the boat.'*

Beneath us, the screaming whine of the engine rose and fell like a wailing siren, giving voice to the vibrating prop as it spun through layer upon layer of white-water cavitation.

Any moment now, a few more seconds . . .

I kept waiting for the diesel to return to its labored but steady *chug-chug-chug.* It would confirm the helmsman had regained the ability to steer the ship. But the cries from the overstressed engine were only a prelude to an even more ominous high-pitched metallic pinging now saturating every deck plank and sideboard.

"What the hell is that?" I searched Annie's face, waiting for an answer.

I could almost hear Carl's voice in the background . . . *every mechanical system has limits, every engine and drive shaft designed to operate only a short time in situations exceeding maximum overload thresholds.* He'd repeated the phrase more times than I could remember—as if it were some kind of nautical mantra—usually while chastising one of the locals for abusing an old power-plant until it was reduced to 500 pounds of scrap iron.

I felt a sudden rise, as if the hull had hit a bump in the liquid road. Compared to previous swells, the pitch of the wave was comparatively gentle—at first. In seconds, the subtle lift of the bow gave way to an alarming angle of ascent, confirmed by the clatter and crash of shifting pots and pans echoing from the galley.

I tried to stay calm, reassure myself. Although the boat was over a half-century old, it had been designed for trans-oceanic crossings, its hull and superstructure built to withstand the harshest extremes of weather. Certainly it had been through other storms, no doubt far worse than this.

With the boat continuing to climb, I said, "Jesus, Annie, the ship's trying to fly."

I waited for her to dismiss it, tell me she'd experienced the same harsh buffeting on other crossings.

Instead, I saw only worry on her face.

"We'll get through it," she said finally. "It's a bad one, but we'll get through it."

I wanted to take comfort in what she said, but alarmed by the ever increasing angle, I held her tight, fearful we'd reach a point at which the boat would begin to slide backward down the building mountain of water.

The boat moaned in a tormented cry for relief.

I said what I was sure Annie was thinking. "It can't take much more of this."

"Shush," she whispered. "We'll be fine. Just hold on."

The torturous climb ended as quickly as it began. Breaking the crest of the wave, the bow began to drop. Although my heart was pounding, I told myself the ship and the ocean had finally reached a truce.

But just as the boat had endured the full onslaught of a near vertical wall of water, it would also have to negotiate the downslope of the same huge breaker. The next moment brought a rush of confusion and panic as the sound of the hull cutting through the sea was replaced with an eerie and foreboding silence.

I froze, bracing against the odd sense of weightlessness, the surreal absence of gravity releasing a surge of sickening dread—one that sent me crouching halfway to my knees.

But Annie's instincts had been honed from over two years at sea. Grabbing my wrist, she lunged for the mattress. "Jump for it, now!"

We never made it.

Released from the peak of the huge rogue wave, the boat dropped bow first, plunging into the open mouth of a hungry ocean.

Flailing against the abrupt change in gravity, Annie's fingertips slipped over my skin. She did her best to hold on to me, but like the rest of the unanchored items in the room, I was already sliding across the floor, my near free-fall ending with a crash into the lower wall of the cabin.

The sound of shattering glass and breaking wood filled the room, yet the din paled in comparison to nature's explosive blast on the exterior of the ship. Like a belt sander stripping a rough board, the monstrous wall of water roared over the boat, ripping away the sails and rigging, devouring everything not intrinsic to the ship's mainframe.

The *Kelsey* shook violently, each tremor accompanied by the sounds of straining metal and splintering wood. The hull began to roll, the upper decks dipping toward the sea. In seconds, the boat was broadside.

Intense pressure on my chest spawned the purest form of terror, and it momentarily blinded me to the real cause—Annie was sprawled on top of me.

In her leap for the mattress, she had managed to grasp the edge of the bed frame. Not bolted to the floor, the bed had followed her down, joining a landslide of lamps, books, and half-a-dozen loose drawers that spilled from the dresser like pieces of an exploding jig-saw puzzle.

She'd landed hard, confirmed by the unmistakable hollow crack of bone. As still as stone, she lie heavy and limp across my ribs, her dead weight restricting my breath.

A jabbing pain erupted from my back. I was pinned against something sharp—the corner of a cabinet or a broken piece of furniture.

"Annie, get up, you've got to move. Something's stabbing me. If you can roll to the side, then I can—"

I saw the blood trickling from her scalp. "No! You have to be okay. You have to tell me what to do!"

She moaned, a pitiful gut-launched cry, and I mistakenly welcomed it as a sign of returning consciousness. I did my best to sweep the hair from her face, my fingers leaving a smear of crimson across her forehead. "Annie? Can you hear me? Say something."

The echoes of breaking timber and the relentless pounding of the waves filled the cabin.

Straining against the claustrophobic pressure of Annie's motionless form and the burning ache in my back, a new fear gripped me—would the boat be able to right itself?

If I had been able to view our situation from the eye of the storm, I would have realized my question was born from hopeful expectation, and about as likely as reanimating a corpse. What had previously been a stable sailing craft had been reduced to a broken hulk of wood and fiberglass, its direction as aimless as that of a bobbing cork.

From what I could tell, the cabin was still dry. But I had no way of telling how much longer the few inches of hull separating us from the raging ocean would remain intact.

My concerns were well-founded.

Below the waterline, the keel had nearly separated from the ship. Only a brittle overcoat of shattered fiberglass maintained its connection to the hull. Once that bond was severed, the vessel would be free to roll completely over. With the boat already taking on water in the forward hold, it was only a matter of time before the sea would fill the interior and send the *Kelsey* below the waves.

I had to move. The pressure against my back was unbearable, the throbbing ache penetrating deep into my flesh. I prayed it was only a blunt object pressing against a nerve, and not an embedded shard of wood tearing muscle from bone.

Ignoring the sting from unseen cuts and scrapes, I scuttled my feet over broken glass, struggling to find leverage.

Another groan from Annie. I knew she might have internal injuries, but I had no choice. I needed her awake—and conscious. Otherwise, there was a good chance neither of us would get out of the cabin alive. I began easing out from beneath her, shifting her weight a little at a time.

The violent roll of the boat announced another crashing swell, the impact stirring the room's contents like bingo balls in a Vegas spin-cage. As the motion turned Annie on her side, I held on, shielding her from shifting debris and showering glass from broken mirrors and what once was her prized collection of perfume bottles.

Relieved of her weight, I sat up to get my bearings. Thankfully, the batteries were maintaining power to the lights, confirmed by the two wall-mounted sconces throwing amber-edged shadows against the walls.

Were we still on the surface? Or had the *Kelsey* already begun its decent to the ocean floor?

I glanced around, searching for the brass-framed porthole that had been a conspicuous fixture in the cabin wall.

I was looking in the wrong place. With the ship was on its side, the porthole was *under* me.

Scraping through the rubble, I located the twelve-inch circle of tempered glass and peered through the thin streaks of viscous oil slithering across the outside surface. A fraction of an inch beyond, weak flashes of storm light illuminated fragments of swirling wood and fiberglass. It was like looking through kaleidoscope, except this view offered a terrifying invitation to the dark water below.

It took me a moment to connect the staccato winks of light on the other side of the glass to the near-constant barrage of background thunder. Compared to the blazing white spiders of fire streaking across the sky, these refracted traces of lightning were feeble and muted, but they confirmed the *Kelsey* was on the surface, or at least close enough to it that Annie and I could make our way off the ship—*if* she regained consciousness.

I thought about the men who had been topside, wondering if they had seen the enormous wave as it approached in the distance or if it had arrived out of the blackness, catching them by surprise. By now one of the crew should have found us, helping us to the life rafts. Maybe they were fighting the elements, struggling to keep the ship afloat. Or worse, they were already in the water, their priority focused on self-survival.

With or without their help, I had to find a way off the *Kelsey*. And I was taking Annie with me.

Chapter Fifteen

The sea continued to hammer the broken ship with unimaginable force. Like an angry, vengeful giant, the elements tore at the *Kelsey*'s underbelly, the ragged splintering of laminated beams and teak decking rising up into the wind like a death rattle.

It was an impossible challenge—getting Annie into the hall, up the stairs, and outside to safety. But if I didn't act quickly, the cabin would soon become both coffin and grave.

I remembered the advice of an old military man I'd met during my first week in Sri Lanka. He'd told me how he used to pinch the cheeks of soldiers who'd passed out from fatigue, dehydration, or both. 'Unless something is seriously wrong, it'll wake 'em long enough to get some water down their throat and get 'em back on their feet.'

I gathered a knot of skin on Annie's face and squeezed, hoping I wasn't bruising her.

Whether it was the result of the old man's seemingly simplistic remedy or the normal resumption of brain function following a minor concussion, I was relieved to see Annie's eyes shoot wide open.

My words came fast and furious. "A huge wave flipped us over. The boat's on its side. We have to get out now!"

Her vacant stare told me she was still dazed, unable to comprehend what I was saying.

I tried again. "Annie, listen to me. We're sinking. We don't have much time. You have to tell me what to do." I continued talking, explaining our situation, unsure if any of it was getting through. "We can't stay in the cabin. We have to get topside. Can you get to your feet?"

Leaning back, I reached out, ready to pull her up. Her expression changed from confusion to unmistakable fear.

I was unprepared for the blow that came from her right fist. Lying on her back and unable to control the angle, her knuckles glanced off my jaw. If she'd been able to make a solid connection with my head, her punch would have easily knocked me out.

More startled than hurt, I screamed at her. "Annie, stop! It's me, it's Jewel . . ."

The panic in her eyes was not unlike that of a wild animal ready to fight for its life. I had to keep her from hitting me again. If she managed to effectively land another punch, I could lose consciousness and the sea would take us both.

I grabbed her wrists and leaned forward, pinning her arms flat. Bringing my lips to her ear, I whispered. "Annie, it's me, Jewel. Please Annie, I need you to remember." I waited for a few seconds and then added, "Say it. Say my name."

The creases in her brow relaxed. I felt the tension in her arms subsiding. I had to take the chance. Slowly easing back, I released some of my body weight. Her arched back eased down against the rubble, her resistance gone.

The change in her expression was painfully slow. But it was definitely there. As I released my grip, her hands rose toward me, this time in a gentle but desperate reach.

"My head is killing me," she grumbled.

Annie was back.

I gave her the bottom line. "The boat's sinking. We have to get out of here."

She fumbled for a handhold. "Help me up."

Getting Annie to her feet would have been hard enough, but fighting the heavy wake from the storm made it twice as difficult. As I lifted her to her knees, it was obvious she was too shaky to stand on her own.

"I need a minute," she said. "I'm dizzy."

We didn't have a minute. For all I knew, the ocean was waiting for us right outside the door.

I wrapped my arms around her waist. "I'm going to get you on your feet, and help you into the hallway."

"Wait!" She began to shake her head then stopped, grimacing from the pain. "There's a lifejacket in the top of the closet. Get it and put it on."

"There's no time. Put your arms around me and—"

"Get the jacket," she argued. "We're not leaving the cabin without it."

I couldn't tell if she was being stubborn or justifiably concerned for our safety. It didn't matter. I scrambled over the bed-frame, kicked a dresser drawer out of the way, and turned the closet latch. As the door fell open, Annie's belongings—clothing, shoes, belts, and a few small boxes—rained over me. The orange life vest was tightly wedged into a storage space above the top shelf.

Ignoring the bite of metal belt buckles and hard rubber heels digging into my knees, I dragged the vest back to Annie. "You wear it. I'm a good swimmer."

She waved her hand in disagreement. "You have no idea what the ocean will be like. Put it on and if we wind up in the water, I'll hold on to you."

"No, Annie, you're hurt." I pushed the vest toward her. I could see her forehead was beginning to swell, the skin turning a light purple.

She stopped me cold. "Listen to me. We don't know what condition the rest of the boat is in. I don't know how easy it'll be getting to a life raft. I can't be worrying about you slipping under the water."

We were wasting time. I slid my arm through the shoulder strap, then stopped. I realized all I had on was a T-shirt. "We need some clothes."

"Over there," Annie said, pointing to the spilled contents of a dislocated drawer. "Grab something for me too."

She shrugged the terry cloth robe off her shoulders, grimacing from movement. "Make sure it's something light," she added. "Nothing that will drag us under."

I scooped up some shorts and a couple of pullovers.

I had them on in seconds.

While I buckled the lifejacket, Annie methodically dressed herself, finally tying a knot in the bottom of the shirt after cinching up the loose material.

"I don't want anything restricting me once I'm in the water."

She spoke as if talking to herself, repeating a step from a survival checklist—another symptom of her impaired focus.

Another large swell broke against the ship. I reached out and grabbed Annie's arm, waiting for the wave-quake to subside.

"Ready?" I felt like an impatient mother coaxing a reluctant child to leave for school.

She ignored my question, a glazed look in her eyes. "As long as we don't run into rising water," she began, "we'll go slow. Always move toward the surface. If we get swamped, if a compartment begins to flood, don't wait for the water to lift you. Get to the nearest hatch. And don't wait for me." Her stern expression was impossible to dismiss.

I drew a finger across my lower lip, slightly stunned. There was no way I would leave the boat without her. "Uh-huh. Sure."

"I'm serious," she countered. "If the water gets any higher than your ankles, get your ass out of here and don't worry about me. I can take care of myself."

The hull shook from the impact of another wave. Feeling the boat settle, I grabbed her hand. "I'm scared shitless and I need you to point me in the right direction. So if you're all done being heroic and everything, let's get out of here."

She started to nod, then winced, the pain too much to hide.

"Annie?"

"I'm fine," she said finally. "Let's go."

Whether my attention had been so focused on Annie's injuries as to make me unaware of the angle of the cabin floor or the topsy-turvy condition of the cabin had disguised the boat's severe listing, the slope of the deck was disturbingly obvious as I opened the cabin door.

I guessed the angle to be at least twenty-five degrees. It meant the ship was taking on water—fast. We would have to climb *up* the hallway.

With my arm around Annie's waist, we worked toward the stairs. The sound of rushing water was everywhere. Although I couldn't see the point of the entry, the steady splash and gurgle confirmed the sea's relentless effort to fill every vacant inch of the boat's interior.

In spite of the unnerving hull-shake, our ascent up the hallway was relatively easy. But as we reached the base of the stairs, our situation changed. The steps were useless. With the boat on its side, the angle of the stair treads made it impossible to gain footing. We would have to climb the railing like monkey bars.

"You go first." Annie pointed toward the hatchway at the top of the landing.

I began to object, but she cut me off. "Don't worry. I'll be right behind you."

She was as good as her word, one moment pushing me forward, the next locking an arm around my legs to keep me stable.

Making good progress, I asked, "Annie, where's the crew?" Since the ship first rolled, we hadn't seen or heard another soul. And I refused to believe the captain and his men had all perished in the first massive wave.

Annie answer was short and dismissive. "We'll find them. Keep going."

She doesn't want to distract me with conversation, I reasoned.

I'd easily adjusted to the side-squalled cabin, even retaining my sense of up and down as we moved into the outer hallway and up the staircase. But reaching the top of the landing was like entering a carnival fun house. Nothing made sense. The hatch leading to the outside deck was at my feet. The stairs I'd climbed looked more like a munchkin-sized hallway leading down to an alternative and broken universe. I needed another point of reference.

Annie noticed my confusion. "Don't pay any attention to the way things look. We're going out that hatch. And that's all you need to think about."

I looked down through the window seated into the top of the doorway. Our exit was directly over the sea, the boiling ocean lapping below us. For the first time since the wave hit, I felt trapped.

"We have to find another way out," I said, my voice beginning to tremble.

"This side of the deck is nearly under water."

Annie took me by the shoulders. "There *is* no other way." She nudged me to one side, giving her room to straddle the hatch opening. "Help me pull this up and slide the foot-pin into that rubber cleat." She pointed overhead, showing me how far the door would have to be lifted. "That cleat-lock will hold it open . . . keep it from slamming down on us."

"But there's no deck out there to support us. We'll be dropping directly into the ocean."

"We're not jumping into the water. We'll crawl along the sidewall, using the roof tie-downs as handholds to climb up and over to the opposite side of the boat."

I froze. "I don't think I can do that."

"We'll do it together," she promised. "I'll go first, and then I'll pull you up."

The *Kelsey* shuddered, forcing us to reach for the sidewalls. The loss of Annie's touch left me disconnected, the unsteady footing sending me to my knees. Immediately the stairwell interior resounded with the vicious slap of a cresting wave, reminding me I was kneeling in the shadow of death.

I could stay and let its eclipsing pall cover me—or I could fight.

"Let's open it," I said.

She bent down and grabbed the hatch handle. "Get ready." I heard the determination in her voice—tempered only by the blood trickling down her temple.

She released the lock.

A blast of water-laced wind exploded into the compartment, the outside pressure lifting the door several inches above the jamb. I wanted to step on it, push it shut and rethink our plan. But I knew I'd be closing the lid on our own coffin.

As the ocean's wet breath swirled around us, we lifted the hatch and set the retaining pin into the cleat. Annie tested the connection, making sure it would hold. Below us, a black and unforgiving ocean lapped against the hatch-jamb.

Annie yelled over the chorus of howling wind and clattering rain. "Now watch me."

Dropping to her hands and knees, she positioned herself over the opening. "Keep your legs spread wide for support, then lower yourself head-first to the outside. The tie-downs are within easy reach. Just feel for them."

Releasing one hand at a time, she dropped through the hatchway. For a moment, she hung there, dangling inches above the waves, her upper torso fully exposed to the elements. Swinging at the waist, she began building momentum, each time coming closer to the first handhold.

"Got it!" she yelled.

Seeing her legs snap together and drop through the opening was like watching an acrobatic dive, leaving me stunned, anxious—and alone.

I realized my hand was stretched out in front of me—*frozen*. I had instinctively reached out, as if wanting to prevent her from being sucked from the cabin by some monstrous evil. I had to remind myself she had plunged through the opening on purpose, to escape from this tiny cubicle that was now a deathtrap.

Dropping to my knees, I crawled to the edge of the hatchway and lowered my head toward the ocean until my hair floated on the waves. I caught a brief glimpse of Annie's feet, skimming the whitecaps, scrambling for a foot-hold. They disappeared as she scaled the side-squalled roof of the compartment.

Using the brass tie-downs like pylons on a mountaineer's scaling wall, she made her way to the opposite side of the hatchway, the thumping of her arms and legs against the cabin walls confirming her progress.

"Okay, Jewel. Your turn." She was right above me, yet her voice seemed to come from somewhere far more distant, a place outside my reach. "Straddle the hatch and spread your legs across the opening," she yelled. "When you're sure you can hold your weight, let go one hand at a time and drop through."

It looked easy when I'd watched her do it. Now it seemed insane—hanging headlong over the raging ocean, searching for a grip in the stinging, wind-driven rain.

The *Kelsey* trembled, tilting a few more degrees forward. I retreated back into the compartment, waiting for the ship to rebound from the clutches of the sub-surface currents. But this time, the hull settled deeper into the sea. The bow was taking on more water.

Chapter Sixteen

I'd never considered my fate to be aligned with that of the ship. I knew the boat was sinking, but I thought I would remain safe simply because I had the will to live. The truth was as dark as the ocean waiting impatiently at my feet—the distance between the water and the hatchway was quickly shrinking, and soon, the sea would pour through the opening. Once I was trapped inside, I would have no protection against the inrush of water. The likelihood of the rising ocean rushing into my lungs was now a very real—and terrifying—possibility.

I was frantic.

"Annie? I'm not sure I can get out."

"Yes you can," she scolded. "Drop through the doorway. I'm right here."

I wiped at the tears streaming down my face. I was as angry as I was afraid. On the brink of death, I was hesitating, refusing to do what was necessary to save myself. My only option was to follow her example, use my legs for support and hang headfirst through the hatchway. From there, I could grab her hand—I hoped.

Cautiously straddling the opening, I lowered my head toward the ocean, inching my way through the hatchway until I felt the waves licking at my forehead. I had gone as far as I could without relinquishing my grip on the hatch-jamb.

"I can't see you." I tried to disguise the panic in my voice, but it broke from pure terror.

"Look up, beyond the edge." Annie said. "You've got to come out farther."

I was fighting against the incessant rocking of the ship, my muscles straining against both gravity and fear. The thought of abandoning my handhold and stretching out over the ocean was...

Paralyzing.

I clung to the exterior projection of the hatch jamb like a frightened child, waiting for someone to chase away the nightmare and save me. But as the seconds ticked away, the reality was agonizingly clear. If I stayed where I was, Annie would never be able to reach me.

I remembered how shutting my eyes had helped me control my emotions the first time Butch forced himself on me in the engine room.

Maybe it would work now.

"Jewel, where are you? Say something." Annie's voice was faint, muffled by the rain and twisted on the wind. I felt the distance between us growing, the cruel hand of nature creating a barrier that could easily separate us forever.

Then it hit me—with my very survival at stake, I was acting like a baby, my closed eyes offering no more protection than if I covered my head with a blanket, trying to shield myself from goblins in the night. The next few minutes would determine if I lived or died, and how I used those minutes was up to me.

Whether it was a burst of adrenaline that pushed the fear from my muscles or I'd finally realized letting the ocean take me without a fight would be the last—and most regrettable—decision I'd ever make, remaining frozen with panic was no longer an option.

"Annie, I'm coming!" I yelled. "I'm coming."

Annie's voice cut through the howling wind. "We don't have much time. You have to get out NOW!"

Her plea carried the raw threat of an ultimatum—*move or die.*

I had watched Annie drop through the hatch with deft precision, as if every agile movement was part of a well-choreographed dance routine. I left in a graceless, gawky tumble, my legs slipping through the wet door-frame in spite of my efforts to keep them spread across the opening.

Plunging headlong into the sea, I surfaced in a flailing panic. Grabbing at the hatch jamb, I pulled myself up, the pressing cabin sidewall trapping me under the exterior of the sinking compartment.

I had anticipated the icy water and the pounding impact from the breakers. I never imagined my most horrifying enemy would come from deep within my own mind. With the sheeting rain restricting my breathing and the rocking sidewall of the ship looming above, I felt the suffocating clutch of claustrophobia.

"Look up! Reach for me. I'm right above you."

Annie.

Retaining a fingertip hold on the hatch jamb, I managed to peer around the sidewall and look straight up. Through the flashes of storm-light, I saw her hand dangling above me. She was lying flat on top of the compartment, ready to use her weight to offset mine.

A large swell rolled across the length of the boat, the crest swamping the hatch and filling my remaining air space with water. My sudden gasp drew the ocean into my nose and throat. Coughing, unable to breath, I acted on instinct, releasing the hatch jamb and pushing myself out from under the side-squalled cabin.

I reached up into the wind.

Annie's hand met mine in a clumsy scramble. "I've got you," she shouted. "I won't let you go."

Although I couldn't see her face, her voice penetrated the storm with sheer determination, her resolve confirming a bond between two souls, ready to live or die—together.

At most, Annie weighed a little over a hundred pounds. Lifting me out of the water with a single hand would take herculean strength—beyond her physical capability while maintaining her balance on the lurching ship. The best she could do was prevent me from being dragged away from the wreck by the current.

"Feel for the tie-downs," Annie yelled. "Use them like a ladder."

I ran my free hand over the slightly pitched surface. The metal fittings she'd used to scale the upturned roof seemed impossibly small, offering only the dull impression of raised metal against the water-soaked wood. I had no idea how I could put any weight on such a tiny, oddly shaped projection.

Unable to stabilize myself, I slid back and forth against the roof of the partially submerged cabin like a flailing fish, unable to escape the grip of a merciless sea.

Lightning tore across the sky.

Cringing against the blinding flash, I opened my eyes in time to see cobwebby streaks of fading plasma dividing the darkness, filling the air with frozen raindrops. Moments later, a deafening crash of thunder arrived with percussive impact.

Beyond the artificial silence of my stunned senses, I heard Annie's voice breaking through. It took several seconds before I could make sense of what she was saying. "There's a half-dozen cleats right at your feet. Keep trying!"

Even with her encouragement, I couldn't locate a useable foothold. And now I knew why. My feet and hands were turning numb. More than a symptom of the cold, it inferred a disheartening—and likely fatal—prognosis. With the loss of feeling, my odds of climbing up and over the roof were fading.

I looked up, knowing Annie was a only a few feet away, hidden in the black rain. As the waves continued to bounce me against the sinking wreck, I had no choice—I had to tell her.

"Annie, I can't feel my legs."

For the longest time, she was silent. Perhaps she was calculating the odds of my succumbing to hypothermia or estimating how much time remained before the ship dropped below the surface.

When she finally spoke, her voice was subdued and artificially calm, the way a passerby talks to an accident victim, attempting to disguise the true extent of their injuries.

"We'll use the swells for lift. We need to wait for one to raise you high enough. The boat is dropping lower in the water. Either way, it's just a matter of time before I can pull you out. Then we'll make a run for the life raft."

A quick streak of flame dropped from the heavens, revealing her face—a frozen flash of labored worry against a black canvas. I knew she would never willingly release me. Yet I also knew there was a limit to her endurance.

I tried to think of other options, a piece of rope, a life preserver, anything we could use to bridge the gap between us. I even considered letting go, waiting adrift in the sea while she located the raft. But the odds of her being able to find me in time—before the current dragged me away from the wreck—were small. Even if I were able to find a something to hold on to, it would be temporary at best, forcing me to abandon it as the boat continued to sink. And to make matters worse, the flotation jacket's built-in strobe had failed to activate upon being exposed to the salt water. A dead battery was most likely the culprit and, without the light, I would be a floating needle in a dark and endless haystack.

Annie's suggestion was the only one offering some chance of success. We needed a large wave, one that would lift me high enough for her to raise me onto the tilted cabin sidewall. It was a cruel irony—the storm was our obvious enemy, yet we would have to rely on its random cooperation.

As I bobbed against the boat, I realized Annie was timing her efforts with the rise and fall of the sea. More than tired, she was nearing exhaustion.

While a nonstop barrage of wind-whipped rain peppered my back, I knew Annie was receiving far worse. Her position on top of the wreck left her exposed to the angry elements. I hated it—the agony I knew she was enduring, and worse, the risk she was taking by refusing to abandon me.

A few hours ago, I had felt uncomfortable concern—even guilt—over Annie's suggestion of a committed relationship.

'Nothing else between us. Forever,' she'd said.

Now a single thought overwhelmed me—*I didn't deserve her.*

I felt Annie's fingers tighten around my wrist. My mind raced to the worst possibility—the boat must be turning, beginning its final rotation to a fully capsized position. In moments, she would have to release me and swim to the stern, dive below the surface and find the submerged storage canister. Then somehow, in the darkness, remove the tightly packed life raft, find the activation trigger and release the CO_2, allowing the chambers to inflate.

And I would be left floundering on the surface.

My racing heart set my brain to throb.

I yelled into the wind, hoping my voice would carry far enough to reach her.

"Annie, you need to get to the stern before the boat rolls over. I want you to leave . . . now!"

Her answer came through the pyro-clipped darkness. "We'll use the surge for lift. If the water's high enough, I'll bring you in off the top of the swell."

She hadn't heard me.

It was just as well. My panicked conjecture of a rolling hull had been wrong. Annie had correctly interpreted the rapid recession of the ocean from around the ship as signaling the approach of another huge wave.

From her position, and with a few well-timed bursts of sky-fire, she would see it first.

She confirmed its advance. "It's nearly on us, hold on."

I turned to see the flame-scarred sky reveal a towering fringe of seething foam devouring the horizon with eerie fluorescence.

"Get ready, and hold your breath," she added.

My body was numb. With the open jaws of the sea enveloping me to the chest, my fate relied on Annie—and a huge dose of luck.

I feared the inrush of water as much as I welcomed it. While the lift might bring me closer to her, it could also pin me against the hull, counteracting any boost I might receive. Worse, the sheer power of the wave could tear Annie and I from the ship, dooming both of us to nameless graves at the bottom of the sea.

"If we're separated," I yelled, "you swim toward the life raft. I'll hang on here."

I was giving her permission to leave me behind, and regardless of what happened, she was not to blame herself.

I regretted it immediately. It was placating, a get-out-of-guilt-free card. The realization that it might be the last thing I would ever say to her filled me with shame.

But there was no time to take it back.

A barrage of thunderclaps shattered the air, demanding our attention, as if nature was setting the stage for one of its finest performances.

A curtain of wicked lace crackled across the sky, the blazing web spearing the earth with ladders of white-hot fire. For an instant, night turned into day.

In the receding filaments of illumination, I saw it: A thirty-foot wall of water bearing down on the wreck. With artifacts of blue-white corona sparkling off the white-capped crest, I inhaled deeply and braced for it.

It hit with far more impact than I expected, completely engulfing the ship. As the wave broke high over our heads, I worried Annie would lose her grip and the churning current would sweep her from the boat. But she managed to hold on, and before the swell could recede, she hauled me in, refusing to let go even after I had surrounded her waist with my free arm.

"Breathe with your head down," she commanded. "There's less chance of getting a mouthful of water."

I nodded, deciding to thank her *after* we were in the life raft.

The pain of being dragged across the exposed edge of the roof was mercifully delayed until the ship rose into the trough of the next wave. While the cuts and abrasions were minor, their sting was intensified by the brine-infused water.

I ignored it, knowing tomorrow my aches and pains would surface as bruises—temporary badges to commemorate my victory over fear.

Tomorrow.

Under the circumstances, the word seemed impossibly optimistic.

Annie's face drew close, her breath reaching my mouth as warm wisps of hope. "Let's work our way to the stern. The raft is in the storage compartment under the seats."

I glanced toward the rear of the boat. A curtain of pounding rain had rendered the stern deck invisible, as if absorbed by some monstrous storm-cloaked apparition. But Annie knew the ship inside and out . . . where to step, when to jump. If the raft was there, she would find it.

I spread my hands for better balance and scooted back a few inches, ready to follow. "Wish we'd grabbed a flashlight," I said.

Annie hesitated.

I reasoned she was waiting for the waves to shift the boat, to put the wind at our backs. But her reluctance had nothing to do with improving our ability to resist the elements. The culprit was fatigue. And as the lightening-scored sky illuminated her face, I saw signs of exhaustion—her eyes glazed, her head bobbing slightly. The injury she'd received when tumbling through the cabin had been aggravated by her efforts to keep me tethered to the ship. By ignoring the debilitating effects of what was surely a concussion, she had depleted her physical reserves, the strain of saving my life now endangering hers.

Perhaps her second wind would come.

But when?

We couldn't risk the wait. We had to move toward the stern of the ship—and a fiberglass container holding one hundred and fifty pounds of inflatable polyurethane-coated nylon—our only means of survival.

"I'll go first. We'll take a few feet at a time." I tried to sound confident.

"Okay," Annie mumbled.

"Stay low and crawl," I added.

I was terrified. Less than a minute ago, I had thought Annie would take charge. Now she would have to follow *me*. She was, in the most literal sense, putting her life in my hands. Somehow I had to find the courage to lead, and that meant making split-second decisions of when to advance and when to wait. As the raging cycle of waves continued to rise and fall around us, I prayed Annie's instincts would remain sharp so she could warn me before I did something stupid—and dangerous.

Crawling on our hands and knees, our progress was excruciatingly slow. My vision was limited to a few precious feet, and then only when a ribbon of fire set the ocean to boil with a flash of blinding white light.

The raindrops pummeled our flesh like steel rods, its impact magnified tenfold by the driving wind. There was no rhythm, no sense of timing to the storm's onslaught—only wave after pounding wave, each cresting peak a prelude to the next wall of screaming ocean.

Above us, the traumatized sky had become a living, breathing monster, its dark eyes launching shards of white-hot plasma raking the heavens in blasts of ear-splitting fury.

As we continued plodding toward the stern, I couldn't believe the ship was still afloat. Only a few hours ago, the sails had captured the wind in the same way a tailored gown drapes the body of a fit and graceful woman. Now the sailcloth hung over the mid-ship like a death shroud, while all around us, thick cotton lines thrashed across the deck, ready to coil around our hands and feet, eager to sacrifice our souls to Poseidon.

It's just rope. It's not alive.

I repeated it over and over, under my breath. And yet I occasionally brushed away a particularly threatening piece of line, as if the woven fibers might rise and attack, possessed by the most primal and demonic forces of nature.

Underneath us, the irregular surface of routed oak repelled our advance with shards of peeling varnish, the thin slivers piercing our hands and knees as effectively as glass. With our progress measured in pain rather than distance, I told myself each stinging puncture brought us nearer to our destination.

The end of the ship came unexpectedly—and much too soon. Until now, we'd taken advantage of make-shift bridging and scalable roof overhangs. Those were gone.

"There, against the railing." Annie pointed into the sheets of rain.

Light from the constant volley of sky-borne fire confirmed the location of the partially exposed stern. Inside the aft railing, a good forty feet away, the bench seat rhythmically rode the waves. It was our final destination. Under that seat cover we would find a fiberglass barrel, and inside, a life raft—our only way off the *Kelsey*.

There were only two ways to get there. Climb the wet, vertical deck to the side rail and work our way to the stern or take the direct route and swim the distance. It wasn't a hard decision.

Large portions of the side rail had been torn away when the mast and rigging separated from the ship. Without a handhold, the shifting hull could easily shake me off and drop me into the ocean. And if I fell into the sea on the opposite side of the boat, I'd be gone forever.

A forty-foot gulf of furious ocean stretched before me, daring me to test its cold currents and head-topping swells. I considered a running jump, using the four or five feet of relatively flat cabin sidewall that lay behind me to build momentum. If timed correctly, and the wind cooperated, I might cut the distance by ten feet. But with each lightning-fired glimpse, I saw more of what waited under the water—a submerged trap of twisted steel and broken sheet metal, the remains of the canopy structure. With no way to avoid the sharp edges and pointed end braces of the wreckage, a bounding leap was too dangerous.

I would have to swim the entire distance, carefully testing the area ahead of me before taking a deep stoke or kick.

I can do this. It's not that far. I've covered much longer distances in choppy seas before.

I reminded myself of the time I swam the one-and-a-half-mile stretch of ocean between the eastern shore of Sri Lanka and Pigeon Island. The weather was good, the sea calm, and there were ten of us—all with fins, masks, and snorkels—and a guide boat within easy reach. Starting out, I was scared. With the island too flat to present any kind of silhouette, it appeared as if we were swimming into the open sea without a fixed destination. But the others encouraged me and, knowing my husband was a strong swimmer, I took my first strokes, wanting the memory—and the victory of having completed the challenge.

But this ocean was different—a vicious predator, outraged and violent, anxious to suffocate its victims with a blanket of liquid death. As it continued to drag the *Kelsey* lower with every surge of wave-wash, it reminded us we were living on borrowed time.

I hadn't noticed Annie coming up from behind. Quickly sitting on the edge of the structure, she dropped her legs over the side, her feet disappearing into the dark, simmering ocean.

"What are you doing?" I sounded like a horrified mother shrieking at a child who was about to jump off a roof in a naive attempt to fly.

"I'm going for the raft." She said it without hesitating.

"You can't! Your scalp is bleeding. I've got more strength."

Annie shook her head, slinging drops of red-tinted water in both directions. "There are two latches on the canister. I know where they're located and how to open them. You don't."

"Tell me where there are, how to work them."

"Listen to me. The inflation trigger has to be activated. And as the raft inflates, I have to make sure it doesn't get caught or wedged in the wreckage." She paused, looking at me with silent desperation. "Do you understand? I'm the only one who can do it."

I couldn't argue with her. I would be a floundering neophyte, unfamiliar with the canister or the operation of the raft. She would have to go.

I unsnapped the front catch on the lifejacket and began pulling it off my shoulders.

"NO! Leave it on." Annie was reaching for the straps, threading them back through the loop-rings, fumbling to re-secure them.

"But you need this more than I do," I argued.

"It will only slow me down. Promise me you'll keep it on."

The urgency in her voice should have alarmed me. Instead, it was the most reassuring sound I'd heard since the huge rogue wave swamped the boat. In spite of her head injury, she was demonstrating her usual logic and keen perception.

Taking my face in her hands, she kissed me, and without another word, slipped into the water. She looked up, about to say something. But the raging ocean would not permit it, and in a cruel reminder of our diminishing odds of survival, the next wave swallowed her whole.

"Be careful," I shouted. In the same instant, she sprang forward, skimming the top of the water. But the intensity of the storm was as brutal below the surface as above, and before she could cover half the distance, the sea attacked her with a choking web of fluid tentacles.

In seconds, she was gone.

On the verge of panic, I clawed at the closures of the lifejacket. Freeing it from my arms, I flung it toward the spot where the current had taken her under.

It disappeared into the staccato-quick flashes of light and dark.

I wanted to follow her. Save her.

There was no time to do either.

With the screaming wind and crashing thunder masking its approach, I didn't hear the distinctive roar of the huge swell until it was nearly on top of the boat. With only a single tie-down within reach, I grabbed the anvil-shaped piece of brass and braced myself.

It hit the boat broadside, the impact tearing into the very core of the ship. Hugging the tilted cabin structure, I held on as the wall of water exploded over me with the power of an artillery burst. The *Kelsey* shuttered, trying to shed me the same way an animal attempts to rid itself of an unwanted parasite.

Completely submerged, I felt the bump and brush of swirling scrap, no doubt some of it the water-soaked possessions of the crew. Knowing I might also be feeling the intractable touch of a lifeless body, I kept my eyes shut, determined to lock out the lightning-fired shadows of the restless dead.

I prayed for the boat to rise, to again find the surface of the rain-swept sea. But there was only the unceasing draw of the ocean—and darkness.

A few more seconds, that's all I can stand.

The thought of abandoning my connection to the ship was terrifying. It had been my protector, an island of relative safety in a ferocious sea. Even now, as logic and reason told me it no longer offered deliverance from death, the thought of letting go was synonymous with surrender to the grave.

As panic and fear threatened to render me a catatonic fixture on the stern cabin, I realized staying with the ship would produce a singular outcome: Immediate drowning.

Thoughts of imminent death pounded at my temples. But inside my brain, I was haunted by something my father had told me many years ago: *'No matter how bad the situation, always keep looking for the best course of action. And never decide on anything important until you find it.'*

My life—and choosing to fight for it—was an important decision. And while I didn't have any influence over the wind and water, I still had control over my own actions.

I released my grip on the tie-down. Using muted flashes from the heavens as a guide, I began kicking toward the surface. My natural buoyancy was useless against the strong current, and I silently repeated the obvious and inescapable conclusion . . .

I should have let go sooner.

It was difficult to tell if I was making any headway. The water was refracting the light, bending it into confusing images, luring in me one direction, then another.

In a final surge of adrenaline-laced panic, I made a frenzied charge toward what I hoped to be the surface. I was met with a flash of overhead shadow, followed by the disorienting shock of severe impact. A wrenching burn tore through my wrists, adding agony to my searing hunger for air.

Had the current pushed me back into one of the ship's submerged compartments? Or worse, had it trapped me under the hull? In this purgatory of blackness, it was impossible to tell.

Railing against a fate that would condemn me to die inside a boat dedicated to human slavery, I gathered the last of my fading strength and punched at the overhead barrier. The surface rebounded with soft pliancy.

It felt like . . . rubber.

I was seconds away from drawing the sea down my throat. Frantically clawing at the obstruction, I felt something smooth and curved, like the rounded edge of a pneumatic chamber.

The life raft?

I reached up, desperate for a handhold.

A sudden vice-grip around my wrist sent a jolt of fire deep into my shoulder. The water fell away from my face and I sucked in the air, my expanding lungs distracting me from the pain.

I could breath.

While the fleshy hold on my arm was firm, it lacked the leverage to lift me into the raft. I brought my leg up, scrambling to find footing.

"Don't try to climb up. Drop in from the waist. Then bring in your legs."

The words fell on me like an unfamiliar noise, the sound unable to compete against the clattering storm.

It took several attempts, but I finally managed to scale the slick nylon tube and tumble into the bottom of the bucking raft.

I grabbed the hand-straps and pulled myself tight against the sides, gulping down the air, barely aware of the water sloshing back and forth over my legs. Being plucked from the sea brought more than relief. It delivered an unexpected reprieve from death.

"Stay low and hold on to those straps."

There it was again—that sense that something was wrong, out of place. It was like coming home to an empty house and noticing an unrecognizable footprint on a freshly vacuumed carpet.

It took another few seconds for my muddled comprehension to finally give way to the unwelcome, yet inescapable conclusion—*the voice was not Annie's!*

I looked up, keeping my eyes fixed on the rain-shrouded figure. I had to know who had taken Annie's place—who had dared assume her role as my savior.

Blinded by the thick curtain of side-blown rain, the blitzkrieg of wind and water was as effective as a funeral veil, obscuring every feature, every detail of my raft-mate. Worse, the life preserver's strobe lights had activated on inflation, their staccato flicker distorting my vision with a slow-motion blur.

It didn't matter. The heavens would eventually reveal his identity. All I knew for sure was that the person sitting on the opposite side of the raft was a man, and Annie was nowhere to be seen.

His act of heroic mercy demanded I thank him. While I didn't want to appear unappreciative, I saved my voice. With each swell threatening to capsize the tiny craft, it would be like attempting to exchange pleasantries while fighting off a ferocious enemy—at least, that's what I told myself.

The selfish truth was more to the point. If I was going to shout loud enough to be heard over the crashing thunder and screaming wind, it would be to ask the singular question consuming my very soul: *If Annie didn't make it to the raft, where was she?*

A new barrage of storm-light caught his face at the wrong angle, adding only shadow to form. It also illuminated the arrival of a large swell, top-heavy with debris from the ship. Pieces of wood the size of my arm rained down on us with all the power a twenty-foot wave could muster. I winced as my legs absorbed the full impact of a four-inch timber the length of a chair leg, grateful that none of it caught my head.

With nature continuing to telegraph its relentless message of fear, I refused to take my eyes off my companion. Even as he leaned forward to rake the broken wood and bits of fiberglass over the side, I strained for a clear glimpse of his face.

I made out the tip of a nose, the top of an ear—that's all the storm would allow.

Clutching the side-straps, I waited.

It was nearly another wave-bucking, rain-soaked minute until a blue-white strike penetrated the thick curtain of rain with enough illumination to reveal my raft-mate's identity. This time the angle and timing were in my favor, the light falling on him as he turned his face to mine. While it didn't make any difference who had pulled me to safety, his familiarity struck me with an odd sense of irony. Most of my contact with the crew had been limited to a few minutes with each man during the training sessions. I'd learned very little about their individual predispositions or personalities.

R.J. had been the exception. He was manipulative, devious, and cunning—traits that were as much a part of his personality as his pretentious arrogance.

Above all, I knew he couldn't be trusted.

The window of light had been short. I waited for the next discharge to expose his calm and deliberately composed expression. But as an unexpectedly bright burst rippled along the bottom of the clouds, I saw his face etched with equal amounts of fear and desperation.

He knew our situation was deadly serious, and he saw no point in trying to hide it.

I struggled to sit higher, to see over the inflated main tube. The strobing illumination that initially masked R.J.'s face had the opposite effect on the scene outside the raft. Lighting the sea to a distance of thirty yards, I saw the wreck had resurfaced at the very edge of visibility. A broken hulk projecting just above the broiling froth, I was drawn to one end of the debris field, where a portion of deck rode slightly higher than the rest of the doomed vessel.

I prayed for it—a close and lingering assault of lightning that would expose every inch of the stricken ship. Perhaps atmospheric conditions made my plea an easy one to answer or it was the storm's way of tempting me with possibility before torturing me with hopeless despair. In either case, the next discharge arrived in seconds, striking near enough to set the raft tingling with static electricity.

And in that moment, as the eruption of light spread across the water . . .

I saw her.

Clinging to one of the damaged canopy supports, Annie had taken refuge on a section of the stern railing. With the whitecaps lapping at her knees, I knew she would soon be forced to abandon the sinking hulk.

A few yards away and attached by a safety rope, the empty life raft container bobbed like a rambunctious sea creature, anxious to free itself. The image revealed a devastating truth. Annie had needlessly risked her life to swim to the rear of the ship, only to discover the storage compartment under the bench seat was empty.

R.J. had gotten to it first.

Why hadn't we seen the empty fiberglass cylinder floating on the surface before Annie jumped into the raging ocean?

Maybe the raft canister had lodged on something below the surface. Or maybe it was there all the time, and with our vision hampered by the rain, we'd simply missed it.

"Over there!" I screamed. "It's Annie! Take us toward the wreck. We'll pick her up."

R.J. shook his head. "There's no paddles, no way to move the raft."

"We'll use our hands," I pleaded. "If we can get half-way, she can swim to us."

Even through the back-flashes of strobe-lite, I saw his resigned expression. "Annie knows," he said.

"What the hell does that mean? *What* does Annie know?"

"We're being dragged away from the wreck faster than she can swim. By the time she made it this far, we'd be twice the distance."

I was stunned, my mouth gaping open, unable to speak. Finally, I said, "We're going to leave her?"

R.J.'s silent stare confirmed it.

I couldn't believe it. She was right there, separated from us by a scant fifty yards. And although the storm had surely taken a lot out of her, she was a strong swimmer.

So why wasn't she jumping in?

Because R. J. was right.

As I watched Annie's crouched form growing smaller, I didn't need instruments to tell me what was happening. The wind and current were quickly pushing us away from the ship, the distance between us increasing by the second.

"Jewel, look over there, to the right!" R. J. was yelling, pointing to a spot some forty feet or more from where Annie was stranded. I ignored him, unwilling to take my eyes off the ship's stern. As long as it harbored a trace of movement, I knew Annie was there—still alive.

R. J. called out again. "Jewel, listen to me. *There's someone else in the water.*"

Reluctantly glancing in the direction of his pointed finger, I expected to see the flailing arms of a desperate, near-drowned sailor. Instead there was an eerie spot of muted iridescence originating from a partially submerged emergency beacon, probably grabbed by one of the crew before he was washed overboard.

I shook my head, ready to dismiss his claim of another survivor as wishful thinking. But as the powerful spotlight caught me directly in the eyes, it was obvious the light was not responding solely to the rise and fall of the swells—it was being directed with frantic intention. There *was* someone else in the water, fighting to stay alive.

Despite my pupils contracting from the bright light, I could see the bobbing, twisting beam was attached to a thrashing limb. As if to magnify his desperate need for rescue, the newfound survivor suddenly turned the light on himself, the wave-wash across the sealed lens producing the surreal image of a human figure. At that distance, his features were indistinguishable, but it was definitely a man—*a man who appeared to be standing on the surface of the water.* For an instant, I considered the possibility of Divine intervention, but in this chaotic and storm-churned hell, the angel of death seemed the more likely architect of this strange apparition.

A blazing salvo dropped from the sky, confirming my suspicions.

The condemned soul was riding the surge, standing on what I reasoned to be the submerged sidewall of the bridge. Gripping an extension of broken mast rigging, he was using his free hand to direct the light.

He was in no position to help Annie, but I was sure she could see him. I hoped she took comfort in knowing she didn't stand alone on the edge of a watery grave.

"I can't tell who it is," R. J. yelled. "But at least someone else was able to survive the first wave. I thought I was the only one."

"Well, you weren't!" I screamed. "And you left Annie to die."

He shook his head, denying my accusation. "When the first wave hit, we were all amidships, tying down the sails, securing the rigging. We didn't see it coming. It washed most of the crew overboard. I was thrown against the mast and was able to hold on."

"But you took the only raft," I shot back, wiping at the mix of water and tears.

"The only other one was forward, on the starboard side," he argued. "But that side of the ship was submerged and covered in sailcloth. I managed to get this one out of the stern locker."

I managed to get this one out of the stern locker. It might as well have been Annie's eulogy.

As the wind pushed us further from the wreck, the man clutching the marine spotlight continued to illuminate the horrific scene, first targeting the raft, then pointing to the rear of the boat, where Annie clung to the railing. He completed the rotation by turning the light on himself, as if confirming the location of the only survivors.

Each time the lantern's spot found the stern of the *Kelsey*, I searched for the faint outline of Annie's form, the sight of her shadowed silhouette confirming she was alive, holding on to the last projecting piece of the ship.

Then the light would move, and the darkness would reclaim her.

It was devastating . . . leaving Annie there to die. The thought of losing her was inconceivable, my need to be with her overwhelming my own survival instincts. For a moment, I considered swimming to meet her halfway, even if it meant our last embrace would be shared in death.

A dozen times I started to wave, wanting her to know it was me in the inflatable, and that in spite of the distance separating us, we were still connected—still together. But each time, the sea took advantage of my momentary lack of a handhold and threatened to toss me from the raft.

My flailing hand never rose above the upper side tube.

I tried to imagine how alone and afraid she felt. I wanted to cry—just for her. But my own fear was a selfish and shameful excuse for the tears streaming down my face.

We were several hundred yards from the stricken ship when I noticed the spotlight's narrow amber beam growing feeble. Even so, I kept my eyes on it, watching it advance and retreat over the rain-swept surface, pretending I could still see Annie's profile against the twisted wreckage.

Blinded by a strike of blue-white fire, I slumped lower into the raft, cringing against the pounding concussion.

The cold, salty ocean splashed over my face, momentarily blurring my vision.

I was missing the last few moments of Annie's life.

I sat up, waiting for the next discharge to reveal the distant outline of the floating hulk. In moments, a blazing cobweb lit the sky. I scanned the surface where I had last seen the puny light from the marine lantern. Now, only huge crashing whitecaps rode the surface of the sea.

"Stay low, Jewel. We have to keep the raft stable."

Without realizing it, I had risen to my knees, my hands knotted around the safety rope, blood weeping from between my fingers. For a moment, I wondered if offering myself to the sea would redeem me from eternal oblivion, if my sacrifice would reunite me with Annie. By now, she had surely found her way to the other side of the storm, where I hoped she'd discovered a far more tranquil ocean.

"It's getting worse," R. J. yelled. "If the raft flips, try to stay with it. There's a chance it might right itself."

With my thoughts focused on Annie, I'd been oblivious to the storm's increasing intensity. A quick glance told me the wind and waves had become dedicated allies, working together in perfect concert.

Tossed about like a cork on a volcanic sea, the lifeboat bucked and dropped without warning. Often pushed to the edge of capsizing, the raft filled and emptied with its own tide, each inrush and spill threatening to wash us overboard.

Straining to maintain an inseparable bond with the rubber, I held my breath with each assault, hoping the air chambers could withstand the crashing impact, praying the tortured nylon would bend and not break.

All around us, streaks of fire joined the heavens to the earth. Some strikes were so close I was sure I heard the sizzle of boiling water. But what I thought was the sound of steam was an indication of a shocked inner ear, stressed to the point of damage from the collective bombardment of deafening thunder.

With the storm showing no signs of diminishing, each minute was like the one before it—a fight for survival. I had no idea how much time had passed since the *Kelsey* disappeared from sight, no way to measure the distance we'd traveled when I noticed something unusual on the horizon. At first I dismissed it, thinking it was a pulse of refracted storm light momentarily frozen in the rain. But in minutes, it grew steady and predictable, independent from the storm.

The possibility haunted me . . . *could it be the Kelsey?*

I waited, making sure the throbbing yellow star-point was a persistent fixture on the horizon before bringing it to R.J.'s attention.

"Over there. Do you see that?" I tipped my head toward the blinking light, then realized my voice had failed to penetrate the solid curtain of rain. I tried again, almost screaming. "Look on your left. Is that the wreck?"

R.J. scanned the distant junction of ocean and sky. "No, that's a buoy." He must have seen my anxious expression, because he added, "It's not her, Jewel. The ship's gone."

Deep down, I already knew the truth. He didn't have to say it. I just wasn't ready to believe it. The appearance of a light—any light—was enough to unleash a surge of irrational hope that Annie was still out there, clinging to a piece of floating debris, determined to survive.

I looked back at the pulsing yellow dot. While I didn't know much about navigation, I'd often overheard Carl simplifying the basics of map reading and course plotting to novice boaters. He would explain how yellow beacons typically identified a NOAA weather buoy, with platforms as large as thirty feet in diameter. Others—the much smaller tsunami detection units—might have hull spans of only six feet.

A red or green light would have been more welcome. Both colors typically indicated a navigational buoy, often marking the entrance to a harbor or the beginning of shallows.

In our situation, the weather buoy offered no advantage. And yet, I kept watching it, letting it distract me, even smiling as the flashing beacon eventually appeared as a collection of winking stars, the dancing lights conveying an almost ethereal presence. I knew it was only swells causing the platform to bob back and forth, yet it was easy to imagine those fuzzy points of yellow light were intended as a message, a steadfast reminder that some things would survive the

storm. And if I was lucky, I might be one of
them.

Chapter Seventeen

Without a watch, it was impossible to know how long we had resisted nature's best efforts to claim us as hapless casualties. My shoulders ached from the strain of keeping myself pinned against the pneumatic chambers of the half-flooded raft. My hands had long ago lost all feeling, and with my nerves numb from the cold, I could only estimate the depth of the lacerations revealed by the crimson-tinted water lining the spaces between my fingers.

R.J.'s voice broke through the wind. "Behind you."

I twisted around, craning my neck. "What?"

"Wait for it."

I wasn't exactly sure where he wanted me to look, and as I turned into the wind, a large swell breeched the upper tube and slapped me squarely in the face. I was spitting brine when he yelled again.

"There it is! Directly behind you."

I'd grown accustomed to the slight trace of fear in R.J's voice, seeming to hint at the inescapable conclusion that we were living on borrowed time. Now I heard something else—excitement.

Blinking furiously to clear the salt from my eyes, I peered into the rain-spiked gale. At first, I discounted the glowing pinpoints as retina-retained artifacts or a freakish break in the clouds revealing a slice of the heavens. It took several seconds to recognize the display was neither an illusion nor a fragment of distant sky. Shining steadily through the liquid darkness, the lights rose and fell in a constant, even rhythm, the motion a tattletale clue to their origin.

They were the running lights of a distant vessel.

I speculated on its size—maybe a transport or small tanker, certainly a ship large enough to withstand the storm's punishment.

Through the heavy rain, it was difficult to estimate the stretch of ocean that lay between us. A mile . . . maybe more.

The abrupt pop of the flare gun startled me, the noise driving me flat against the rubber.

Believing the ship was near enough to see our signal, R.J. had retrieved the gun from the emergency kit tethered to the raft's interior and fired the first of three available rounds. But the combination of wave-shake and fatigue had caused him to pull the trigger prematurely, his aimless trajectory sending the shell skimming across the surface into an approaching swell.

Through the relentless downpour, I saw him fumbling with a second round, struggling to reload with a single hand.

Even as I anticipated the next shot, the sharp report made me flinch as the sky's own fire was momentarily challenged by the flying streak of reddish-orange brimstone. Although the strong *whoosh* of the shell provided a persuasive testament to the promise of discovery, the projectile's final altitude and length of burn was limited by the downpour, and as the expanding blister of flame erupted into a weak, pallid light, I knew it was a feeble signal at best.

Apparently it was enough.

What had been a sketchy and disconnected skeleton of earthbound stars on a roller-coaster horizon began to take shape and form as exterior floods illuminated every inch of the distant ship's superstructure. With the additional light, I could tell the ship was much closer than I had originally thought.

The beam of a powerful spotlight shot from its deck.

R.J. retrieved the last shell from the flare case. In seconds, it was aloft. Again the burn was short. But this time, the crew on the would-be rescue ship was waiting for it, and they immediately pointed the searchlight in our direction, sweeping the ocean in tight passes.

"They've seen us!" R.J. seemed almost giddy with relief.

I wasn't ready to share his enthusiasm. "Why do they keep scanning the water? Can't they see the flashing strobes?"

"They're searching for anything floating on the surface to avoid hitting what they can't see, especially survivors who might be in the water. It's standard procedure when responding to a distress signal."

Only after the vessel turned directly toward us did I begin to exchange my skepticism for the real possibility of rescue. Now I could get help from the authorities. Maybe someone in the next port could put me in touch with the American embassy and I could work my way back to the States. At the very least, I could find a place where the *Kelsey's* captain and his network of nefarious associates would never find me.

The captain! The threat of his continued pursuit instinctively raced through my mind.

My memory of him had been unaffected by the catastrophic events of the last few hours. For all I knew he was dead. And with his demise, there would be no one to claim ownership, no one to initiate a search or offer a bounty for my return.

I should have felt a sense of relief or at least a hint of promise after prevailing over my captors. But the wind's incessant howl, punctuated by the unrelenting firestorm streaking across the night-canopy assured me it was much too soon to celebrate.

It was difficult to estimate the ship's speed. While its lights appeared to be approaching, its bearing had changed. No longer on an intercept course, its original turn toward us was exaggerated and, after a few minutes, the vessel had shifted back to our opposite side.

Now I was sure something was wrong. The ship was turning again—away from us.

"R.J! They've changed their mind! They're moving away. The sea must be too rough . . ."

Thick rivulets of rain flew from his face as he shook his head. "They can't come at us in a dead run. They have to keep the bow pointed into the waves. They'll zig-zag until they get within a hundred yards. Then they'll drop a lifeboat and work their way over to us."

It seemed like an eternity before the ship was near enough to present its full profile.

R.J. struggled with a set of binoculars secured by a rubber strap to the raft's accessory pocket. He finally succeeded in holding them against his eyes long enough to scan the vessel.

"I know her. The *Kochi Mar*. Carries cargo." In spite of the erratic bounce of the waves, he was able to read the ship's name on the bow.

Without thinking, I asked. "What kind of cargo?"

I'd never thought it necessary to qualify the integrity of a ship's captain and crew by the nature of their consigned property. Now, every ship—every ocean going transport—would be suspect. Until I was sure the bill of lading consisted of nothing more than computers from China, tires from Japan, or containers packed with the furnishings of ex-patriots, I would always wonder if there were young girls shackled and caged below deck.

Either my question had failed to penetrate the storm or R.J. had intentionally ignored it. "What kind of cargo?" I repeated, this time raising my voice.

He lowered the glasses and dropped his chin. "I . . . don't know."

R.J.'s hesitation was obvious. Maybe he *didn't* know. But in this part off the world, any ship on the same route as the *Kelsey* warranted suspicion.

I tried again. "Do you know the captain?"

"I've seen him in port."

He was hedging.

"I want the truth. Does the captain of that boat buy and sell girls? Does he transport them to auctions?"

R.J. was silent.

I felt a chill—much colder than the icy water surrounding me—crawling up my spine.

Finally, he opened his mouth, but before he could speak, a wave broke from behind, providing him with a convenient distraction. Already on his knees, he reinforced his grip on the safety rope and leaned out to counterbalance the threat of capsize. Caught in the spill of backlight from the strobes, a series of freeze-frames revealed the tight creases in his brow and the stilted contortion around his mouth. Unlike the captain of the ill-fated *Kelsey*, R.J. was unpracticed at deception, and his face disclosed the truth as plainly as if he'd revealed it in neon script—*the approaching ship was a slaver.*

Whether he realized his refusal to answer had aroused my suspicions or he knew his attempt to produce an innocent façade had failed, he tried to fill the uncertain caution between us with invented assurances. "Don't worry. Once we get onboard, I'll negotiate something with the captain."

*You bastard! You have nothing to negotiate with .
. . except me! I'm your currency, your ticket to safety.*

It was all I could do to keep it inside.

While the approaching ship would provide
rescue from the storm, it would not offer
sanctuary. Once onboard, I would again be a
captive, at the mercy of a captain and crew who
would no doubt expect me to demonstrate what
I'd learned aboard the *Kelsey*.

I laid my head against the raft's upper tube,
not caring about the elements full assault on my
face. In that instant, in that moment of absolute
heartbreak, I dismissed the relentless wind and
stinging rain. I could no longer feel the waves as
they breached the sidewalls of the raft. My short-
lived freedom was about to come to an abrupt
end.

Overwhelmed by despair, I turned away
from the lights of the *Kochi Mar* and absently
searched the horizon.

Although much weaker, the blinking yellow
beacon atop the weather buoy was still there,
continuing to signal its presence through the rise
and fall of the ocean—a dancing firefly on a dark,
flame-etched canvas.

How far could it be?

Based on the intensity of the *Kochi Mar's*
lights when they first appeared, I estimated the

buoy to be three to four times as distant—at least two miles away, probably more.

I remembered my swim to Pigeon Island. The distance had been shorter and the weather calm, and I'd worn fins to triple my speed. Even if by some miracle I was able to reach the buoy, then what? Sabotaging the electronics would eventually bring a maintenance crew, but their arrival could take days or even weeks. And if the floating marker turned out to be one of the tsunami detection units, its scalable platform could be smaller than the interior of the raft. I'd have little or no protection from the ocean—or its inhabitants.

The idea was insane. The amber beacon had never implied the suggestion of rescue. To think it offered a better option than taking my chances aboard the approaching ship was absurd.

Illogical.

Foolish.

Still . . . I wondered.

Chapter Eighteen

With my emotions drained from the loss of Annie and my fate surely sealed by the approaching cargo ship, my decision was a basic reflex of survival. If there was a moment of hesitation—to weigh the risk, estimate the odds—it was quickly overshadowed by raw determination.

I waited, keeping an eye on R.J.

I wanted him to believe my disappearance was accidental, that I was a victim of the storm and not an escapee from the designs of the approaching slaver.

No second thoughts . . .

Concentrate on R.J. . .

Wait for the right moment . . .

He turned away from me, taking another bearing on the *Kochi Mar*.

In one smooth motion, I swung my legs over the top of the raft, took a last reference look at the distant speck of yellow light, and slipped into the icy sea.

The water received me with open arms, sucking me below the surface with spinning, cyclonic force. As the darkness closed in around me, the raft's strobes became the only light in a rapidly diminishing window. Like a signal fire on the surface of the ocean, they marked the location of air, the meeting of sky and sea— where I had to return if I was going to live.

Caught in the twisting grip of an undersea vortex, I felt the unnerving disorientation of being tossed end-over-end as the brutal turbulence battered me without mercy. I finally managed to wrap myself into a ball, breaking the water's crushing embrace.

Kicking hard against the downward draw, the sub-surface currents made my ascent surprisingly difficult. And yet, it wasn't my slow progress that filled me with fear. It was the threat of R.J.'s grabbing reach. He would be waiting, watching for me. He might have already tied a line around his waist, ready to retrieve his "bargaining chip." To him, my body represented coin of the realm, and he wouldn't hesitate to trade me for his passage to the next port.

The frigid bite of the water-laden wind confirmed I'd broken the surface. As I drew a frantic breath, I shielded my eyes to create a window in the pelting rain. All around me pulsed light bounced off a sea of whitecaps, the quick bursts of illumination clouding my vision with blurred shadows—especially the one in front of me, a dark silhouette mimicking my every move.

It made no sense, unless . . . *the projected shadow was mine!*

The raft was directly behind me.

Quickly filling my lungs, I stopped my frantic treading and let the drag of the ocean take me under.

I'd been lucky—this time. What about the next? What if R.J. had seen me and, armed with the assurance I was alive, was waiting for the air in my lungs to turn stale and useless?

It was a situation I never had to face. The swift current pulled me away from the raft as it drew me deeper. A vicious opponent, I let it take me, praying I could hold my breath until I could return to the surface.

It was nearly a minute before I extinguished the pain of my aching lungs with a draw of heavy, waterlogged air. Kicking against the churning down-pull, I turned in both directions, searching for the pulsing strobes. When I found them, I was surprised at how far I'd traveled. Appearing as thumb-sized circles of refracted illumination, they looked like the distant headlights of an oncoming car in night-cast rain. I guessed the distance to be sixty, maybe eighty feet. From R.J.'s vantage point, I would be on the very edge of visibility. Even if he saw me bobbing on the surface, there was nothing he could do.

The immediate threat of recapture was gone.

With grueling effort, I managed to flip onto my back to float. Even with the rain strafing my face, I felt a welcome respite from the exertion.

The relief was short lived. The next wave fell on me without warning, engulfing me with pounding intensity.

Deciding to ride it out on the surface was a poor choice. Vulnerable to the storm's most severe punishment, the rolling water tossed me about like a ragdoll. Staying below the waves offered protection, but when submerged, I had no sense of up or down. Relying on my natural buoyancy to lead me to my next breath, I balanced my desperate need for air against the staggering crush of a raging ocean.

As the currents carried me further from the raft, the strobes quickly fell from sight. Each time I broke the surface, I used the precious seconds to scan the darkness for the weather buoy, feeling a sense of relief as I located the dancing yellow pinpoints of light.

Until they vanished.

I had just broken through the waves, waiting for the peaks and valleys of water to cooperate and grant me a brief glimpse of the distant amber dot of pulsing light.

This time I couldn't find it.

I panicked. The only illumination came from a lightning-scored sky, its constant display revealing an endless seascape of white foam spread across a furious ocean.

Being left without direction was terrifying. Without a point of reference, the truth was as callous as the tempest that surrounded me: I was no longer struggling to reach a destination. I was fighting for my life.

Preparing for each assault was impossible. There was no symmetry in the attacking waves, no predictable formation that could be timed or anticipated. Often surfacing at the leading edge of the next collapsing breaker, I took its full impact, enduring another cycle of lung-burning, gut-twisting agony.

I tried to calculate my odds of outlasting the storm. How many more times could I battle my way to the surface? How much longer could

I endure the thrashing waves and the numbing cold before fatigue and oxygen deprivation delivered me into the waiting hands of death?

I couldn't let myself speculate.

With each hammering onslaught pushing me deeper into the freezing depths, every return to the surface was a desperate battle against exhaustion—and it was taking its toll. Until now, I'd been acutely aware of the surface wind and sheeting rain—clues to having emerged from the waves, my signal to take a breath. But my senses were becoming numb to the elements, my powers of awareness and recognition dazed by the relentless battering.

No longer sure when it was safe to breathe, I began opening my lips slightly to test for the presence—or absence—of salt water before drawing in the precious air.

I surfaced to an unexpected calm. Knowing my senses could not be trusted, I was immediately suspicious of the sudden change in my surroundings. Eerie by sheer contrast, the sea's angry temperament had transformed to that of a tranquil lake, set upon by a summer storm.

It didn't make sense. This was a different ocean, where an unpredictable and often erratic

Mother Nature lie exhausted and spent, unable to continue her seething tantrum.

Illusion or not, my muscles were aching, my heart pounding from exertion. I wouldn't question my good fortune. I rolled onto my back to float, thankful for the chance to rest. As I repeatedly filled my lungs, I was aware of a strong surface current, as if being carried in the quiet rush of a quickly draining lake.

At first I dismissed it, thinking it was a trace flow from subsurface turbulence.

Then I remembered—I'd felt it before, when clinging to Annie's hand as the water receded from the wreck to feed an approaching wave. This was similar, but more pronounced, the very air permeated with an ominous threat that the elements were gathering themselves, mustering their strength for a new and more vicious attack.

I realized my surroundings were not a fortunate break in the weather, but the effects of a forced draw, a coastal phenomenon usually preceding an enormous swell. If the change in the sea's disposition was the harbinger of an approaching wave large enough to gather the open ocean, it would be a gigantic freak of nature, the off-spring of a so-called perfect storm—and it would strike with the weight of a falling mountain.

I scanned the rain-splattered surface, searching for a rising liquid foothill on the flash-lit horizon.

I *heard* the approaching behemoth long before I saw it.

Like the sounding of the seven mythical trumpets announcing the arrival of the apocalypse, the massive breaker approached not with the silence of a stalking predator, but with the raging frenzy of a maniacal killer.

From the escalating roar, I knew it was close—and moving fast.

The resting sky flickered, then crackled, signaling a resumption of its pyroclastic assault with high bursts of cloud-fire. The soft light revealed the beast—an exploding barrage of water six stories high, its shock waves so violent, the sea around me began to vibrate.

From disjointed glimpses provided by staccato stitches of lightening, the wave appeared to jump across the surface of the ocean, growing larger in size with every leap.

It would be on me in seconds.

Desperate to escape the initial impact from the ocean's iron fist, I dove. Below the surface, the crash of a thousand tons of falling water was deafening. Yet the sound only hinted at its power—and the depth the wave would take me. Plunged into a liquid night, I felt the pressure building on my eyes and ears. Seconds later, the crushing weight began squeezing the air from my chest, releasing a stream of bubbles from my nose.

The purest form of terror tightened around my neck. I tried to fight back, but at that depth, the freezing ocean had stilled my muscles, contracting them into useless sinew.

My senses dulled, my perception waning, I waited for the inevitable, a slave to the current.

Now it was only a matter of time. In a few seconds, I would no longer wonder if the distant voice breaking through the ocean's icy coffin was real or a product of my own delirium.

Don't give up on yourself . . . Don't give up . . .

I'd heard Annie say it more than once. The last time she'd been wiping the tears from my cheeks, assuring me she would be waiting after the auction, promising to help me escape.

If allowed to live through this hell, I knew I would always look back at this moment as her final reach across the great divide, touching me from the heavens, telling me my surrender was premature.

I felt a change in pressure—the weight of a brutal ocean relaxing its grip. The temperature was also changing, losing its freezing edge.

My body is shutting down, I reasoned. *I'm experiencing a delusion or suffering from a final burst of hopeful deception before slipping into unconsciousness.*

It struck me as odd—my ability to rationalize what was happening to me with such clarity. Why wouldn't my cognitive skills also be affected, my ability to reason as faulty as my perception? While I might be experiencing the symptoms of hyperthermia and oxygen deprivation, what if the unlikely sensations were real? It would mean I was no longer being driven toward the seabed, but *away* from it.

That seemed impossible.

Yet in illogical contrast to nature's dispassionate rule over life and death, I *was* being lifted toward the surface and into the wave's newly forming trough.

But there was no benevolence in the storm's true intentions, and instead of pushing me toward life-giving air, it was hurling my battered body toward something else.

The blow to my left arm was severe and punishing, as if my flesh had been struck with a two-by-four wrapped in barbed-wire. The unexpected strike penetrated my forearm like a salvo of razor-edged quartz. I winced against the fiery bite of the ocean's salt burn.

There were few possible attackers, and my mind immediately centered on the most deadly.

A shark!

The storm would not take me after all. The final victory would belong to the most brutal of coldblooded killers. On the brink of panic, I recognized the symbolic irony. If there was another living creature equivalent to the heartless bastards who bought and sold human beings, there was none more fitting than a shark.

I was plagued by a rush of memories—stories told by men who had witnessed an attack. The victims were usually unfortunate crewmembers knocked into the sea by a swinging boom or a loose cage-trap skidding across the deck, the resulting scramble to save them always coming too late as the hungry monsters turned their last few seconds of life into sheer terror.

I tried to shut down my brain, force myself to pass out, rendering me oblivious to the agony of needle-sharp teeth sinking deep into my legs, to the sea turning blood red as the thrashing creature ripped them from my torso.

What if I'd stayed in the raft with R.J.?

It was a haunting epitaph—the belated regret of a hopeless choice. My decision to swim to the buoy had become a death sentence, sealing my fate as effectively as surrendering my soul to the heartless Reaper.

Yet I would not go to my grave as just another unfortunate victim. I would accept my passing as a method of travel, a transition from his world to the next. I hoped I would find a place without pain, fear, or loneliness.

With my fading consciousness masking the agony of my bursting lungs, I counted down toward oblivion, the future falling away from me like the discarded pedals of a hastily plucked rose.

But the Angel of Death would not permit me to leave this world in such a blissful state.

Again, my deadly adversary slammed into me. Wrenching pain tore through my right shoulder, the intense burn of salty brine on an open wound agonizing confirmation that my skin had been left ripped and bleeding.

Writhing against the attack, I heard the pitiful sound of my own screams leaving my mouth as a useless eruption of bubbles.

Instinctively covering the area with my hand, I prepared myself to find loose flaps of shredded flesh and the raw edges of exposed bone. Even with numbed fingers, I could tell my arm was mostly intact. At worst, I was suffering from a deep abrasion resulting from a collision with something heavy and jagged.

The truth was a confusing relief—the wound was relatively benign. A shark would have struck without restraint or hesitation, determined to rip me apart. This second assault had come without intention or targeting, suggesting my attacker might not be the instinctual killer I'd imagined.

In fact, I had scraped against *it*.

As impossible as it seemed, my ascent from the depths of the ocean had driven my floundering body into an obstruction large enough to block my access to the surface.

With my lungs holding back a persistent ocean, I reached out, trying to determine what it was, and how to get around it.

Like a heartless captor seizing the opportunity to escalate his cruelty, the ocean's currents reacted with abrupt and unbridled dominance, slamming the living into the dead, bringing us together in another intense collision.

Although dazed from the blow, the taste of sea-brine told me the first trickle of water had squeezed its way into my mouth. Only the involuntary clamping of my throat muscles prevented an immediate inrush of water.

A shudder of light and shadow, a gray shroud, severing my connection to the pain, panic, and fear.

. . . on the brink.

. . . almost done.

Onset hallucinations began to swirl in the darkness, my subconscious preparing to display its handiwork. Texture and color gelled into virtual substance, creating a desperate manifestation of symbolic escape—the wavering image of a door. Unsupported by walls, it floated on a canvas as black and eternal as a starless night.

I saw myself reaching out to open it, as I might in a dream.

The reality of my nitrogen-induced illusion was far less peaceful. The hyper-driven current had catapulted me into a large, waterlogged timber. With involuntary convulsions driving my arms in reckless and violent spasms, I was frantically clawing at its splintered edges, driving tiny shards of wood deep under my fingernails.

In my altered state of awareness, the pain was slow to register— the searing punctures cutting through my delirium, beckoning to me like a lifeline, drawing a scream from my fading consciousness.

In a sudden and fiery reawakening of my senses, I realized the truth—I had collided with a piece of submerged debris, possibly from the broken ship.

But it was too late.

The building implosion in my chest had become a contracting vacuum forcing my throat to open, engorging my lungs with water.

Hold it! Don't let it in.

They were orders my body could no longer obey. My nose drew first, the sea filling my throat. My mouth opened in protest, coughing up the invading intruder.

My wheezing scream could barely compete with the howl of the wind. But it did provide gut-wrenching confirmation that, without realizing it, I had made my way to the surface.

The exchange of water for air was excruciating. Taking shallow breaths, my lungs expelled the liquid despite the painful contractions. I had come dangerously close to drowning, and I was not about to risk accidental suffocation from a few spoonfuls of ocean dribbling down my windpipe.

My presumption of having struck a piece of the *Kelsey* had been right. Partially submerged, it appeared to be a section of the ship's hull. Flashes of storm-light revealed the promise of a make-shift platform—one I hoped was large enough to support my weight.

As desperate as I was to pull myself from the water, I was exhausted. I needed to rest, to gather my strength. But with each new wave threatening to rip me away from the floating hull-scrap, I quickly realized I was growing weaker.

If I was going to save myself, I had to act now.

My first efforts to climb onto the surface were frightening, and more than once, I nearly lost my grip. I began to time my movements, establishing a new handhold only when I was certain I could brace myself against the next head-swamping breaker.

After several failed attempts, I learned to use the swells to my advantage. Dropping the upper part of my torso onto the wooden float, I brought my legs up one at a time, maintaining my balance as I tested the stability of my new life raft.

Each new ragged discharge from the blue-fired canopy provided another glimpse of the wreckage. Barely twelve-foot square, the panel of wood had stayed intact due to several large cross-beams maintaining its integrity. Perhaps it had been torn from the ship's skeletal frame as the *Kelsey* was hit with a final and fatal onslaught of water.

My heart caught in my throat. I hoped that Annie—

It was too late for hope. I could only pray that Annie hadn't died alone and afraid.

Straddling the center-most beam, I shifted forward a bit, then from side-to-side, searching for the point of balance. With my additional weight, the wooden raft rode much lower in the water, yet with the longer trailing lengths of timber acting as submerged pontoons, the section of broken ship was relatively stable.

My tears mixed with rain as the support of something solid relieved the strain on my muscles. I ached to lie down and rest. But I knew how easily sleep would overtake me. And if I fell from the floating wreckage, I would lose the only thing separating me from a frigid ocean—and death.

I remembered the lifejacket I'd tossed toward Annie as she'd disappeared under the sea. From the shape of her profile as she'd stood on the stern of the *Kelsey*, the waves had swept it from her reach. Even so, I didn't regret my decision. All I could do now was rely on what stamina I had left to keep me stationary on this fragile platform of broken wood. If my grip failed for even an instant, I would never have the strength to pull myself from the water a second time.

I thought about the *Kochi Mar.* I was certain the ship was still out there, and by now, R.J. was surely enjoying the hospitality of his new captain. I hoped he was telling the crew about me, ending his story with the gruesome details about how I'd been bounced from the raft and drowned. It was a meaningless conclusion to a promising life, but one I desperately wanted the network of slavers to believe.

A chance to survive—that's all I was asking.

I rode the continuous rise and fall of the ocean for what seemed like hours, hoping my floating refuge would withstand the next pulverizing crash of water. Often submerged by the rolling waves, I held on, ironically knowing my life—or death—would be determined by how long I could stay connected to this remnant of a broken slave ship.

The realization the angry breakers had been replaced with the gentle rocking of three-foot swells came to me slowly. I wondered if I had dozed off, miraculously staying on top of the wreckage in spite of nature's best efforts to separate us.

I quickly dismissed the possibility of having fallen asleep. Assuming a prone position would have allowed the heavy sea to sweep me from the platform. And yet, I could not remember exactly when the wind began to subside, nor could I recall when the rain had ceased its drenching downpour.

I never considered I might be suffering from the effects of shock. And although my confusion wasn't the near-death hallucinations I'd experienced beneath the surface, it was definitely an indication of my diminishing resistance to exposure.

Whether an instinct of survival or a flash of logical insight, I kept my exertion to a minimum, saving my remaining physical reserves to maintain my core temperature.

I laid my head on the highest projection of the center beam. Even there, the sea continued to taunt me, licking at my face in a repeating cycle of wave-wash. Unlike its biblical counterpart, this ark was of accidental design—never intended to keep its lone occupant dry.

Feeling the fall of light rain on my back, I twisted to my side, welcoming the opportunity to rinse the salt from my lips. A few hours before, the sky had soaked my skin with a flurry of tiny whitecaps. Now it touched me like a gentle shower, the distant pulses of lightning freezing the drops in a kaleidoscope of color.

Jewels floating in the night . . . like me.

Directly overhead, the gradual appearance of the first stars began to replace the remaining traces of storm-light, and with it came an intoxicating sense of calm. I ached to roll onto my back and give myself the gift of sleep.

Not yet. Too soon. Too risky.

So far, I'd been lucky. I'd beaten impossible odds to survive both the sinking of the *Kelsey* and extended exposure to the sea. In a few hours the rising sun would light the horizon. Maybe it would reveal a coastline or the profile of a passenger liner—one that offered rescue rather than a return to captivity.

But regardless of what waited for me, I'd been given what I'd asked for . . .

A chance.

To Be Continued . . .

Next in the Series. . .

Reunion

Book Two
"World Without Love"

In *Reunion*, Jewel's story continues as she finds herself alone and stranded in a far-flung corner of the world. Struggling to elude her captors and the network of bounty hunters, she meets her would-be savior, a man who promises to provide protection and comfort. Jewel believes her nightmare has finally come to an end. But greed raises its ugly head, and the terrifying future she thought she'd evaded becomes a reality—one that seems impossible to escape.

Reunion **is available December 2015 from Amazon in kindle ebook and Paperback**

About the Author . . .

Jaye Frances is the author of the erotica suspense series, "World Without Love," including *Betrayed, Reunion*, and *Redemption*. Her other books include *The Beach,* a sci-fi supernatural tale about the possibilities—and horror—of wishful thinking; *The Kure*, a paranormal-occult romance novel; *The Possibilities of Amy*, a coming-of-age story of first love; and *Love Travels Forever*, a collection of poignant short stories. When not absorbed in her writing, Jaye enjoys cooking, taking pictures—lots of them—and sipping a glass of merlot with a side of dark chocolate. Jaye lives on the gulf coast of Florida, sharing her home with one husband, six computers, and several hundred pairs of shoes.

For more information, visit Jaye's

Website:

www.jayefrances.com

Facebook Page:

www.facebook.com/jayefrancesauthor

Amazon Author Page:

www.amazon.com/author/www.jayefrances.com

Other Books by Jaye Frances

The Beach

Alan loves the beach. More than a weekend respite, it is his home, his refuge, his sanctuary. And for most of the year, he strolls the sand in blissful solitude, letting nature—and no one else—touch him. But spring has given way to summer, and soon, the annual invasion of vacationers and tourists will subdivide the beach with blankets, umbrellas, and chairs, depriving Alan of his privacy and seclusion—the fundamental touchstones of his life.

Resigned to endure another seasonal onslaught of beach-goers, Alan believes there is nothing he can do but prepare for the worst.

But fate has other plans.

Delivered to him on the crest of a rogue wave, the strange object appears to have no purpose, no practical use—until Alan accidentally discovers what waits inside. Now he must attempt to unravel an ageless mystery, unaware that the final outcome will change his life, and the beach, forever.

In the companion novella *Short Time*, you'll meet a respectable but bored middle-class executive, who exchanges his future for six months of excess and extravagance, only to discover out the price he must pay for his hedonistic indulgence is beyond anything he could have imagined.

The Beach is available in kindle ebook and paperback from Amazon

The Possibilities of Amy

Amy is the ultimate trophy girl—gorgeous face, killer body, and a vivacious personality. But there's something else about her, something that makes her even more special. Amy is new. A transfer student from out of state, she's starting her senior year without knowing a soul. And that means she's up for grabs, available.

Infatuated from the moment he sees her, David is determined to meet Amy, and if the fates are willing, to spend the rest of his life with her. But his shyness prevents him from approaching her—until his friends devise a contest to determine who will be the first to prove their manhood by seducing her.

The Possibilities of Amy is available in kindle ebook and paperback from Amazon

The Kure

John Tyler, a young man in his early twenties, awakens to find a ghastly affliction taking over his body. When the village doctor offers the conventional, and potentially disfiguring, treatment as the only cure, John tenaciously convinces the doctor to reveal an alternative remedy—a forbidden ritual contained within an ancient manuscript called the *Kure*.

Although initially rejecting the vile and sinister rite, John realizes, too late, that the ritual is more than a faded promise scrawled on a page of crumbling paper. And as cure quickly becomes curse, the demonic text unleashes a dark power that drives him to consider the unthinkable—a depraved and wicked act requiring the corruption of an innocent soul.

The Kure is available in kindle ebook and paperback from Amazon

Love Travels Forever

In *Love Travels Forever*, Jaye Frances captures the reader's heart with an inspiring collection of seventeen stories filled with romance and passion, the hopeful innocence of youth, and a love so strong that it transcends the mortality of life. Here are just a few of the people you'll meet:

Evan and Frankie, a loving couple traveling through life hand-in-hand, are unaware that the shadow of fate is about to tear them apart. Helpless to change their shortened future together, one of them makes a promise—a promise of devotion and courage, honoring a love that surpasses the boundaries of time.

Mark and Janice, the perfect couple with the perfect life, are on the threshold of finally seeing their dreams come true—until an unexpected circumstance changes their lives forever.

Danny, a young soldier fresh out of boot-camp, is desperate to find a way to travel home and marry his sweetheart before being shipped overseas. Stranded in a train station on a three day pass with no hope in sight, Danny meets Wanda, an incredible woman who vows to find a way to bring Danny and his fiance together.

Nora and Georgia are two eight-year-old best friends who share giggles, dolls, and secrets. But when one of them faces sudden danger, the other responds with an unconditional act of love and forges a lifelong bond between them unaffected by fear or prejudice.

So find a quiet spot, get comfy, and grab a box of tissue. You're about to take an unforgettable journey of the heart, to a place where compassion and hope have no limits, and where love continues to travel forever.

Love Travels Forever is available in kindle ebook and paperback from Amazon